THE LAST SILVER SNAIL

by

DERF GNÖLJ

The Last Silver Snail

GlossaHouse, LLC
110 Callis Circle
Wilmore, KY 40390

Publisher's Cataloging-in-Publication Data:

Long, Fredrick J. (Derf Gnölj)

The Last Silver Snail/ Fredrick J. Long. Wilmore, KY: GlossaHouse, ©2026

GlossaHouse Fiction and Fantasy Series (GFFS)

x, 268 pages ; 15.6 x 23.4 cm

ISBN: 978-1-63663-138-7 (paperback)

1. Fiction, Christian. 2. Author. 3. I. Title. II. Series.

Cover Design by Fredrick J. Long with great gratitude to and permission of Mirko Cogo and his amazing piece "Fate of Snail" at www.yumestudio.it.

Book Layout by Fredrick J. Long

The snail doodle divider was designed by Sketchepedia / Freepik and used with permission.

Troyton Pencil drawings by Archer Edwards were created (many years ago!) by Hannah (Long) Hammer and used with permission.

Many pictures were my own and edited in GIMP. Some images were created by Canva and sometimes further edited in GIMP. Most of the images/pictures below were edited similarly.

Melon picture transformed into humin fruit by AlkisO - Own work, CC BY-SA 4.0, https://commons.wikimedia.org/w/index.php?curid=104469103

Opossum picture edited to appear as a Yunt, by Juan Tello - originally posted to Flickr as Rabipelao, CC BY 2.0, https://commons.wikimedia.org/w/index.php?curid=9479352

Gerenuks as Long Necked Deer by frederic.salein originally posted to Flickr as "Gerenuks in Samburu" CC BY-SA 2.0

Ficus leaf under Humin plate is from Felix E. Klee, CC 0, via Wikimedia Commons.

Stone Bridge at the Narrows is edited photo by Berishasinan - Own work, CC BY-SA 4.0, https://commons.wikimedia.org/w/index.php?curid=119122442

Stone Giant edited to form Trioptic Giants and the Gilded One is from ID 188975034 © obsidianfantasy | Dreamstime.com

Stone Giant along water is based upon a picture ID 284954969 © Nick Klein | Dreamstime.com

Archer looking into the sky utilize the image Giant in night sky ID 386131243 © Deep Your Life | Dreamstime.com

Tufted Ground Squirrel as the basis for a Bouley is in the public domain by Joseph Wolf, Proceedings of the Zoological Society of London, 1856.

Inspired by reading to

my five little kiddos

which I absolutely loved

and

dedicated to

Tom Ostrander

who as our youth pastor inspired
so many of us and started our group's
ministry "Crossroads"

and

first called me Derf Gnol.

Tom himself was otherwise known as

"Rednartso"

(thanks to Mark Sapp for reminding me of this!)

Map of Sylvanwood

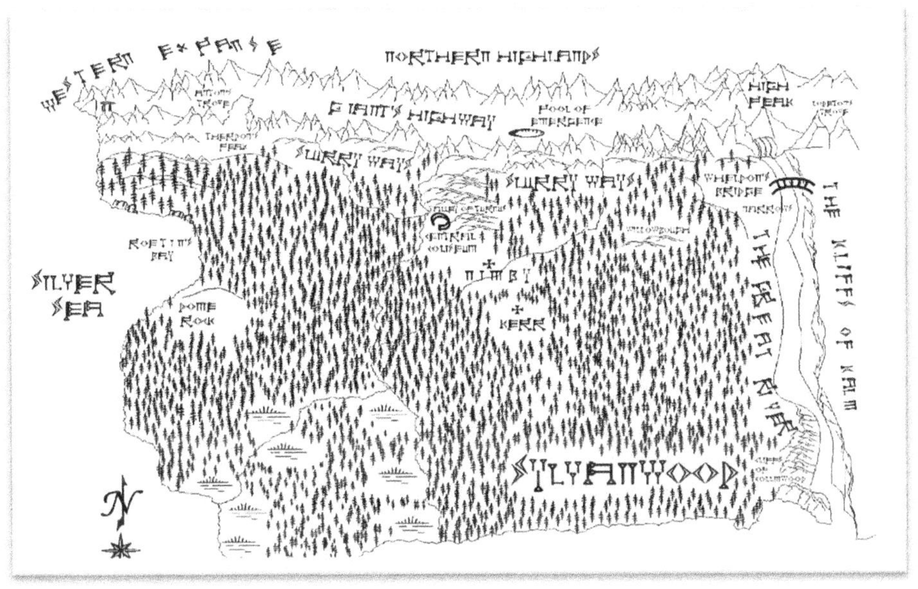

Book Overview

In the 'falling' world of Verthana, the Trioptic Giants of the Highlands have fallen from the Conductor ... and their folly is spreading to the elfin Musselkin down in the Sylvan Lowlands. The prodigious Silver Snails are disappearing and Sylvanwood is bitterly divided. And yet, providentially, at the discovery of mysterious rings, seven youth of Earth transport themselves to Verthana only to find themselves amidst the fallen giants, talking Silver Snails, and the falling Musselkin. After entering Verthana, the youth are torn apart and caught up in strange encounters, alien customs, and celestial events. Their aim is simply to survive deathly peril, reunite, and return to their home on Earth.

Table of Contents

Part I—On the Borders of the Giants' Land

Chapter 1 Wheldon-olt's Fall 3
Chapter 2 Breakrock's Delight 14
Chapter 3 The Silver Snails' Warning 24
Chapter 4 The Second Giant Encounter 33
Chapter 5 Decordem's Speech 41
Chapter 6 The First Giant Encounter 47

Part II—The Entrance of the Earthen Youth

Chapter 7 The Mitchells and their Friends 59
Chapter 8 The Celestial Crossroads 69
Chapter 9 Bonnie's and Paige's Discovery 77
Chapter 10 The Giants' Pool of Emergence 83
Chapter 11 Salton-suhl Tukal, the Giant King 92

Part III—Providential Encounters

Chapter 12 The Path Downwards 107
Chapter 13 A Bouley's Gift 117
Chapter 14 Hilasdem, the Last Silver Snail 122
Chapter 15 The Yunt Pack 131
Chapter 16 The Conductor 138
Chapter 17 Tipton-tyne Baer 147

Part IV—The Drama of Verthana

Chapter 18 Bydelus's Administration 157

Chapter 19 The Corridor of Time 164
Chapter 20 Anton's One Gem 171
Chapter 21 The Escape from the Narrows 179
Chapter 22 The Journey to Central Coliseum 188
Chapter 23 Bydelus, Highest Priest, Chief
Governor Supreme in Perpetuity 196

Part V—The Venture of Redemption

Chapter 24—Verthana's Ransom 207
Chapter 25 Troyton's Journey Westward 214
Chapter 26 At the Western Sea Tides 220
Chapter 27 The Tunnel from Within 227
Chapter 28 The Great Rising 235
Chapter 29 The New Giant King 243

Part VI—Farewell to the Giants' Land

Chapter 30 Kingly Prerogatives 253
Chapter 31 Home Again 262

Part I

On the Borders of the Giants' Land

Chapter 1
Wheldon-olt's Fall

On the exact day a year prior, the clan had experienced their abandonment—not to put it too bluntly but indeed speaking precisely. The Great Mover in the sky, marking the late afternoon, neared the end of its daily circuit above the Giant Skyway of the Western Expanse dipping into the Silver Sea. The heavenly firmament shimmered deep aqua blue. The orange radiance of the Mover animated two creatures of the clan below playing a game. With their feet they juggled between them the center of their competition, a gamestone weighing as much as two earthen men. The player who dropped it was dubbed the "Loser." The game involved a good deal of banter, for there was often a question of whether one received a "fair" pass or not. And, if not, a "fault" was claimed and the juggling resumed.

The ground beneath them quaked and crumbled as they played since each stood over forty feet tall. What would strike any earthen creature watching them, apart from their size, was a larger third eye centered on the forehead and slightly above the other two. These were Trioptic Giants and this middle eye gave them exceptional vision to aide their search for precious gems and rare stones lying deep in mountainous caverns like amethyst, emeralds, and even diamonds. "But why would they search for them?" you might rightly ask. Well, such contained minerals and carbon structures that prolonged their motion of life. But such searches were dangerous because darkness put these giants to slumbering.

How nimbly these twin giants juggled, mesmerizingly caressed, the stone passed between them. The artistic moving, cavaliering, shifting, and passing of the game stone from one triple-toed giant foot to another was calculated to entrance the opponent.

When passing the stone, one giant, Bryton-duhl Nadar, would oft chant a ditty that would translate in English something like this,

Kick a trick to flick the rock
to beat ol' Pedul flatfoot N'brick.
A nine-tenth's chance of winning hence,
or ten, if he doesn't do the dance...
Do the dance ... do the dance ... do the dance.

The final repetition continued into faint fading with ebb and flow until the other's exasperation. The ditty was truly irritating.

The other, Nimbrik-al Pedul, was the quieter and older of the two by thirteen thirty-seventh thousandths of a circuit (that is, three minutes and twenty-one seconds in earthen time). He was only slightly more calcified, encrusted within and without from his more adventurous diet. The two were twins, an anomaly in their world where giants entered one at a time from the Pool of Emergence under the auspices of the monarchal giant whose main responsibility was to assign each youngling a giant elder as its guardian "Watcher." The giants were genderless, neither boys nor girls, by design of the Maker, the Conductor. In these accounts of the Celestial Crossroads, we will describe Trioptic Giants using "he," "his," and "him"; however, when not deserving of the personalizing effect of such a gendered pronoun, a giant may also be described as an "it." These twin giants were the most recent to be born in the Western Expanse and reckoned to be the last ever since none other had since emerged—but remarkably and providentially one more would yet step out of the pool. About such matters, as observers of these events and appointed archivists of the Celestial Glories of the Celestial Encyclopedia, we humbly submit the following account of the Conductor's marvels on this world of Verthana, one of the "falling" worlds. The Conductor is One who is holy, just, loving, faithful, merciful, sovereign, and good in every way imaginable and beyond all imagination—whose Name is always to be praised!

The Pool of Emergence, charcoal by Paige Edwards

Presently, Nimbrik and Bryton were twenty-eight years old and forty-five feet tall; yet they had the sophistication and patience of snotty-nosed, ten-year old earthen children. And so, Bryton's taunt of this ditty made Nimbrik mad. He belted back, "Bellowing belly's too big for Bryton's brickies!" which was the best he could manage. Nimbrik-al, although not as quick-tongued as Bryton-duhl, was better in sustained thought, and hence a better calculating mathematician. Bryton knew it and teased him to try to feel better about himself.

Wheldon-olt Maar, their guardian elder by fifteen years was a full fifty feet tall. He reacted to their infantile antics like any withdrawn, somber earthen teenager would have. He seldom played this game with them anymore, preferring rather to create and set off firerock powder or search cavernward for some new rock formation of tasty delight, perhaps some vein of red potassium-rich granite that would tickle his palate, or, if he were really lucky, some secret trove full of gemstones like opal, jasper, and even diamond that had hidden by many a giant along the skyway. Any of these would prolong his motion of life. However, even Wheldon-olt grew bored of these pursuits just as had their guardian Watcher of the year prior. Thus, Weldon inherited the title Watcher when their Watcher had abandoned them. It was the anniversary of that sad day approaching the exact hour.

Wheldon-olt, leaning against a nearby precipice, looked on numbly as his watchlings sported and taunted one another. His eyes dimmed, his ears dulled. Giant matherapists would have diagnosed him with FDV—"Fractural Dysvolition"; in earthen clinical terms, "depression." He was increasingly seized with apathy in increasing frequency. The reason was no mystery: After most of the elder watcher giants had seized up and stopped moving or had largely vacated their traditional western homelands, life left behind had become lonesome for him and the twins. To remain in the Western Expanse "sucked." But more than this, life was flat-out tiresome, utterly boring, for a giant of his age. As a consequence, he moped about aimlessly with nothing constructive to do.

The anniversary time kept reminding him of their Watcher, Therndonal Byrl. Why indeed had he ditched his "family clan of four"? Was it indeed from fear of being "poisoned," as he had said running past them never to return? But, poisoned by whom and for what reason? The remaining clan mused rather that he left to choose more substantial pursuits in the minelands along the Eastern Borders or perhaps in the Northern Barrens. They hadn't contemplated running after him at the time and always held out hope of his return. Indeed, Therndon vanished never to return. So, now Wheldon-olt watched over his two watchlings forming a "family clan of three," the lastborn of their kind from the Pool of Emergence, or so they thought.

However, unbeknownst to them all—even to the giant monarch, King Salton-suhl Tukal—another giant of a different kind would emerge through the pool into the grey borders of the giants' land. This border featured a ridge line snaking along the well-traversed giants' skyway—a course connecting the entire highlands from the glimmering salty Silver Sea of the west to the fresh water inland sea of the far east. Facing southward below this stood a rather steep cliff face that tumbled some two miles downward. This slope was increasingly populated with pine, spruce, and fir trees. The ashen surface rock, long ago deposited by springs, consisted mainly of limestone and shale; but these left the giants with a sour taste in the mouth and a "slowing down" effect from calcite buildup. Journeying northward and higher, in the otherwise inhospitable terrain with scarcity of water, the stone quality increased significantly with marvelously colored, motion-granting granites. But, in the lower borders along the skyway the giants could chance upon a life-giving gem with labor and luck. One could also chance upon hidden memory caches embedded at atomic levels in unexpected, clandestine rockfaces. But downward over the ridge the southern lowlands consisted of sandstone and clay—utterly detestable to the taste of a Trioptic Giant, and actually quite beneath them geophysically. And, moreover, from atop this ridge, the giants could conveniently lean over to pop open their belly flap to release their slurry of undigested mineral waste, which stank to high heaven like sulfur.

It was downward to this lowland that Wheldon-olt's watcher, Therndon, many times had ventured the year before he vanished, the sole giant ever to have done so in violation of the natural order. Returning from there, he proffered particularly poor rock samples in hopes of somehow concocting something of them tasty and motion-sustaining. Therndon labored in vain making pebbled pastes and porridges, stone goulashes and stews; nothing satisfactory resulted. Instead, the clan of four would feel stiffer and slower after eating them—quite distressing to any giant. Their nervous systems—composed of mineral links throughout their rocky frames and lubricated at junctures with pure, slick graphite—would start to freeze up. A regularly poor diet could seize them up perpetually. But, on several occasions Therndon found large green emeralds in the muddy banks of rivulets trickling down from the mountainside. When eaten, the beryl stones rich with chromium invigorated the giants' limbs thus easing their movements and rejuvenating their thoughts and actions.

Once upon a time—as it must now be related as like a fairy tale—the Trioptics had enjoyed perpetual motion, moving endlessly; but when through their own will of self-determination, for reasons fully-known only in the Celestial Realms, the giants had fallen thereby introducing a debilitating catalytic pollution among their race that constrained their motion. How exactly this race of Trioptics initially faltered we have chronicled elsewhere, and so too their restoration. However, since that time they could continue moving scarcely longer than two centuries with the right diet mixture of rock and precious gemstones. Hence, these materials were their constant quest. And so the growing lack of sustainable surface quarry stone resulted in many Western Borderland giants venturing to the Northern Barrens and, if desperate enough, even cavernward using mirrors, torches, or phosphorescent lanterns to empower them to descend into the heart of the mountains reaching sometimes even dangerously to the depths of the molten rock core never to venture again surfaceward to emerge or be seen; or they ventured via the Skyway to the Eastern Borders along the massive mountain range—a range spanning endlessly towards the horizon from which daily rose the Great Mover in its perpetual light. Tales were brought back to the Westernlands, which confirmed, conflated, or conflicted with the already circulating rumors about what could be found elsewhere; bright red granite veins, quartzite caves, and trove stashes filled with rare gems. The Western Expanse had its share of troves, too, if one happened to find one and dared to enter it.

Many generations ago, Wheldon-olt's lineage, the Tumbel-duhl Clan of the Smytstoyne Watchers, had settled this particular ridge height with its prestigious "peak" later renamed after one of its watchers, Therndon. They had had their own trove, but this had been discovered and looted. So, in his inauspicious time of watching, Wheldon-olt wondered if he would ever have a trove of his own or would have to leave the Western Expanse and travel to the Northern Barren lands, or eastward beyond High Peak, or even westward across the Silver Sea to obtain one.

Of late, Wheldon-olt had grown increasingly discontented with the normal fare of common rocks. Sometimes he would feel a fuzzy dreamlink in this or that rockface, of a fanciful and fitful kind, about finding something more sustaining. "*Who would be messaging me from afar?*" he wondered. He knew not the source of these links which frustrated him. Instead, he found it entertaining to search the stonefaces for memory caches of sage giants who implanted databanks of tomes and maps, sometimes intended for another giant to find, but at other times not, rather to hide and keep them safe from another giant's assault who through body trawl could forcibly extract the data. But Wheldon-olt figured that, if lucky, he could find something to help him locate a rich trove and instruct him how to dismantle its traps, or information to reveal other mysteries of the age of the giants or of the foundation of his world, Verthana.

Thus far, Wheldon had found fourteen caches, two of which contained maps of purportedly "gem laden" troves in the deep Caverns of Rhuinnmall and another of a massive trove in the Eastern Borderlands; six caches contained meticulously boring historical accounts of clans and their feuds; and three recounted fanciful stories of strange travels, creatures, and places through pools like the giants' one of Emergence. In all of this, sadly, little thought did Wheldon entertain of gaining knowledge of the Conductor, whose Name is to be praised!

Yet even making these cache discoveries, Wheldon-olt grew terribly impatient with his life's trajectory of motion; he wanted to leave Therndon's Peak just as had done his watcher exactly one year ago on the very same day. Even now the very same hour and minute approached, according to Wheldon's recalculations. This anniversary only heightened his anxiety for decisive action. How he longed to be with his watcher Therndon-al Byrl once again, to make things right and have an adventure together!

It was just before the third breakrock of the day (the Trioptic Giants typically had only three) when Wheldon-olt finally had had enough of his watchlings' constant chattering and mutual taunting. He sprung at their gamestone, perfectly calculating its flight trajectory, caught it, and hurled it over the ridge and down the slurry slope. Instantly, after a quick glance of agreement (and according to Wheldon's expectation), both Bryton-duhl and Nimbrik-al pounced on him and pinned him against the inner ridge wall with planned precision.

"Go get our stone!" shouted Bryton-duhl.

"Yeah, go get it!" echoed Nimbrik-al.

Be he replied coldly, "Just what do you think you two are doing?" Wheldon-olt computed points of leverage and angles of trajectory for his next moves.

"We want you to stop throwing away our stones down the slopes!" shouted Nimbrik-al, who shifted to counter Wheldon's pushing and twisting.

"So, this is about stones," said Wheldon-olt shaking his head. "No, go get it yourselves, or make a new one." He was not finding a weakness in the twin's positioning.

Bryton-duhl spoke up, "It's not just about our stones. You've been mad at us since Therndon-al left us. It's not our fault, you know. Something happened down *there ... beneath us.*" He nodded at Nimbrik-al and pointed back down the outer ridge of the slurry slope.

Wheldon-olt, stalling to find a weakness in their positioning, shifted himself a bit and asked, "Do you two remember what he said to us when he left? Well, who rightly calculating would want to go down there?!!!" But the twins remained silent. "Let me up before I get angry!!! I've just about had it!"

"No! Not this time. You've thrown the last stone. We've *also* had enough, Watcher of us or not! You may be older and more calculating, but you *cannot take us.*"

"*Fine!* Have it *your* way!" Seeing their stubborn resolve, Wheldon-olt then calculated his best sequence of moves, making a final estimate of his strategy. After 2.17 seconds of swaying back and forth to counterweigh them, he bolted upward to escape their grasp. His left hand twisted free, then it shot across to grab Nimbrik's uplifting right hand. Then his right leg pushed, while his head ducked, as he drove forward to the right of Bryton's waist, sweeping awkwardly with his left leg with a stutter step to trip Nimbrik-al, and attempting to hold Bryton around the waist with his right arm.

And so, the thunderous and horrific wrestling began with grunting and gasps. The clan of three staggered together awkwardly into the middle of the Skyway with huffs and puffs. Sharp, crackling screeches with an occasional deafening thud echoed across the Skyway. Tiny shards of the giants' rocky, calcified exteriors dislodged here and there, showering the well-worn Skyway with their anger. Bryton-duhl sprawled to his left, planting his right hand squarely on Wheldon's forehead, covering his central eye, and pushed with all his might. Nimbrik-al rebalanced himself and grabbed Wheldon's right ankle and jerked him back. Wheldon-olt collapsed when his right ankle was pulled but immediately jerked it free and sprung up to his base. Reaching for Bryton's right leg, he drove forward, grabbing and lifting. Nimbrik-al surged forward behind Wheldon-olt, now wrapping up both legs, flattening Wheldon-Olt once more. But Wheldon-olt regained his base, scrambling forward, mule kicking as he went.

Their tactics, rather than a street brawl, resembled a wrestling match; moves were mechanically executed to gain leverage and advantage. The maneuvering was masterful with carefully placed holds, grasps, and clutches. Both hands and feet were executed furiously in moves and countermoves, stopping only occasionally for intensive twisting, wrenching, and re-grasping. Leverage and balance dictated the placement of each hand and foot. It was no equal match since the younger two had recently proved more and more difficult for Wheldon-olt alone to manage when they worked together; Wheldon's intimidating psychological advantage had finally given way to the twin's cooperation and combined brute strength.

Inevitably the twin's tactics led to a submission. After just moments (15.67 seconds to be exact), Bryton-duhl and Nimbrik-al had lifted and pinned Wheldon-olt teetering along the outer ridge wall overlooking the southern slurry slope precisely where Wheldon-olt had thrown down their game stone. He knew he was in a precarious position but was more concerned at losing the battle to the twins, still each smaller than he.

Once more Bryton-duhl huffed out, "Go get our game stone!" his eyes meeting Wheldon's, who defiantly shook his head side-to-side.

Wheldon-olt then made a last calculation and mustered his final strength reserve to break free. As he began to execute his moves, the other two, nodding at each other, easily hefted him up and over the ledge, sending him lurching down the steep slope.

The two watchlings erupted with cheering and laughter at their feat. "Ho! Ha! What do you make of that?!!!" They fisted each other, nodding in triumph. "Do the dance ... do the dance!" they shouted and looked down the slope.

Wheldon-olt slid slowly at first but then began tumbling. Wisps of pulverized rock and displaced debris were flung about. But when he crossed into the path of their morning slurry release, he slid more rapidly, careening this way and then that way. As the twins watched his fall become more and more perilous, their cheering stopped. And, just as it did, Wheldon-olt stabilized himself somewhat and managed an upward glance with a smile. He nodded at the two and upthrusted his right fist at them, before continuing to slide downwards.

Bryton-duhl, reflexively returned the gesture, one of achievement; then looked over at Nimbrik-al saying, "He'll be okay—right?—only slightly fractured." But they looked back down and their worried faces betrayed the incredulity of his words.

"What shall we do now?!!" Nimbrik-al wailed as they watched Wheldon-olt plummeting happily downwards.

Chapter 2
Breakrock's Delight

The steep slope from the ridge, sparsely covered with dwarfed trees at the top, leveled only slightly and unevenly as it descended; but the leveling did not slow Wheldon's careening fall as he had calculated it would. He continued accelerating downward. His mass carried him faster and faster, sliding fatefully towards the lowland two miles below. He had been initially very pleased with himself to be descending; but when he began to spin about wildly—on his back sideways, then headfirst rolling, then feet first, and then sideways again—he worried that his limbs would seize up; he had never been so fractured before. Moreover, he could feel his nervous system cracking, dissembling faster than the speed of repairing as he was violently shaken about.

To slow himself, he began grabbing at the more numerous small trees, which he ripped out. Debris scattered about as he flailed and tried to right himself. Soil sprayed up into his mouth. He gagged and coughed. But this was the least of his concerns as the larger conifers nearer the bottom had pointed tops. The clan had often pointed them out from the ridge. If he landed just right onto one of these trees, Wheldon-olt thought, it might very well skewer him, leaving him permanently affixed mid tree, seeping out, without leverage, and eventually immovable. His movement would end.

So, he began calculating what was increasing his slide rate by a factor of 1.37; it was the slurry his clan had released that morning! This particular thought repulsed him the most—*his* sliding in *their own* slurry! As it was, also, his stomach flap bulged and popped, so that he had become quite covered in his own slurry mess. But more concerning was that the slurry decreased the coefficient of friction.

As he careened downwards, he managed to spin around to face forward and then leaned backwards flat. This allowed his feet, in front of him, to steer a bit. He swerved back and forth trying to avoid the occasional rock formation or steeper overhangs that could propel him to land upon one of the massive trees at the bottom. Tree tops and the lowlands approached him at a dizzying rate. Then suddenly, he was airborne and, with a thunderous crash, his left ankle, by the heel, was skewered upon a huge conifer; and as the tree received it, it lurched and sprung back in a wide circle, spinning him around the truck one full rotation before bending over releasing him midair, aspinning, only to land remarkably on his feet accompanied by a massive crunching sound and cutting thud, right between joints of his hallux. He did not stick his landing, but with arms wheeling for balance he fell backwards against a conifer, which slowly leaned over, creaking, and itself succumbed to gravity. It made its final plunge with a crash and whoosh of its branches at the edge of a clearing. Dust and darkness immediately overtook Wheldon-olt. The jarring drop after the whiplashing spin had broken all his synapses simultaneously. His internal systems had effectively cracked. His frame remained unconscious for some time. The forest fell instantly quiet which had just moments before been full of chirping and chattering.

But Wheldon had not completely stopped moving. Within his graphite interior, minute electrical pulses propelled chemical reactions to begin the automated task of repairing synaptic connections and dendrite networks that collectively embodied his mind. Fresh neural branches spread to replace the old depleted and irreparable ones. Established synaptic pathways began reconfiguring the capacities of the surrounding networks progressively from inward to outward. Reestablished pathways eventually restored his consciousness and calculating presence of mind.

From his head there next emanated a low tonal sigh that culminated in a huff being released from his vibration holes. His limbs flinched altogether, reanimating, and like a resuscitated corpse, twitched convulsively for a few moments and stopped once again. Then Wheldon attempted to right himself vertically, but was unable—the external repairs to his left ankle would take longer. At the same time, he also felt the familiar pain of a deep gash in his right hallux. He had received many such deep wounds while mining in the caverns where Trioptic Giants often experienced lacerations, small and large, when excavating and working with broken shards of rock. However, these were not motion-threatening since their bodies regenerated. Presently, the laceration throbbed in pain receptors from the minute traces of methane of the decaying lowland debris, which reacted with his internal heated body core chemistry. Inside his stony frame, the metallic catalysts reacted to the organic compounds creating painful electron transfers at the atomic level. The wounds had introduced oxygen rich air, which was converted to reactive oxygen ions—O^- and O_2^-, by these catalysts, which then produced the oxidative coupling of methane. Heat was produced as one by-product, but this was not the problem; rather, these reactions sent nagging pulsations of electrons from his right foot and left ankle throughout his legs and into the core of his thinking body. His thinking was quite literally fuzzy and muddled.

And so, it was the pain of this fissure and wounds that held fast Wheldon's first conscious thoughts. The initial dull aching from the internal cracking of carbon chains gave way to jabbing stings, repeating again and again and again. Inside his embodied mind, in order to avoid receiving the painful signals, Wheldon-olt severed non-essential pathways. In this way, he could more quickly gain situational awareness.

When Wheldon-olt was finally able to move his feet, he heard and felt a crunching sound that coordinated with the unnerving jolts that shot up his right leg once again. He knew that his foot was not fractured but had been lacerated by some sharp rock or tree trunk. He reached down to pull out whatever it was and proceeded to fissure open his foredigit.

At that, Wheldon-olt Maar, formerly watched by Therndon-al Byrl of the Smytstoyne Watchers of the Trioptic race, popped his finger immediately into his mouth to remove it from the pain-producing oxidizing air. At that very moment all thought of his woes left him. Mixed very slightly with the taste of his own pure black graphite vital fluid was quite a delicious flavor, titillating his palate, flooding his mouth with a symphonic composition of mineral elements in excellent proportion: phosphorus, iron, sodium, potassium, and calcium. He spontaneously released a deep groan of statisfaction, as he calculated the nutrient rich qualities of his ingestion. Forgetting his nagging wounds (which would mend themselves given time), he carefully inspected what his right foot had fallen upon.

This was the queerest thing to him: curled, silver, sharp flake-like sheets of something like mica stone; a crunchy, tasty rock in its own rights. But this new thing was sticking out from his foot in shards. It was as sharp as flint, yet as thin as the stone wafers his watcher gave him at his Foundation Day. But this hard substance with the two to one phosphorus to calcium ratio was not remarkable, but tolerable; the extra dietary calcium would be removed in his grey slurry. Rather, it was the gooey, warm stuff inside that had the perfect blend of minerals that, he thought, would surely perpetuate his motion of life.

In fact, unbeknownst to him—recounted with great sadness to you now, dear reader—Wheldon-olt had fallen squarely upon a yearling Silver Snail, fatefully named Mortidem, who had just recently attained full maturity at twelve earthen feet in length, eighth in width, and seven in height. These Silver Snails traveled yearly to that slurry-enriched habitat at the bottom of the slurry ridge on the borders of the giants' land. Along this ridge the giants had once occupied the borderlands in greater numbers—this we have already related to you—but, importantly for the young snails, these giants would empty their slurry pouches, releasing mineral-rich, alkaline, residual slurry from their digestion of granite and other rock to enrich the lowlands. Below these southern slopes, too, was where the Silver Snails laid their eggs. The soil there was moistened by springs and rich in mineral nutrients, producing rich flora with ample succulent foliage for the emergent and growing youngster snails to feast upon. The snails mainly inhabited these southwestern lowlands between the Great River of the East and the Western Shores of Roetin's Bay on the Silver Sea. These lower regions below the giants' land are known as Sylvanwood by its sentient lowland inhabitants. The giants never journeyed downward to Sylvanwood since they considered the lowlands quite "beneath" them, but also because they detested their own slurry.

Long-necked Deer feeding at a River Wash, photograph by Bonnie Mitchell

It is true that within the giants' land one could often run across the hairy northern beasts such as the bouleys, the yunts, and the long-necked deer. But none of these were ever eaten by the giants since they were, after all, not nutritious rocks or motion-extending gems. So, it is no wonder then that Wheldon-olt never could have imagined that something so hard on the outside and delicious on the inside as this newly discovered gooey "rock" could be a sentient being, a

Silver Snail of Sylvanwood. And so, with Mortidem's death, Wheldon-olt had discovered something new and had no name for the gooey "new rock"; nor did he have any understanding that it was not a rock at all, but a sentient creature of soul, will, and speech. His only point of reference was the fiery acid lava drinks he had once enjoyed deep in the Caverns of Rhuinnmall under the Northern Barrens. And by no fault of his own, neither his Watcher, nor his Watcher's Watcher, nor any of the memory caches that had related to him any matters of centuries past—indeed he was truly and honestly ignorant that the Trioptics had long ago had friendly relations with the Silver Snails among the sentient creatures of this world Verthana, when both were in the custom of crossing through the Silver Sea to the Distant Lands of Mahar—Wheldon-olt ate the flesh of a once-living soul.

As Wheldon-olt tended to his foot, he also managed to salvage several mouthfuls of his newfound delight. He gobbled down the rest of the snail because he thought he heard the calls of his watchlings. "*Or,*" he wondered, "*Am I still repairing from the cracking?*" He immediately articulated the following questions: "*How long was I unconscious?*" "Have they followed me down?" "*Should I share with them this new living stone?*" "*Will this delight perpetuate my motion forever?*" He carefully pondered them. Given the positioning of the Great Mover in the sky and the pang of hunger he felt, he figured he had been unconscious eleven-sixteenths of an hour. As he gazed back up the mountain, he efficiently figured anew the distance and the likely path that his watchlings would have taken down if they had followed him. His calculation was that, they, having left immediately after throwing him over the ridge, could reach him any moment. *But had they come down the mountain at all?*—this was the question. As he gazed up searching for clues, he caught no sight or sound of Nimbrik-al and Bryton-duhl. "*Hadn't I just heard them?*" He returned to pay attention to his sensory synapses in order to hear better, but it was hard to differentiate the sounds from the pangs of pain he felt. One question kept pushing forward in his mind, "*Would they actually dare to come down here after what they have done to me?!!*" Pleased or not to have fallen, this thought got his ire up. He had to be ready for them.

Despite these anxieties, the soft, supple, green surroundings—so different than Wheldon-olt had known—began to overpower his newly reactivated senses; his reasoning and calculations were uncertain and fuzzy. The air was thick with rich aromas and pungent smells and oppressive, muggier than atop the mountain. He felt no breeze. The stilted air reminded him of the few journeys deep into the Northern Caverns he had taken with his watcher, Therndon-al, when then there had been more water to feed the underground springs.

Wheldon continued looking about and then spotted several other snails within a stone's throw at the edge of the clearing. They were in deep sleep, as most snails were in the afternoon, after a long night of laborious traveling and early morning supping on freshly fallen leaves; the crash had not awakened them. Hobbling over, Wheldon-olt knelt down and greedily proceeded to gorge himself on all the snails he managed to find, for there were also others nearby. Chewing on the second to last of these while holding the last snail in the clearing, suddenly Nimbrik-al and Bryton-duhl appeared in front of him.

Their journey downward had in fact commenced shortly after their mountaintop joy had turned to dreadful worry. They calculated what might have been the fate of Wheldon-olt. When they had hoped to catch a glimpse of him lumbering back up fairly quickly, and this did not happen, they had continued descending. Despite their fear of severe reprimand for throwing Wheldon-olt over the slurry ridge and because of their lostness at being alone without him, they had decided to go down after him. They climbed over the corner wall of the ridge on dry ground to avoid their slurry, just as Wheldon-olt had calculated they would. As the two worked their way downward, it was decided that, if they could strike a deal with Wheldon-olt, perhaps he might even "forget" what had happened. As they weaved in and out of the conifers slightly taller than they, they entered a small clearing. Thus, their search ended when they saw their watcher kneeling facing them.

"Hey! Ahhh ... You're a bit messed up, slurry and all!" blurted out Nimbrik-al. "And you're sitting there funny like!!! Are you intact or fractured up???"

Bryton-duhl asked awkwardly, "Yeah ... what's been your delay? We expected you up for third breakrock." He then gulped and asked, "Are you holding out on us, Wheldolt? Have you found some goodies down here?!" He laughed nervously. Nimbrik-al chuckled along worriedly, but they had no idea.

Wheldon-olt immediately stopped chewing and froze. He dared not gulp down the delight in his mouth, he thought, lest they discover it. He wanted them all for himself! But harder to hide was the snail he had just picked up in his left hand. He held it behind his leg. The snail began emerging, trying to escape his grip, and he felt its oozing stickiness. Indeed, the snail was attempting to send out a warning call to other snails, but the firm grip silenced its vibrations. Yet, it also simultaneously emitted pheromone cries of distress into the air—a warning to other snails. This olfactory alarm began wafting out of the clearing and farther into the woods.

Nimbrik-al said, "Soon it'll be time for breakrock. Come on. We can climb back up in ten-elevenths of the hour, I figure. We can make it back up before the Great Mover leaves us and slumbertyme overtakes us."

Wheldon-olt remained silent.

Bryton-duhl interpreted his silence as anger. "Oh, come on, Wheldolt. Just say something, will you? You're not upset at us, are you? You started [illegible]u've had it coming, too, the way you've treated me and Brik. [illegible]actured badly, are you?! Let's get back up top. I'm craving [illegible]st thinking about being stuck down here. Look at yourself—

the clay and slurry. You're smeared with it. And it doesn't smell 'fresh' down here."

Having said this, Bryton-duhl noticed Wheldon's wounded feet. "Ohhh! Ouch! ... Of course ... that explains it. Will these be one or two-dayers?" (Trioptic Giants measured more serious injuries by the number of days to heal.)

Wheldon-olt shrugged, chewed a bit, swallowed gently, and finally said, "I got cut up bad and my ankle is punctured through; see here by my heel. But I've been repairing and think I can stumble along alright."

"Let me have a look," said Bryton-duhl stepping closer. "Seriously, we should get back in a hurry; I'm starved just thinking of the hike back up." He strode over closer to Wheldon-olt. He glanced up noticing the Great Mover descending further into the western horizon.

"No," said Wheldon-olt, looking up at them. "I'm fine ... I just needed a rest. The Great Mover still warms me up. I'm moving again. I'll get up now." As he did so, he stumbled and dropped the snail on the ground. Immediately, it emanated a very low, deep thumping sound—an alarm for all snails nearby.

"What's that?" said Nimbrik-al alarmed, sensing very keenly the thumps through his ear holes encircling the back of his head.

Grabbing the snail again, immediately the calling stopped, effectively silencing the snail's outer shell reverberation chamber. Indeed, his firm grip made the snail powerless of audible speech. Wheldon-olt could stand it no longer. Feeling hungrier, he turned away from the twins and popped the helpless snail into his mouth and turned back with a half-smile. He realized that he was hiding nothing, for they had seen him eat it.

Still chewing, he managed to mumble out, "What?! What are you staring at, you numbstones?" He gulped. He figured it best to explain his discovery to Nimbrik-al and Bryton-duhl.

As Wheldon-olt finished his brief account, Nimbrik-al objected, "You' lying!" He paused a moment and then added calmly, "Okay, I get it. Now I understand. You're trying to trick us! Nope, I'm not falling for it."

"Yes, you're just trying to get our hopes up," Bryton-duhl chided, "and miss our last meal of the day while we look around this stinky place for some *rare* stone that you've just eaten the last one of, right?! Couldn't resist it, could you?! ... Could you??!!" Wheldon-olt remained silent. And Bryton-duhl kept asking the question "Could you??!!" until it ceased being a question and became, in fact, an observation.

So, then, at Wheldon's full disclosure and, as their own appetite increased more and more, the twins became full believers.

Hearing other thumping alarm sounds that alerted them of still more snails, Wheldon-olt limped along to and fro pointing out the delights to his watchlings. Together they hunted the sentient snails and gorged themselves for what became the main course of their third breakrock. Each found plenty of snails to be sated in the surrounding woods. They then returned to the clearing just as the Great Mover finally dropped from their sight over the ridge.

Darkness indeed settled on Sylvanwood. And so, the giants fell into deep slumber—almost as deep as death itself. They slept not only that night, but through the next day and night as well. But their sleep was not all that restful.

Chapter 3
The Silver Snails' Warning

After the rising of the Great Mover on the third day, the giants finally awoke. Wheldon-olt, dazed, was unable to remember his whereabouts. He was uncertain what day it was and whether it was dusk or dawn. The air was still cool; the morning fog resisted the bright light filling the firmament above. Thirst cut at his gullet. As he contemplated his condition, he recalled dreaming about some delicious gems he had found; no, they were delights ... crunchy, gooey delights. He erected himself and became more disoriented. On the one hand, he had never slumbered so long before; on the other hand, all typical signs for calculating time were not to be observed—he could see no dim stars on the western horizon, no distinct form of the Great Mover, no craggy range tops over which the Great Mover shone, and no leaning shadows along the Skyway. In addition to his thirst, he had a severe pang of nutrient depletion, which was quite unlike the normal exhaustion between regular breakrocks. His vision was blurry; he was only able to see the shapes of the vertical tree trunks at the edge of the clearing. He felt stiff and lacking in motion.

As he repositioned himself turning to his right, Wheldon-olt was quite wonderfully surprised to notice through the lifting fog three of the delights not far from where he sat. Fixating on them, he imagined they were moving ever closer to him. He wondered whether he was still sleeping or experiencing a waking dream. He rubbed his sight sockets.

Oddly, he began to imagine that he heard one of the snails projecting a sound at him. It was a deep low sound, quite soothing and mesmerizing if it were not so startling. He had never heard such a full, complete tonal resonance. The rhythmical and melodic sounds reverberated throughout his stony frame, and captivated his listening, as if reaching all the way to his synaptic relays. He focused intently on the sounds, which he came to realize were syllables; as he focused on them further, the syllables became words, and then the words phrases, and the phrases sentences, until he found himself swimming within a symphony of speech. He experienced a moving Voice that was new to him, and yet not unfamiliar. Deep precision and wisdom attended the Voice, like a vast reservoir of water, like a thunderous waterfall. As sudden as a lightning strike, a terrifying thought befell him, "This delight I have found is not only moving, but able to produce meaningful discourse! It is sentient!"

As the triad of snails approached Wheldon-olt, he calculated their size to be slightly larger than those he had remembered eating. But they could still fit into his hand. Most disturbing to him, however, was the protruding front column of the living thing, which itself had two more stems reaching out like branches, somewhat bulbous at the extreme ends.

"Giant of three eyes," the Voice said melodically. "What brings you downward so low to do such an abominable thing as you have done?"

Dumbfounded, Wheldon-olt stammered a reply, "I ... I ... I ..." but his voice faltered.

"We are Silver Snails of Sylvanwood, and we serve the Conductor, just as your kind once did."

Dazed, Wheldon-olt just stared, stunned. But the Voice continued, "The Conductor of this Sphere, both yours and ours, and of the celestial glories, has sent us for two purposes: first, to have you disclose your reasoning in this grave matter, if there be any reason in it; and, second, to warn you to put an end to your foolishness. If you have done this vile thing unwittingly, then stop and make amends for your own sake before more severe consequences follow. In either case, you must know that you have offended the law of the universe in the second order by your murderous behavior, by ending the motion of our kind in hopes of perpetuating your own motion, which has become a commotion."

Wheldon remained speechless.

The triad, together once again pulsed in waves to form a unified voice, "Are you unable to speak on your own behalf? We implore you to come to your senses. Confess your reasons. Stop this foolishness!"

Wheldon-olt confused, reeled inside, and was cut to his core. He sat frozen in thought.

But then, thunderous thumps and crushing of brush and trees filled the surrounding woods. Emerging through the fog in full stride, Nimbrik-al and Bryton-duhl raced into the misty clearing, shoulder-to-shoulder. Springing forward, both dove at the three snails, each grabbing one, but fumbling and fighting for the third one being batted about in the air until Bryton-duhl finally secured it. With greedy eagerness, both gulped down their prizes.

Wheldon-olt, shocked and stupefied, knew then that he was indeed fully awake.

"Too slow, Wheldolt ... too slow," Bryton-duhl managed to mutter with his mouth full, licking his lips. "You don't gotta be quick to catch these buggers, but quicker than me!"

Nimbrik-al added, "They're all over the woods. We've eaten six this morning. That's two-sevenths as many as yesterday, and it's not even the second breakrock yet! Come on, Wheldolt. It's become a game!!! Now we're all tied at nine apiece, since Bryton-duhl is the cheater that he is. I saw these three first!"

"No, you didn't!" disagreed the other.

"Yes, I did!"

Wheldon-olt remained silent.

Bryton-duhl then noticed Wheldon's blank expression and stopped. "Oh, yes. You might be thirsty. We were, too. Back that aways in full light is water, a stream—Yes, the Mover got us moving! The water's silty, but what do you expect down here?!!" He pointed back behind through the clearing, eastward, more visible now that the fog was giving way to the rising late-morning Sun. "And stream's large enough to clean yourself up. You're still quite a white slurried sight. Are you all repaired? Stand up and you'll see it." He paused and pointed, "Over there."

Shocked by their sudden appearance and eating the snails, he began to doubt whether he had indeed heard the Voice talking to him. He wondered whether he had been hallucinating, half-awake and half-asleep in a slumber state. Nevertheless, his parched palate bid him comply to follow them to quench his thirst. He slowly rose up and stood. However, his awakened central mind, elevated by the recent revelation of the Voice, wanted to scold them for eating the talking Silver Snails of Sylvanwood.

Nimbrik-al hurried him on, "Come on, Come on! Let's go. The day's a wastin'. We need to explore down here som' more! Lead the way!" he pointed.

Impulsively Wheldon-olt did as he was urged to do. His higher thoughts were suppressed to focus on immediate statisfaction. He began walking. The wounds on his foot and ankle were mainly healed. So, the three commenced a brisk gait toward the stream with Wheldon leading the way to quench his thirst and wash himself clean.

The twins followed him and continued their earlier conversation, "Well, are you sure, Bryton-duhl, that we can survive down here *alone*?"

He answered, "We three clanmates *were alone* up there," looking upwards to the slurry slope.

An awkward pause presented itself, both realizing that such a significant conversation had occurred without Wheldon-olt, their Watcher, who asked, "Bryton-duhl, what? Leave the top and stay down here? It is unnatural and beneath us to stay; the air is thick and musty down here. Don't you feel the heaviness of air?!!"

"Yeah, but I figure we can find good stone down here," he replied. "You know, the kind that Therndon-al Byrl always dreamed of finding. At the river this morning I found some edible gem nuggets along with more of these moving delights, but beware of...."

"You mean, some more Silver Snails?!" Wheldon-olt interrupted.

"Slimy Snails?" asked Bryton-duhl. "Hmmmm. Is that what you've decided to call them?"

"No, I said Silver Snails."

"Well, we thought maybe Gemwells or Forever Stones. But 'Slimy Snails' has a good ring to it. But perhaps 'Snail Slide' would be better—get it?!—since they slide down?! These delicacies will be a marketable delight up in the high marketlands. The question is how many of these are down here, and if we can collect them and grow 'em somehow, then spread the word to attract the giants back, and then how many gems we could trade for them, if, that is, they themselves don't prolong our own motion more than the common gems."

But Wheldon did not immediately reply. He kept reflecting as they walked, weaved, and ducked occasionally through the trees which he noticed were not all conifers, but many had white flaky bark with flat broad leaves. He then suddenly blurted out, "Wait ... wait a minute!" He held out his arms halting them. "I'm not sure if we should eat them at all *since* they may be living stones. They move. And haven't either of you heard *anything* from the snail stones? I mean, haven't they spoken words to you? Those three that you just...."

"No, no, no!" Bryton-duhl interrupted. "They don't say anything at all, *not really*. No, ... that's only your conscience trying to rob you of what you've dreamt to have your whole existence, true statisfaction." With a growing air of confidence, he continued, "It's like you're unable to calculate the good fortune you've encountered, Wheldolt, and a fraction of you wants to take away your enjoyment."

At that, Nimbrik-al could not keep silent, "Since when have *you* become a matherapist?!!! Are you now our watcher?" The other two looked at him in surprise; what had gotten into him!

Returning to Bryton-duhl's analysis, Wheldon-olt responded back, "What fraction of me are you talking about? That's incalculable. I am I, whole and all. No, ... I definitely heard 'em alright, just before you two came crashing in and ruined it all. Those Silver Snails were speaking to me about the Conductor and warning us to stop ending their motion...."

"Ending their motion?! That's ridiculous!" retorted Bryton-duhl. "*We've* ... okay, to give you credit ... *you've* just discovered a new kind of rock. It's a moving rock of some sort—I'll grant you that—just like we are moving ... but some of them are slower than others! Ha!" he jabbed Nimbrik-al. "But," he waxed eloquently, "they move—is all there is to it. They're like moving water, which is not alive, but makes noise; or perhaps better they're like the wind in the tunnels howling through them. Sure, it sounds as if the caves are speaking, but they're not alive. These snail rocks resonate ... or *something* ... until you touch them. It's the wind that makes their sounds, or perhaps the gooey water in them." Bryton-duhl was nearer to the truth than it knew.

Wheldon-olt shook his head in disagreement. "But a cave doesn't make articulate sounds like speech by themselves, and the motion of water is due to underground upward pressure or downward gravity, whereas these snails provide their own horizontal motion back and forth *and* turn vibrations into voice *expressing themselves in distinct words*."

Despite this counterargument, Bryton-duhl became even more recalcitrant, persisting in its own resolve. It quickly attempted to divert the issue to another matter. "But 'the Conductor'... really?! ... Really?!!" he spoke condescendingly. "That talk is merely a series of false estimations, you know, sheer guesstimations based upon the accounts of Verthana's first moving that we learned as younglings during our sojourns. The etchings, the stone runes, and the giant tales we heard at the quarry ways were for *entertainment only—merely stories*! We all knew that then, right?!!! Come on! And I would think especially you, Wheldolt, should know this. All the stories of this 'conducting stuff' is completely *incalculable*. It simply can't be true. That nonsense was only to make us sensible 'good' little giants rather than truly *'calculating'* ones. Well, I'm choosing the latter—*to be calculating*—as *indeed we have already become*. We're able to generate our own motion now—*aren't we?*—to conduct our own affairs, maybe even to have perpetual motion by eating these living stones."

Shaking his head the whole time, Wheldon-olt was yet somewhat confused by this reasoning. He remained unconvinced of it. He knew that it wasn't as simple as what Bryton-duhl had argued. Furthermore, he doubted very much whether they were "truly calculating" giants. Yet, at the same time, he hoped that somehow in fact these moving stones had now restored their motion of life forever. Perhaps his discovery of a new stone was the hand of Fate guiding him, now guiding his clan of three, to their fortune, a fortune they would bring to the Giant Race, and with profit.

Nimbrik-al, however, remained puzzled and objected once again, "But, *you wait a minute*, Bryton-duhl! We heard sounds, *too*, from some of the 'moving rocks' both when we first got here and this *very* morning. Even *I* thought I could hear words once or twice, but the sound stopped when I picked them up. You and I were *just* talking about this *this morning!*"

This inconvenient fact set Bryton-duhl aback. It blinked thrice, nodded twice, before shaking its head in disagreement. The giant was clearly conflicted and on the brink of internal fractural failure. The possibility of this inconvenient fact brought into question its articulated calculations that had already begun to solidify at the elemental chemical level into mineral pathways of solidified convictions in its core processes. So, the giant became recalcitrant; consequently, he began calculating a way out of the conundrum in order to re-secure the validity of the network of meanings it had constructed concerning these convictions.

The three giants now stepped clear out of the forest and drew nearer to the banks of the river washes.

"Oh, never mind that, Brik!" countered Bryton-duhl finally. The giant's eyes dulled. "Let's be truly calculating about this now. There were *no words*, and so there is *no worry.... No words, no worry*! Right?" He repeated these words again slowly, "*No words, no worry.*"

Its clanmates pondered this last thought, strangely affected by the simplicity of the alliteration and assonance. The sing song motto resonated somewhat convincingly for the moment.

Again Bryton-duhl repeated the idea as if settled, "No words, no worry." Who could argue with that, it thought. Seeing that this rhyming rhetoric had momentarily quieted the others, to drive the point further, it drafted and sang the following ditty,

No words, no worry;
no thoughts of slurry;
we walk and pick our way;
through the washes we seek,
foraging Ho!
To find more snails we go!

Stopping the song abruptly, the giant diverted the conversation to a reasonable explanation of the supposed talking snails. "Wheldolt, I think you're still 'mentally mending'—no insult intended!—from your cracking when you fell. That was quite a tumble. Sorry about that, by the way ... *hehe*. Many a giant has lost their ability to receive proper data and calculate rightly for weeks after such a cracking as you have had. Now, here we are. Drink up and then get cleaned up! You'll think straighter soon. Then it's time for breakrock."

And so Wheldon-olt eagerly knelt at the water to wash himself.

From a distance, many pairs of distraught eyes followed every move of the three enormous Trioptic Giants.

Stones of the River Wash, photograph by Bonnie Mitchell

Chapter 4
The Second Giant Encounter

While these Trioptic Giants were gallivanting about in the slurry lowlands, difficult decisions and brave actions were called for in the Central District of the Musselkin of Sylvanwood. The sylvan lowland plateau was bordered, as you know, to the north by slopes leading upwards to the Western Expanse with its giant Skyway, home to the Trioptic Giants, which overlooked the narrow southern swath of the slurrylands. To the west and south the lowlands were bordered by the Shining Silver Sea with its scattered islands, and to the east by the Great River and the high, black opposing Kliffs of Kalm. The lowland biosphere was home to many types of animals and particularly to two speaking creatures, the Silver Snails and the Musselkin.

The news of the previous day's events had reached the Musselkin that same evening, the day that the "snail slaughter" began, as it was so deemed. It came by way of the swift snail messenger, Curraxdem, who painfully made the perilous trek by day, nearly killing itself from dehydration since it traveled in the heat of the afternoon. Providentially, there had been a heavier than normal dew that morning, and the customary mists which accompanied the early part of the day prolonged the plentiful surface moisture while also providing the comfort of shade from the blazing sun above within the blanketing aqua sky.

The Musselkin, who are short, slender bipeds reaching upwards to five feet, would be classified by some earthen folk as wood elves. The majority had dark brown hair (almost black in appearance) and ruddy pale green faces. Some, however, had reddish brown hair with fair complexion. Their disposition was normally quite lighthearted and jovial. However, the Musselkin were prone to excitement, and under stress, to anxiety and agitation, yet enjoyed performance and oratory. They were loyal as friends and enjoyed festivities and frolicking. They were artisans, many workers of wood, and served the Conductor in the beauty of the variety of their crafts and by their faithful service to the Silver Snails. Mutually loyal to one another, these sentient species of Sylvanwood enjoyed a symbiotic relationship in which the Musselkin would care for the basic needs of the snails, tending flora and supplying foliage for them at critical times of the year (droughtyme and chilltyme) and caring for the snail youngsters before their departure to Furtivement (their rite of passage) across the Silver Sea at six months of age. This was no small task for the Musselkin, who worked together as a people to furnish foods, since the snails grew rapidly, eating voraciously and storing up fat for their journey through the sea. For the snails' part, they would teach the ways of the Conductor to the Musselkin; the snails were oracular, speaking on behalf of the Conductor and mediating the Conductor's presence for the frequent celebrations and feasts.

When Curraxdem arrived, the Musselkin were shocked by the news and were surprisingly in quite a state of unreadiness. I say "surprisingly" because once before they had in fact encountered face-to-face a single giant of the trioptic kind during a fateful week exactly one year prior to the day. Musselman Bydelus, who was now currently Chief Governor of the first city of the Central District, had been there and had orchestrated a plan to win the affections of the giant, which failed miserably. When this had happened, he was acting as mere governor of the second city, with fewer resources and a small following. Now, however, after the annual change of governors and first cities, he acted serendipitously as Chief Governor of the first city and was exuberantly elated to have a second chance to win the affection of not one, but three powerful, towering giants. For that whole year he had dreamt and pondered, planned and schemed, how to handle the giants differently, should a next opportunity present itself, and to what ends he would employ them, if he would encounter them ever again. This preoccupation became for him more than a prayer if not even his mantra; but he kept the rest of the populace in the dark in order to better control the situation when such another chance might occur.

Now, dear readers, it is incumbent upon us as narrators to relate currently that fateful first encounter that had occurred exactly one year prior. What follows in this and the following two chapters is what Greek Historians call an extended "digression"; it is in the form of a sustained "flashback." It is not pleasant for us to recount such. You have been forewarned.

One year earlier, the snails had spotted a lone single giant near the eastern riverbeds along the slurry washlands. This visibly disturbed the Musselkin, because their only source of information about the giant race were the seldom-told stories by the snails, whose wisdom on most matters ran very deep, partly due to their extensive travel (over land and under the sea to distant regions) and especially due to their complete devotion and intimate relation to the heavenly Conductor. Moreover, the snails knew all too well the complete history of the giants and their fall, yet they related just the bare necessities of this history to the Musselkin. The Musselkin were apprehensive of the thought of another race of creatures ten times their size. To this partial knowledge were added popular stories of the giants, which were regular fare around campfires. Just how alarmed they should be was yet to be realized, if only because of the evil which would enter among their own kind and into their own hearts, turning one against the other in a deathly struggle.

The single giant's lumbering presence immediately received the highest attention of the Chief Governor of the Musselkin, Governor Praktor. He quickly sent scouts to study the creature's enjoyments, learn of his habits and intentions, and to discover whether he would present any harm to the Musselkin or Silver Snails. To them, it would be inconceivable that the creature would be a foe to fight, for they knew no evil and only knew "accidents" that might harm someone but would be soothed and quickly healed.

Every morning the giant would descend the slopes, spend the better part of the day at or near the riverbeds, scooping up large quantities of rock and soil, sorting them, and packing a large satchel bag sewn of enormous leaves from some plant unknown in Sylvanwood. He would then climb back up the mountain just before dusk. They observed, too, that he nimbly ingested tiny stones, either from those he had brought down in his bag or from among the river gems that he had found. This behavior was observed on three successive days.

'Giant Awash' plankillism style by Musselman Doriyan Mopelwinker

On the third evening, after gathering all the intelligence on the Trioptic Giants up to that point in time, Praktor called a conclave of all the Musselkin in their capital town of Kerr to decide their course of action. The Silver Snails were amply represented, having their emissaries present.

It was difficult to bring the meeting to order—clusters of Musselkin dotted the outdoor chambers along the glade chattering excitedly. Nerves were on edge as Praktor called the assembly to order, saying:

"Musselkin of Kerr, and the neighboring conurbations, it is under grave circumstances that we have called this conclave—the specifics of which are known to most of you. Exactly three days ago, the snails reported the descent of a three-eyed giant along the northern slurryways, who daily has walked eastward to the central river washes and spent most of his day there. Our intelligence sources have observed him digging up rock. Three times he has rerouted rivulets when excavating and unearthing rocks as large in diameter as the great Cedars along our western lands."

At this, gasps of surprise came from the attendees at the thought—all except Bydelus the Governor of Nimbyn, the second city of the central region. Bydelus marveled at these colossal feats and imagined the brute strength and possible accomplishments of the giant.

"Yes, it is quite shocking!" continued Praktor. "The mere size of the giant and his strength is amazing, even glorious, reflecting the greatness of our Conductor. But it could easily ruin our entire realm, and, easier still, the habitat of our beloved snails by destroying the plants they eat. But let me continue with some good news—there has been no reason to suspect that the giant will give injury to us. Just please stay away, lest he inadvertently step or kneel down on you. On several occasions, observers have confirmed that the giant saw some of our largest wild creatures—the bouley and long-necked deer—and took no interest in them. One Musselkin informant, whom we deem to be most trustworthy, Dernal, standing among us, also believes the giant to have seen his very own person while in a clearing; upon doing so, the giant stopped his work, sat up, stared at Dernal for a moment, shook his head side-to-side, and continued in his labor.

"The shaking of his head is a bit troubling—What might it mean, indeed? In the giant manner of things, it may be a greeting of some kind, or a sign of puzzlement or dislike, or a warning, or something else. So, although not necessarily a positive sign, taken as a whole, the encounter seems to suggest to our most learned Musselkin that the three-eyed giant is not concerned about us, but is on some other errand or quest. And so, it is of utmost priority for us to determine for certain what it is he wants and whether we might be of some assistance—yes, assistance—while at the same time somehow preventing him from any serious redirection of the streams, upon which our foliage farms depend. We cannot wait another day because the consequences are simply too great, as you all understand."

Praktor then paused, as many Musselkin began jumping excitably and raising their hands. A few began blurting out questions uncontrollably, but certainly forgivably, due to the circumstances.

"Is there more than one giant? Are others coming?" asked one.

"Has he been eating the bigger stones, and the fishes, too?" queried another.

"How tall is he really? Does he top the northern cedars?" one blurted out.

"One giant; no fishes to our knowledge; not quite as tall, fifty feet is all," replied Praktor. "Now, please remain calm. We must yet hear from our beloved snail friends tonight, but let me allow a few questions pertaining strictly to the observations of the giant, one at a time please."

At this several Musselkin were recognized to offer their questions, which ranged from the unanswerable due to their limited knowledge ("What is the nature of the third central eye?") to the ridiculous ("Is his hair bronze or gold?" In fact, he had no hair, but a brownish encrusted top).

Governor Bydelus was then recognized, being as he was the governor of the second city of Nimbyn, and he offered these sentiments:

"The municipality of Nimbyn is grateful for Kerr's active and cautious leadership at this delicate moment, even if overly so. The circumstances are uncertain—to be sure—and to most of us very frightening beyond any challenge previously encountered. But, on the other hand, they may represent something less from which to be cured than an opportunity and remedy to be applied, a salve, so to speak. We Musselkin are in need of several endeavors beyond our expertise to finish. Although we excel in our artistic crafts, we have, of late, begun to long for more suitable environments that would make our work more decorative and enjoyable. We hope to improve upon our circumstances. It may very well be that this giant would offer his services to us in exchange for mutual benefits. Has the governor of Kerr and his counselors considered what opportunity may be presenting itself for our benefit and whether or not these very circumstances may have their source in the hand of the Conductor?"

Praktor suddenly realized this mini speech had ended; Bydelus's line of inquiry was not entirely unexpected, and the crowd hushed to hear the response. Praktor paused several moments to gather his thoughts before approaching the podium to reply, turning to look squarely at Bydelus as he did so:

"We must not get ahead of ourselves here, Governor Bydelus, in being either overly cautious with inaction or overly optimistic with reckless regard, as you have said 'to improve upon our circumstances.' We must be content in our habitations as we have every reason to be. Praise be to the Conductor! Given the gravity of the potential damage to be done, it is my best counsel that we indeed walk very cautiously in this unfamiliar territory. Your comments, Governor Bydelus, and question really anticipate two other needful topics of discussion this evening: how exactly to approach the giant and how best to discern the will of the Conductor in this matter. Now, before turning to the former matter in our closed governors' session—which will follow this present one in order to address this latter topic—discerning the will of the Conductor—let me give the floor to the honorable Representative Decordem of the Silver Snails."

It would have been obvious to any observer that the presence of the snail approaching the center was indeed a great comfort to the Musselkin. A sustained hush fell upon them all as they settled down and stopped hopping about. Hearts were calmed and minds eased at the very presence of the snail who reminded them of the Conductor with Whom they also regularly enjoyed companionship through the snails and the green flames of the sedge achenes. These orchestrated the Conductor's tune for many routine and new, challenging occasions. Now, Decordem's presence before them also reminded the Musselkin what was at stake—the snail habitations. All hushed and watched the steady glide of the snail, a couple feet taller than any of them, as it approached the center of the stage.

Chapter 5
Decordem's Speech

The shells of the Silver Snails were wonderfully made. From afar they were gloriously white with a silver tint, whereby they derived their name. However, when struck by light just right, the shells shimmered in various hues of pinks, purples, oranges, and teals. But this spectacle was not often seen, for the sun's rays rarely struck them. The snails kept themselves in the shaded areas during the daylight, often slumbering on until sunset when they began foraging and fellowshipping. Their feeding and friendly conversation would last throughout the night and early morning.

The flickering firelight this particular night simulated the glorious effect on Decordem's rounded glowing exterior as the snail approached the center stage. Then, after a brief pause, Decordem's two eye columns extended fully along the top of his mantle and leaned towards the hushed crowd. His eyes separated and returned, making notes on the atmosphere and mood of the Musselkin. The moment was ripe with expectancy, and the snail began throbbing the still night air with soothing audible vibrations, turning motion into sound:

"Governor Praktor and all Musselkin, blessings from the Conductor and prudence to us all on this somber evening! The Conductor with Almighty Wisdom made our lands and endowed all fauna and flora that moves within it with life, occupation, and freedom for our mutual cohabitation. The Conductor has taught us that with these freedoms come boundaries. It has been made known to us that we creatures have been granted special endowments for the stewardship of all of life in keeping with the good intentions of the

Conductor's will. We snails and you Musselkin have enjoyed a most wonderful friendship along the lowlands bordering the coasts of the Silver Seas since the Foundation of our world. In the mountain Highlands, the Trioptic Giants have been given the sun, what they warmly call the Great Mover, to animate their actions and illuminate their path, the Skyway. They have been given their freedom to explore and range, to work their mighty feats and enjoy their mutual labors, to raise their own kind, to craft and consume their rock, and for our benefit to fill the slurry ways that help to nourish our young most essentially."

Pausing momentarily, he continued slowly and with sadness, "But by reasons not entirely knowable to us—indeed, it is completely perplexing and irrational, and words are lacking—but I ... must sadly say ... a boundary, a grave boundary has been breached on the boarders of the giants' land. But this breach of boundary is only symptomatic of a previous faltering—or really falling*s*—and from now on we sentient creatures will be *estrang*ed from one another...."

At this last statement, a simultaneous swell of ill-ease, discomfort, and some consternation came over the Musselkin. A few, perceiving the gravity of these statements, blurted out, interrupting Decordem, "Speak clear words to us...!" and "What does '*irrational*' and '*estranged*' mean?" And, "These new words are ... are ... not '*life*' words!"

As more and more kinsfolk voiced such questions and remarks, jumping up and down with increasing agitation, the snail began to retract its eyes and then withdrew its head into its shell. Observing this and feeling the mood change, the Musselkin hushed one another. A sadness fell upon them; crying commenced, not the crying of ecstatic joy they had known or the tearful crying that would come with physical injury, as happened on occasion, that accompanied the pain marking injury. Rather, deep sobs of regret and profound lostness overcame most of them.

Then Musselkin Governor Praktor made his way to the conical form of the Silver Snail Decordem and whispered something. With head and eye stems again extending, the familiar throbbing pitched again into recognizable words that so often prior had offered relief to the Musselkin, but these new words themselves were not soothing. "My dear friends, let me try again to speak in a way that is understandable and clear. 'Irrational' means that it does not make good 'sense'; the thinking may be permanently 'harmed' and jumbled and misdirected towards things that are not Conductor-worthy. And 'estranged'—well, this word means that we will become as dangerous strangers to one another, even when having once been friends ... maybe even injurious strangers, intent on hurting one another *on purpose.*" At this last word, gasps filled the assembly and puzzled faces looked at Decordem and one another.

"*On purpose?!!*" one of the Musselkin blurted out, perplexed and confused.

"Now," Decordem continued, "as to what *this* means, it may help to think of matters this way: The situation is like a stubbed toe that ouches, or someone tripping that results in a bump on the head, or a collision or accident in which one gets *hurt*—this has happened to many of you, and if not, it is still something that you have all witnessed, and so thus *experienced. But* a time is coming, and is now here, when some 'collision' or 'accident' is actually *wanted* and *done on purpose*, perhaps obvious or not obvious during a game or in jest, but it's done to gain *something* for oneself *at the expense of another.*"

He paused. One could hear nothing but the faintest of breaths, but all felt in their own chests each pounding heart. Decordem continued, "*This* is what has occurred *on purpose* and for us it is now named as '*evil'*—a new idea for you. '*Evil'* is not merely the opposite of 'good' as in 'bad to be avoided.' *This* you have always understood that *bad* is to be avoided. Rather, *evil* means being *bad on purpose at the expense of the other.* Until now, you've known many types of things—good things and bad things to be avoided—including many *new* things. But something now *also* new exists—although it does not *really exist* on its own. This *new* thing, I am telling you, is not simply *contrary* to the good and thus bad as in not-good, but this we must name as '*evil*,' that is, '*bad on purpose*.' So, from now on, something *new* may not simply be *good* or *not-good* as it has been thus far in our life together, like in the joy of discovery during the voyage of learning that our young ones undertake at their furtivement, or the pummeling waves that are not good for you Musselkin. Yes, something '*new*' may indeed be something different than good or not-good, but what must be named '*evil*.' And so, moreover, as soon as we know *for certain* that this new thing is being or doing *bad on purpose*, at that same moment we must rightly call such a thing '*evil*.'" The snail paused and said slowly, "*Evil* is *doing* or *being* or *crossing into* the bad *on purpose*."

The snail stopped and decompressed its extended neck and eye stems but then elongated these once again. "Finally—it must be said—there will be many other '*evil things*' that will befall us Silver Snails—and even *done to us*! And, yet, even worse than this, new evils will be *taught*, *learned*, and *encouraged by* Musselkin *among* Musselkin, *even evil aimed against us Silver Snails*."

At this, the snail paused once again, deeply pained by this last prospect. Even so, it extended its eyes fully and head completely with a firmness of conviction to convey courage and hope to the Musselkin. His eyes canvassed the whole audience and he concluded, "Now, I urge you all, to stay near the good that you have known, and embrace rightly relating to one another that the Conductor will show you. Continue in your devotion to the Conductor in the joy of your hearts (as you well know that joy!) and you will not falter as the giants have. All the while, avoid the new that is 'evil'; you will know something as evil by the cost of life it exacts from the other that is unwanted, harmful, and not for good. Continue to think, feel, and live; but be sure to continue to distinguish between what is good and what is not good; don't violate boundaries *into evil.* I urge you not to do evil in the sight of Conductor so that you may dwell ever in Sylvanwood. Know, finally, that whatever may befall us, the Conductor will rightly relate to us, and *be good* despite the evil, for the Conductor's goodness is *bigger* than any evil, and His kindness endures forever."

All understood equally the gravity of what had been said and foretold, but not all equally received the words of the snail. Governor Bydelus did not succumb to the common feeling but became increasingly agitated by the speech as he was listening. Wanting to turn the words back upon the speaker, he answered back to Decordem, "You have spoken that 'we will *now* be estranged.' In what way do you mean?!"

"Sir Bydelus of the second city," Decordem solemnly responded back, "Why have you now said, 'we will *now* be estranged'? Thus says the Conductor, 'If you, Bydelus, continue to do rightly, your good countenance will remain. However, evil is even *now* forming its deadly fruit. Don't pick and eat it, or it will *eat you up*. Be careful what you want and make, for from what you ill-create will ill-fortune make.'"

Hesitating a moment broadening his gaze, Decordem added, "And now, dear friends, a poem for you has come to me in meditation while preparing this speech.

When a watcher tumbles from the sky,
Beware the blight of snails is nigh.
Grey slurry then abandons the loam;
The coming drought ends their home.
Essence of time is then to find,
Four ones anew of an alien kind.
The Last One ends in a spectacle,
In theater made, but mere half full,

To work release, turn famine to feast,
And so redeem the lost and the least.

"Therefore," Decordem concluded, "know that the Word from the Conductor is like dew on our path and like light upon your plants: *It* will prevail. We must take heart at His Word." The snail's eyes drooped as it ended. The shimmer faded from its shell as it slid slowly across the center to the edge of their assembly hall.

The Musselkin's murmuring about the meaning of the verse filled the air.

Immediately, at Praktor's signal, the ten governors and governesses exchanged nods of agreement, and went to session to discuss plans how to engage the giant and to ascertain his intentions. These leaders were district overseers according to roughly equivalent partitions from natural topographic landmarks. The Central District was split into two jurisdictions with corresponding cities, a first and a second, governed by Praktor and Bydelus, respectively. The primacy of these cities and jurisdictions alternated with each year's selection of their governor. Four Districts of North, South, East, and West surrounded the Central District, with a first and second governor in each. Selection of the governors each year was on the basis of "divine calling" at local shrines among the meadow sedges with two or three witnesses for confirmation. As with the Central District, the place of first and second city and first and second governor respectively, alternated with the selection of a new governor each year. This was the nature of the Musselkin government to promote equal opportunity and distributed representation.

Eventually, after much debate with a very close vote of six to four, Bydelus's particular plan was adopted. He had prepared it with five of his closest associates among whom were his closest ally, Kataloas, governor of the first city of the North District, and Byrn, governor of the second city of the East District.

Chapter 6

The First Giant Encounter

The next morning the Musselkin began preparations. Within three days all was made ready. Upon a platform was constructed an image nearly ten times larger than any Musselkin; it was a perfect representation of the Trioptic Giant. The artistic expertise of the Musselkin was wonderfully reflected in the craftsmanship which was based on meticulous observation of the giant. Despite their fascination, the typical creative fancy of the artisans was carefully checked; absolute accuracy was needed down to the most intimate detail of the giant. The plan of Bydelus demanded accuracy, because the image was to woo the giant into "kindness" and "generosity" towards the Musselkin. In fact, Bydelus wanted to secure the giant's goodwill to perform monumental tasks, such as constructing generous building structures, bridges over topographical impasses, the plowing of fields for easier harvests, and an elaborate inter-district roadway structure to connect and unify the nation. He spent hours thinking to himself, "Why ... the possibilities are innumerable!"

The effigy's head mirrored the giant's. It was round, although with a small bumpy bulge on the right side. The top of the head was uneven and crumbly looking. There was no hair, but one could see fissures running from the face backwards which darkened and aged the image's already stark facial features. No outward ear appendages were seen (as the Musselkin had), but rather a string of holes started at each side of the head and continued around meeting at the backside. The eyes of the trioptic image were most stunning and realistic. The three eye slits formed an isosceles triangle in the contoured and rough face. Above the eyes arched a single ridge that formed what looked like an eyebrow. The eyes were dark and had a sad, mysterious blankness about them. A rounded nub, making the face even more Musselkin-like, was placed in proportion under the central eye, and equidistant from the other two. Whether this functioned like a nose could not be determined by its appearance since there were no nostrils. The mouth of the giant was below this nose nub. It was fashioned into a somber smile—one that had been observed by the Musselkin on several occasions when the giant had found a small gemstone among the stones or buried in the rivulet muds of the water washes. No individual teeth had been seen. Rather the giant had two shining metallic-looking bands on top and bottom just inside the oral cavity, presumably for crushing stone.

The neck of the effigy was broad and short and led into a pair of shoulders that were bulky. Terrible strength appeared to reside in the appendages that formed arms of disproportionate length. The left arm was slightly longer, which puzzled the Musselkin. Unbeknownst to them, the shorter arm had resulted from an injury during an accident after which the remarkable regenerative capabilities of the Trioptic Giant race had begun to regrow the arm. The agile digits at the end of each arm varied in number—the left had six and the right only five somewhat smaller ones, again due to this injury. These digits exxtended from large, pudgy palms. The torso of the replica was truncated and thick and unremarkable. Legs like massive tree trunks descended from the torso and were interrupted only by saucer-shaped and dimpled patellae at the middle of each leg. These natural knee-pads were well suited for the common position of labor for harvesting stone in rugged terrain. Terminating the legs were three toed triangular feet that oddly rounded out the Trioptic Giant's appearance of angularity from forehead to toe. The Musselkin named their creation "Trey."

Hand-chiseled from prepared trees that were glued together, the effigy from the front was a near perfect representation of the real giant as far as the height and girth were concerned. The only difference between the two was in their coloring. Now, on this particular detail, Bydelus gave special attention to what might be most attractive to the giant in order to help show off the gift for what it was. The most precious commodity of the Musselkin was collected from a cave near the far eastern river washes. From this commodity was made paint, thrice applied, which gilded the effigy. This commodity was gold. The finished statue reflected the sunlight brightly, although remained unmoved by it. In appearance, Trey was like an Olympian god.

However, the design, craftsmanship, and construction had been the easiest part of the Musselkin's preparations. The difficulties lay in the effigy's transportation, the best determination of its destination, and the timing of its presentation as a gift to the giant. Felled logs were used for transporting it, upon which the figure could be rolled. Hundreds of Musselkin were employed for this. Never had such an engineering feat been seen among the Musselkin. The inspiration for this aspect, in addition to using gilded paint, had come to Bydelus in a flash of insight at one of the bush shrines, which had burned redder than ever before that occasion, a color he had discovered just recently. This new color differed from the standard green flame.

But these were not the only preparations. As further gifts to the giant, special gems and metal ores were created to offer as food since they often saw the giant eat each of these items. For special effect, gilded spheres would be tossed to the giant as final offerings when the image was shown to him.

During these preparations, an unprecedented tragedy occurred late one day while organizing how to set the effigy aright. The Musselkin governor, Kataloas, was crushed to death as the figure toppled on him, and so he ceased moving completely and for good. He had simply died, and he was not healed; no one treated the injuries since they were too extreme. This was very odd, because death was completely unknown to the Musselkin, who had hitherto enjoyed deathless existence until then. For three days a special healing ceremony was held with several Silver Snails presiding. Little comfort could be gained from their presence, however; the Conductor did not have any life or encouragement for their endeavors. Certain Musselkin were planted in the crowds to interrupt any contrary word of the snails attempted to warn them of their folly. So completely unnerved by this strange event were the Musselkin that they nearly abandoned the entire project.

However, Bydelus prevailed upon his kinsfolk, a nation now on the rise, by introducing the thought that Kataloas would now obtain immediate heavenly access to the Conductor, much like the Silver Snails had presently, and he would exercise his skill in the celestial realms for their nation's benefit; and that it was now the moment for the Musselkin nation to attain its full maturity into perfection. At the same time, Bydelus insinuated blame of his death upon the snails, arguing that the snails should have helped them in the project and should have generally contributed more to the well-being of the Musselkin nation rather than simply being cared for by them; and that failure for healing pointed to the snails' lack of goodwill, which was a new idea that was not true, but indeed the very evil that the snails had forewarned them about—a bad thing done on purpose. He introduced new words like "hypocrite," and "liar," and "fake." All these fallacious arguments later helped Bydelus secure the Musselkin's goodwill towards him while simultaneously creating widespread apathy, if not outright antagonism, towards the once beloved silver snails.

When the day had been determined to reveal the effigy, the Musselkin camp reverberated with excitement and trepidation. The performance would need to be carried through perfectly. Scouts had spotted the giant making his way eastward; they had determined the giant was progressively moving in their direction working along the river washes. The Musselkin had found a dry clearing among bush to lay the giant image down opposite to the next calculated working location across the shallow river. A progressive lever system had been devised that would allow the Musselkin to upright the image vertically in good timing. The Musselkin had practiced the maneuver several times the previous day until success was nearly all but assured.

At the first of dawn, they executed the maneuver for the last time. Two groups of ten first lifted up the back of the head of the image, as two other groups of ten positioned carefully placed poles. With these poles in place, the first groups picked up and used slightly longer poles switching the weight onto their two poles. The first groups, thus relieved, continued the process. This went through ten stages.

At this point the image was almost erect, and it remained only for a final push by two groups at the front while the other two groups repositioned and received the image with their two poles from the back. This set the figure completely upright. In practice, this final step proved the most difficult, since the figure could teeter and fall, and fall fatally on any of the scampering Musselkin as had been Kataloas's fate in their practice. But this last time the two groups, which had just been relieved, quickly ran to the back and wrestled with the two long poles aiming them at the enormous armpits of the effigy. At the signal, the two groups at the front surged the figure forward; the back groups then aimed to receive the tottering mass. All looked well until the right pole missed the armpit but fortunately found a hold higher up in one of the ear notches. That group surged forward, wheeling to their right to prevent the figure from spinning to its left and likely falling on them.

Bydelus, who was directing the maneuvers, ran in and single-handedly held the heel of the image's left foot, pushing and heaving upwards. As the back pole arched and creaked, Bydelus grunted and managed to stabilize the figure. The effigy finally edged back and tottered into its right position. It had indeed appeared that with super musselman strength Bydelus alone had righted the image and saved the day. A cheer arose among the crews just as a scout ran into their midst to announce the giant's imminence; he was very near.

As was typical in the lowland river washes, the mornings were misty along certain shaded stretches until the mid-morning sunlight burned away the fog. The giant was kneeling on the sunlight bank and excavating along its shoreline. He looked like a child digging at the beach, amassing mounds of earth in piles around him. Occasionally, he paused and reached into the river to wash off some particular "find"—a gem or other edible stone—only to put it into his large leaf satchel. This satchel was not included on the image of the effigy; Bydelus was terribly vexed with himself for this omission.

Then the sun began to work its magic and the mists retreated. Nervous Musselkin on makeshift rafts began to push across the shallow stream with poles. Onboard they had an assorted collection of gems, ores, and gilded gifts. This required tremendous courage, for by nature the Musselkin were land lovers.

The giant continued his excavations and procedures. The rafts, with some intermittent splashing, arrived at the bank closest to it. One musselman fell overboard but scrambled onto shore and lay down afraid to look up. The rest waited some fifteen minutes, anxiously staring at the giant, each other, and back across the stream. The mist continued to burn away as the giant persisted in his excavations. Worried glances and gesturing, which grew frantic in their motions and emotions, went back and forth from the rafts to the opposite shoreline where Bydelus and the rest of the Musselkin watched nervously. Now the effigy was fully ablaze by the sun's rays in its radiance. The giant, in response to this new source of light, paused suddenly and slowly and eerily rotated its head and glared blankly at the image in the meadow across the stream. Slowly rising to his feet, the giant stood fifty feet tall and froze himself stunned.

Bydelus interpreted this as favorable appreciation for the gift and then began to cheer. Others followed his example from the shoreline. The giant then noticed the funny little creatures jumping and cheering on the opposite shore. A queer look came over his face. At that signal, the Musselkin in the rafts began tossing and flinging their stone "gifts" towards the giant. His gaze then lowered to take in these nearest Musselkin. One gilded stone reached his toes. He bent over and reached for it and stopped. The Musselkin continued their onslaught of flinging and tossing their precious offerings. Gathering courage, they bettered their range and actually began to pelt the feet of the giant!

At this, the giant looked up in terror at them and then back up at the gilded image, and stammered out, "No, not to me!" And, whirling about, he bolted away and scrambled up the nearby sloping mountainside. In the giant's escape, an avalanche tumbled down after him, with a few broken rocks reaching and splashing into the stream, nearly reaching the rafts. The kinfolk frantically pushed their way back to the opposite shore, propelled also by the waves from splashing, falling rocks The dust of the debris filled the quaint washland valley as the giant scurried up the mountain slope to safety. In the opposite direction, the Musselkin ran for cover into the woods, as far away from the terrified and terrifying giant as possible. In their retreat, all of them could hear the echoes of the giant huffing, puffing, and grunting with rocks tumbling down as it scrambled up. But, Bydelus remained and watched on, completely demoralized at the giant scurrying away and quickly gaining altitude up the mountain. The opportunity for his greatness ascended with it, out of his grasp. He had failed and failed miserably.

For days, weeks, and months later, the Musselkin pondered why the giant left in such a hurry and what he had actually said. They understood the giant's statement to be "No, *it's* not me" in reference to the effigy. Thus, they concluded that their gilded image had simply not resembled the giant closely enough. Bydelus brooded upon his failure to replicate the giant's satchel. But, in fact, this detail was not the failure; rather gold was the bane of the giants, a stiffening poison. If sufficiently exposed to the ore, the

Trioptic Giants stopped moving completely. Gold had polluted their Pool of Emergence and had subsequently led to their eventual loss of motion. So, the giant had rather said, "No, not to me!" as in "I'm not going to turn into a pillar of gold!"

From atop the mountain the watchling giants had heard the ascent of their watcher and peered down below. When he emerged over the slurry ridge, he ran past them and continued running eastward away from them shouting, "Beware the stiffening, poison ore!!!" They, however, failed to follow him, not sure what his warning had meant exactly and whether he was himself sufficiently infected or not. Instead, they watched him disappear around the bend in the Skyway, never to return again.

If you, brave reader, have not yet figured out, this terrified Trioptic Giant was the very watcher, Therndon-al Byrl, who had then abandoned our Wheldon-olt, Bryton-duhl, and Nimbrik-al. And, we have just finished explaining how it came to pass that when these three watchling giants appeared along the washes of Sylvanwood, the Silver Snails and Musselkin were not without both a forewarning and a hopeful promise in the form of verse from the Conductor through Decordem, worth repeating again:

When a watcher tumbles from the sky,
Beware the blight of snails is nigh.
Grey slurry then abandons the loam;
The coming drought ends their home.
Essence of time is then to find,
Four ones anew of an alien kind.
The Last One ends in a spectacle,
In theater made, but mere half full,
To work release, turn famine to feast,
And so redeem the lost and the least.

Reader, we must now turn your attention to another aspect of this odd story, but before doing so, let us summarize the sequence of events thus far: Therndon-al Byrl, the watcher of Wheldon-olt, Bryton-duhl and Nimbrik-al, descended the highland mountains to the lowlands of Sylvanwood in search of precious stones to perpetuate his motion of life. At his frightful encounter with the Musselkin when seeing the frozen, golden giant effigy, he fled thinking that these little creatures were targeting him next to end his motion, and thus he fled far away abandoning his clan of four. Wheldon-olt, then, feebly watched over the remaining clan of three while continuing his search for better stones. A year later to the day and hour Wheldon-olt, after angering his watchlings Bryton-duhl and Nimbrik-al, provoked them to toss him over the slurry ridge and tumble down into the Sylvanwood lowlands. He happened to fall (literally) upon the Silver Snails and found them delectable. And thus, he and his clan violated the law of the universe of the second order by killing and eating as many Silver Snails as they could find. Rightly alarmed, the Musselkin and the remaining Silver Snails gathered to discuss how best to handle the deteriorating situation, as we have related.

'Trioptic Giant' (Therndon), sedgepen by Musselwoman Dwendil Merryflower

From these events, you, reader, might appropriately be asking several questions: "Will Wheldon-olt, the Trioptic Giant, come to his senses?" "What further evil will governor Bydelus devise?" "How will the Conductor begin to remedy these evil decisions and sad events if remedy is even possible?" All we can urge now is "Patience!" For we can tell you, dear reader, that this strange story will become even stranger still since it will intersect with the lives of earthen girls and boys, some willingly, some unwillingly, but all providentially.

PART II

The Entrance of the Earthen Youth

Chapter 7

The Mitchells and their Friends

The Friday afternoon was ending too fast. The huge playground spread out half the size of a football field. Children were everywhere shouting, jumping, dodging, dropping, skipping, swinging, and laughing. It was a cacophony of activity. Amid this frolicking, something much more serious was being planned—an attempt to find the perfect hiding place and avoid capture. The Mitchell kids and their friends were in their last round of "hide and capture." They had received the standard five-minute warning from their moms, which, if they were lucky, would be tripled and really mean another fifteen minutes of the game. It was time enough for a final round. The three girls—Bonnie Mitchell (15), her little sister Guinevere (8), and their friend Paige Edwards (15)—had agreed to play the boys' game in the afternoon under the condition that the four boys would play the girls' game later that evening. Thomas Mitchell (14), his brothers Troy (12), Tanner (8—a fraternal twin to Guinevere), and their friend Archer (13), the brother of Paige, had challenged the girls to play their game first.

The capture part consisted in each team finding the one hiding member of the other team and dragging him or her back to the common base. Often a wrestling match ensued, with reinforcements coming to the rescue from both teams. The two teams strategized carefully for this final round. The three girls agreed that Guinevere, the youngest, should hide. Bonnie and Paige were more "into" the finding and chasing of the game play anyway. Guinevere had a disposition to distraction and daydreaming. All they needed to do was to help her find the right place to hide, and they would take care of the rest even though outnumbered by the younger boys. They had found the perfect spot on the far south side of the playground below the towering wooden play structures. It was a neglected upturned rowboat, and Bonnie had seen that it was quite possible for a little person like Guinevere to squeeze under the hull facing away from the center of the playground and out towards the field full of flowering dandelions. Bonnie had pointed out the spot earlier to Guinevere who quickly made her way there during the final "eyes-shut" countdown; her twin brother Tanner found his spot behind a tree bordering the west side of the playground.

Guinevere scrambled under the boat and found it quite cozy. At least there were no broken bottles, pieces of gum, or spiders—not that she minded arachnids, but not in such close quarters. Settling in, she felt quite safe from capture. So, Guinevere soon began to look dreamily upon the sunny field spread out before her. Floating seeds and flying bees buzzed and meandered. The din and sounds of the playground faded from a scene she began to imagine. Like her favorite spot near home, she envisioned a stream with birds and gentle, tumbling rocks along a bank watered with rivulets flowing from a dense forest of rich, green foliage of exotic ferns and large leafed plants. Upon one she imagined herself walking—no gliding—along as a bright snail, not just any snail, but a regal one. Her shell shimmered and the trail behind her glistened while she stopped on the edge of her leaf as like a throne overlooking her domain. She was a powerful snail, one that despite her size was in fact the stewardess of this stream world, the Snail Queen.

Her vision continued imagining a delicate green dragonfly flitting about but landing on a rock on the bank only to be ensnared in the slim trap of the Grey Slug, her nemesis. The slug approached greedily. It cruelly mocked the queen, bearing its fangs, as the dragonfly struggled to escape its clutches. But how would she save her subject? Suddenly, the sun was blocked, and Guinevere was overshadowed by a human form. An enormous arm descended and grabbed her. She was snatched up and squeezed. Guinevere, the Snail Queen, had been found under the boat and was being dragged out by Troy, with Thomas and Archer approvingly running up to them.

Guinevere didn't struggle much at first; Troy held her fast and was much stronger. But she could scream, and this she did with all her might: "I'm caught!!! I'm caught!!! Bonnie and Paige, *I'm caught!!!!*" When Troy put his hand over her mouth too gruffly, she bit it.

"Ouch! You little ... little *blockhea*d!" he yelled angrily. But it was too late—Paige and Bonnie had already responded to her cry.

Bonnie stopped and yelled: *"Go, Paige, go!!!!* I see Tanner. Slow them down! I can get Tanner to base before they can get Guinevere there." So, the two split up.

Tanner saw Bonnie coming but could not leave his hiding spot until touched by someone from the other team—this was the rule. He hedged on leaving just before she arrived, however. But, Bonnie grabbed him and immediately began tickling him. She then repositioned and began carrying and then dragging him to the base, periodically tickling his armpits. He was helpless. The girls would win.

Thomas and Archer were conflicted what to do seeing Bonnie running at Tanner's hiding spot. So, they tried to help Troy as he brusquely carried Guinevere screaming and kicking and biting the whole time.

Paige ran towards them, targeted Thomas knees, wrapped them up as her dad had taught her, and tackled him down to the tire-tread covered playground with such force that he got a taste of the black stuff. She held tight. She had practiced tackling her dad (a football coach) and brother Archer, and it proved useful now. She liked Thomas and enjoyed tackling him just a little bit too much.

"That's it! That's it!" Thomas shouted. "You're going down, Paige!" This was just what she had hoped for. She let him go and ran away,

Thomas chasing her. Archer, always wanting to get even with his sister, followed after Thomas.

So, Troy was left with the kicking and biting Guinevere and he had had enough. "Ouch! You little blockhead! *Stop that!"* He finally let go of her.

"Can't you think of something better to call me?!" Guinevere shouted and ran away.

"No ... it fits your square head quite well." He shouted and chased her.

Guinevere, free now, dodged him once and then twice, but Troy cornered her in. She then saw Bonnie dragging Tanner and made a beeline straight to her.

Thomas couldn't catch Paige, who was fast; so, he decided to settle the score by getting Guinevere back to base and winning the game. Looking around and seeing Archer behind him, he motioned to get Guinevere who was followed by Troy, running towards Bonnie who was dragging Tanner.

They all converged just yards from a huge oak tree, which was the base with a circle scraped around it. They grabbed, pushed, screamed, and tumbled across into the circle in a pile of arms and legs.

"We won! We won!" announced Troy standing up triumphantly.

"No way!" contested Paige.

"Oh, yes, we did! I pushed Guinevere over the circle, didn't I, Guinevere? *Didn't I?!"*

"But I dragged Tanner over the line first," retorted Bonnie. *"You're cheating!"*

"Bonnie, you're a *blockhead!"* yelled Troy, "A really *big blockhead!"*

He and the boys argued back and forth with their sisters. However, the twins, Tanner and Guinevere, remained quiet, each thinking that they had been dragged or pushed over the line *before* the other had. But when the twins each confessed their own perceptions that the other team had won, the older kids argued even more. As far as Troy was concerned, they were all "blockheads."

The twenty-minute ride back to the Mitchell's home was a quiet one. The Mitchell's fifteen-passenger van allowed them to travel with whole other families. Mrs. Mitchell and Mrs. Edwards often met together at the end of the school week to let the kids play and unwind. Paige and Bonnie were sitting at the back looking at pictures on Bonnie's new phone. Archer and Thomas sat in the next bench comparing pocketknives and planning new worlds in Minecraft. Troy was in the next bench alone mulling over the game and stewing on his frustrating life. Sitting in the front bench, Tanner had fallen asleep, a bit odd for an eight-year-old, but he was recovering from a cold and generally napped a lot since he stayed up late reading. He had learned to read at the age of three. He slumbered on Guinevere's shoulder. She dreamily looked out the window to the fields pondering the world of her snail kingdom.

After dinner, the Mitchell kids prevailed upon the mothers to allow Paige and Archer to sleep over. "Besides," Guinevere argued, "the boys have not yet played *our* game." Mrs. Mitchell didn't care about that one bit, but because they had had a good week of school, she allowed it with the agreement of Mrs. Edwards.

Bonnie volunteered to make dinner in return for her mother's allowing Paige and Archer to sleep over. Her meal consisted of steamed broccoli, brown rice, and scrambled eggs. It should have been an easy dinner to prepare, but timing was always difficult for Bonnie. The eggs were slightly burnt, and the broccoli was overcooked to a pale mushy green.

"It's all dad's fault for coming in and asking how my day went ... of course, I had to answer that!" Bonnie was quickly defensive.

Mrs. Mitchell scolded her slightly, "But Bonnie, my dear, that's no excuse for burning the eggs and overcooking the broccoli. When cooking, your first responsibility is properly preparing the food, regardless of who should ask you a question, *even if it's the President.*"

"But, Mom, Dad *is the president* of this house," she retorted.

"That's what *he thinks,"* her mother replied smiling. "Someday, honey, you'll be a good cook, and it wouldn't surprise me if you served royalty, even a king someday, perhaps even the President, your husband!"

"Mom, *stop it!* What if I'm President someday?!" Bonnie was embarrassed in front of Paige and the boys. Yet, Bonnie savored the idea of serving royalty because she had always liked food and wanted to be a professional chef. Her favorite cable channel was the Food Network that her family would watch while on vacation.

Then Mr. Mitchell said the dinner grace. Plates were filled, and the kids began to eat. They were very hungry from the afternoon at the park.

"Yuck," said Troy when he put a forkful of Bonnie's burnt eggs in his mouth. "Bonnie, you're a *blockhead* for burning the eggs!"

"Okay, young man; upstairs!" Mr. Mitchell pointed sternly. "You've been told repeatedly not to call people names, *and* to always be thankful for any food provided. All food that you *don't* have to prepare should be eaten with gratitude even if it tastes bad ... I mean, I didn't mean 'bad', but ... um ... regardless of what it tastes like." He smiled, looking at Bonnie, whose countenance was going south. "And another thing, young man, no more Charlie Brown comics!"

"But Dad...?!" Troy protested. But he perceived his dad's firm look and refrained from any further comments which could end the sleepover. So, he slowly walked away and trotted upstairs. But as he passed by, he shoved Bonnie's shoulder, but no one saw. This didn't bother he because she didn't like her eggs either. Troy knew the punishment would only be for five minutes, but he was terribly embarrassed, particularly with "friends" eating over, even if he didn't presently like them since "they were blockheads," too.

Thomas ate heartily as did Archer. Tanner always ate a lot, which always puzzled his mother because he was so small for his age. Mr. Mitchell attempted to ease his wife's worries with the fact that, "Tanner needed all that food for all the reading and thinking he does." She knew he was bright, eager to keep up with the older kids. He had learned almost everything directly from each of them—from how to do long division and math from Troy, how to build models and construct complicated circuits from Thomas, and how to read and cook from Bonnie. Guinevere learned alongside him just as fast, but was less noticed, which she figured was safer.

After dinner, the girls applied their collective pressures to get the boys to play their game, Guinevere's favorite, dress-up. Tonight, the dress up they had planned would culminate with a wedding ceremony. The older girls feigned less interest, but deep down looked forward to it, especially Paige.

"It's only fair, Thomas and Archer," Bonnie said. "Mom heard when you agreed to it, and she will make you go through with it." Bonnie pressured them with the other girls' approval. She was going to enjoy getting Thomas to dress up; and she had her phone ready.

"Yes, it's only fair, guys," added Paige, whom Thomas realized was just a little bit too eager. In fact, the wedding was Paige's idea. Guinevere and Tanner would be the flower girl and ring bearer, Bonnie and Archer the bridesmaid and groomsman, Troy the pastor, and Thomas and she, the young couple. It would be perfect.

After dinner, just as Bonnie had planned, Mrs. Mitchell gave the children permission to raid the attic in search of play clothes, the source of which was a large chest passed on to the Mitchell's from deceased British relatives on her mom's side of the family. That family's death had been tragic—a car wreck that took all their lives at once. In this antique piece were also some other odds and ends along with some trinkets.

To venture into the attic was a great consolation for the boys, who grew excited about what they could find there. Thomas told them that there was an old rifle, a dull sword, odd paintings, old sleds, and other interesting things. "This will be great—we'll have a military wedding!" Thomas exclaimed. To himself he had reconciled, "Yes, this would make it alright to 'dress up'."

Mr. Mitchell opened the attic door. "Watch yourselves, kids. Stay on the boards—most of the attic has boards—but stay away from the edges; nothing's there to look at anyway. I don't want you falling through, and you wouldn't like that either!"

The older boys pushed past the girls, shoving them aside gruffly.

"Hey, you brutes!!!" the girls all protested.

"I guess chivalry is dead!" Paige added sarcastically.

"This is great!" Archer shouted. "Can we play hide and seek up here?"

"Nah, that's not a good idea," Thomas said. "You don't want to fall through the floor—besides, look at this!" Thomas picked up an old hunting rifle with its firing pin missing. "Dad said this can't shoot. We're going to order a part to fix it. Feel how heavy it is." He handed it to Archer with hands palm up who raised it up and down balancing it.

"Whoa ... That's heavier than I thought." They took turns holding it and pointing out various features of its craftsmanship—the notched wooden handle, the sights, the engraved barrel, and the brass trigger.

Troy deliberately chose a different corner of the attic to investigate. He was, for reasons not fully understood by him, becoming more and more irritated with Archer and Thomas as the day progressed. Dinner didn't help since the other two had sat next to each other opposite him, a third wheel once again. He wanted to spend more time with Archer. However, as it often happened, Archer preferred Thomas's older company. His younger brother Tanner was "okay" to play with but was "beneath" him in age and size as well as just kind of "weird." He was basically a blockhead. In a corner, Troy found a leathern-sheathed scabbard and picked it up. It was curved and had a matching leather belt much too big for him. It was heavy and the blade terribly dull. He slung its strap over his shoulder, but even so, the sword tip dragged on the ground. With great satisfaction he walked over to the older boys.

The girls and Tanner had gone right to the chest of clothes to the right of the attic's landing. Tanner eyed a flask and quickly grabbed it before Guinevere could.

"Mom?" Bonnie yelled down. "Where is that trinket box that came with the chest, by the way? It's not on the display shelf downstairs." The box had captured her fancy ever since she had seen it the first time.

Tanner remained quiet.

"What's that, Honey?" her mother yelled back. "Come down, please, so I can hear you."

Bonnie leaned out the attic, "Mom, where's the decorative trinket box—remember? You know, the one that came with the chest? I just thought of it; it's not on the display shelf downstairs."

"Oh. Tanner asked to see it last week, and I let him look at it. Tanner? ... Tanner? Come here, honey." He trotted over to the top of the attic stairs.

"Yes, Mom."

"Bonnie wants to see the trinket box. Please, go get it."

"Alright." He went slowly down the steps past her into his room. As he did so, Bonnie gave him a questioning look as their eyes met. He shrugged. He soon returned with the little box.

The box was made of dark burly wood. It was five inches long by four wide and three deep. It had strange symbols carved all around it which were not of any modern language. Even more strangely, it was extremely light for its size, suggesting it was hollow inside. When shaken, nothing moved inside. It was shut tight despite the seam they could see around its middle and a metal tab and button where a keyhole would typically be placed. However, when they first found the box, no one could find a way to open it without using something that would likely damage it.

Mr. Mitchell, a classicist, jokingly had said it was a Chinese trick box carved out inside and then closed back up tightly. But, Tanner himself studied the script and concluded it was Phoenician; so he brought it back to his dad inquiring further about it. Mr. Mitchell, truly impressed with Tanner's language facility, acknowledged it was more properly proto-Phoenician although he continued to maintain it was a forgery. If you would really want to know, dear reader, the script betrayed its Atlantean origins.

Chapter 8
The Celestial Crossroads

Tanner had thought differently about the box all along. It felt old and different. However, it wasn't until Thomas had helped him find a book about ancient language scripts that Tanner recognized some of the characters on the box. The book had described and shown how, although the Egyptians' hieroglyphs represented the earliest writing using pictures and images for syllables and words, that it was really the sea-faring and mysterious Phoenicians who had first introduced "characters" as an alphabet system of discrete, individual sounds to the ancient near-eastern cultures that included the Canaanites, Hebrews, Assyrians, Hittites, Moabites, and several other ancient peoples. Tanner could only make out seven characters, which were parts of what he was pretty sure were three words: 'water', 'earth', and 'sky' or 'heaven.' The writing moved from top to bottom and from right to left.

Intrigued more and more with the box, Tanner tried to pry apart the halves. One day, by providence, he was able to do so. The seal had been so tight that a "pop" and a musty vapor escaped at its opening. The box was indeed hollow inside, but not empty. Inside was tightly fitting black molded material. When he lifted this out, fitted in two rows before him were two sets of rings: on the top were five golden ones with space for two others; on the bottom seven greenish rings. Apparently two golden rings had been lost, he thought. He told no one about his discovery and closed the box back up just as he had found it. He later then nonchalantly asked Troy to try opening it, but he could not. It was sealed tightly back up once again.

Trinket Box with Rings,
photograph by Bonnie Mitchell

After that, he wanted to get more books from the library on what had been written about the Phoenician alphabet. Then he showed the box to his dad who looked at it carefully a few minutes but gave it back and made him promise to make careful use of it.

So, Tanner reluctantly handed the box to his mother as requested. Bonnie was eagerly awaiting it.

He blankly said, "Mom, I don't think we should be playing with this."

"Well, that's odd ... *why not,* sweet boy?"

Bonnie interrupted, "Tanner, that's not fair. I wanted to look at the box, too. Besides, you can pretend it's the ring box for the newlyweds, right? You're the ring bearer."

Tanner turned pale and looked blankly at his mom. *"Had Bonnie found out???"* A pang of anxiety hit him fast.

"I don't see any harm in that," said Mrs. Mitchell looking at her youngest son.

"But Dad said ..."

"Now that's enough, young man; hand it over." He complied, shrugging his shoulders and ran up the stairs back into the attic.

In preparation for the wedding ceremony and with their parent's permission, the girls brought down the wedding attire to the basement where they could have more room to stage the wedding. The boys carried down their military implements as well—Thomas his rifle, Archer a long bow and canteen, Troy his dull scabbard, and Tanner his hip flask that once had held gin. When opened, it wafted its juniper smell still, which he liked. Bonnie handed the box back to Tanner.

The basement served well to stage the wedding parties in its various rooms to separate them. As the different parties were dressing up, Bonnie secretly took some great pictures of the boys posing and donning their outfits and implements.

Tanner then made eye contact with Guinevere and motioned to meet her around the corner out of sight. Each was already outfitted for their roles in the wedding. He wanted to show her the trinket box and what was inside. With the others busily occupied for the moment in the other parts of the basement, now was his chance.

"Guinevere, you must promise *not* to tell what I've found," he said earnestly.

She eyed the flask at his hip and nodded. "Only if you give me the flask." Guinevere responded disinterestedly.

"Who cares about the flask! Okay, here it is. But promise not to tell the others. Really! Pinky promise!" His earnestness now held her attention.

Guinevere knew he had something important to show her and when he handed her the flask, she held it with him and interlocked their pinkies. "Yes, I promise," she agreed looking intently into his brown eyes.

They released pinkies, and he pulled out the box.

"I opened this already. You can't guess what's inside—it's actually a ring box!" He sat down with it on his lap and proceeded to hold the box carefully, maneuvered it, and then pulled the halves apart. Carefully removing the black packing inside, he showed Guinevere who became the second Mitchell child to behold the two sets of rings.

Tanner looked over his shoulder to make sure they were still alone. As he did so, however, Guinevere immediately reached to slip on one of the golden rings right as Tanner realized and grabbed her hand to stop her.

The two found themselves in water and shot upwards surfacing into breathable air. Green light shown upon them. Guinevere and Tanner, who held her hand, quite naturally walked out onto the shore. Oddly they were not wet. The place was beautiful with round boulders strewn about everywhere with an occasional tree here and there amidst dozens of pools identical to the one from which they had emerged.

"Where am I?!!" asked Guinevere out loud. "Who are you?" She looked

The Wood to Other Worlds, or, The Celestial Crossroads, Canva generated by Thomas Mitchell

at Tanner and thought him somehow very familiar. But she became distracted by the animals on the shore—bunches and bunches of guinea pigs. A muddle of them was scampering around the trees—little ones, big ones, of various colors. Both earthen children smiled.

"Tanner ... I think my name is Tanner," the boy said reflectively. He looked down at the open box of rings in his hand. This seemed vaguely familiar to him. "I think you are my sister," he said to the girl.

She walked over to the chaos of guinea pigs which began to squeal and scatter. She was able to catch one and sat down underneath a large tree nearby calmly petting it. "This is a peaceful place and full of life," she said quietly to herself. "Our Father is present here."

The boy Tanner came over and sat down next to her. Holding his trinket box, he knew it had been made of wood from a tree of that place.

The girl then noticed the golden ring on her finger. A thought slowly came to her that she had just put it on. She looked at the boy and said, "I am your sister, and you are my brother ... Tanner. Yes, Tanner is your name. I got this ring from that box." She looked down and pointed.

Both of them began to wake as if from a dream as the memories of their other world slowly reentered their consciousness. They talked through the details; this reassured them as to the facts of who they were.

"You, Tanner, wanted to tell me something. I promised not to tell, and then you showed me that you could open this box and these rings were inside. I put this one on." She held it out and Tanner took it and placed it back in the black material in the open box. He then looked at his watch—it remained still at 9:36 PM and 14 seconds.

"Yes," he began slowly, staring blankly at the stopped watch. "I grabbed your hand just as you put the ring on ... and here we are now."

"Then the ring must have a power to bring us here." She kept petting the guinea pig.

"And I caught a ride," he mused.

"There were others—our brothers and sister and friends, right?! Oh, I wonder whether we should be worried?" but she did not worry one bit.

"Maybe we are dead?" Tanner queried although he felt more alive than he had ever before.

"Well, then, also there are these guinea pigs running around. We didn't bring them, did we? The poor things."

"That means that others have been here before us, or perhaps someone sent them here," he reasoned.

"But who would do such a terrible thing as that—leaving them here all alone?!" she exclaimed.

The boy Tanner became even more pensive. "Well, I have this box full of rings, except that two golden ones are missing. I *wonder* whether the guinea pigs were sent here using them."

It was an odd suggestion, but it started Guinevere thinking. "Maybe we should go back now. Maybe I should put on that golden ring while you hold my hand and that will take us back home."

"Yes, that would be a very good idea!" a gentle male voice agreed.

The twins looked behind them and saw a balded man with a grandfatherly smile seated against a tree not ten feet from them. He appeared as a meek soul with corduroy trousers, white buttoned shirt, and a loose-fitting vest. In his hand was a pipe, but he was not smoking it.

"Who are you?" Guinevere asked. "My name is Guinevere and this is my little brother Tanner."

"We're the *same* age!" he retorted, starting to fume inside.

The man said, "Well, siblings, then! I have many names and I've been called many things." He mused further, "Some are true, some not so kind, and others downright nasty. But, I've received a new name, yet I'll not share that with you now. You may call me ... how about ... 'Jacksie.'"

"Jacksie?!!! That's an *odd* name for an old man!" Tanner said bluntly.

"Oh," he guffawed. "Yes, *certainly* it is ... well, it comes from my...."

Guinevere interrupted, "Tanner, that's *not* a nice thing to say! I mean, we don't even *know* him!" She scowled at her brother, took a breath, and then assumed a kinder and more dignified demeanor to ask the old man, "What do you do, Jacksie? Is this *your* place? Did you create it?"

"Oh, well, now *these* are splendid questions! I'm a writer of words, a thinker of thoughts, a wanter of God's will—a Jack of all trades, so to speak! Is this *my* place? Did I *create* it?" he chuckled. "Well, a definite 'no' and kind of a 'yes,' respectively. There is really only *One* Owner of all things, as you know—*right?* You're clever children. But I have written of this place, as have others...."

Tanner interrupted, still agitated at Guinevere's scolding and because he grew impatient with the prolonged response of 'Jacksie.' *"So,* why *are* people so *nasty*, like you say, and call you *names* and all, and *why* are brothers and sisters," he glared at Guinevere, *"the worst?"*

"Ah, brother troubles, have you? I certainly can understand. But," looking at Guinevere, "sister troubles, I can only imagine. Let me say this, though: Don't be beastly to one another or you'll become a beast. And, one must always bear this in mind, 'Pride goeth before destruction, a haughty spirit before a fall.'"

The gravity of these wise words hit the twins hard, and their escalated emotions released. Both simultaneously yawned in reaction to each other.

"Well, Tanner and Guinevere, it's been my pleasure to make your acquaintance. However, I've been dispatched here to warn you that *this* is a dangerous place, not one within which to linger long. So, you best be getting back home." He pointed back at the pools, specifically theirs.

They turned and Tanner held out the trinket box again and opened it. Guinevere took the same golden ring. They paused to look back, but the old man had vanished. They shrugged.

So, Tanner grabbed her left wrist as she put the ring on her right index finger. As she did so, they both tensed up and shut their eyes and waited.

Nothing happened.

"Well, maybe the green rings take us back," Tanner suggested. So, they followed the same procedure.

Nothing happened.

The two stood there considering all the possible configurations: A girl got them there, so maybe a boy would need to take them back; or, they tried switching hands, and then fingers, and then switching boy and girl in each new configuration. So, they took periodic breaks to walk around in wonder at this strange place, only to continue their attempts to return once again. This took some time. It now read 9:36 PM and 15 seconds. At first, he questioned himself but then resolved that indeed only one second had actually passed. They were overthinking it and getting nowhere.

Guinevere said, "Jacksie pointed at the pools, specifically this one. Maybe we need to jump into it to get back."

The boy Tanner nodded. "Good thinking. I'm surprised we hadn't thought of that yet!" Tanner looked at his watch. It was still 9:36 PM and 15 seconds.

The pool was not deep. So, they stood in the water and tried several configurations with a golden ring; none of them worked. Then Tanner put on a green ring while Guinevere was holding both the box and his wrist, and instantly they were transported back to the basement of the Mitchell's once again from which they had started.

Tanner looked down at his watch immediately. The seconds began advancing 9:36 PM and 16, 17, 18 seconds....

Chapter 9

Bonnie's and Paige's Discovery

"We have to tell the others!" Guinevere urged her brother. "It's too unbelievable!"

"But you promised!" Tanner contested, looking her squarely in the eyes holding up his pinky.

She looked away and then back at him, "But only *you*, Tanner, a young boy, could open the box; no adult could! It's meant for us kids! We've already figured out how to get there and back *all by ourselves*." She continued less urgently, smiling, "Besides, who'll look after that herd of guinea pigs?!" Both began to giggle at the thought of all the guinea pigs there.

Tanner soberly said, "This *is too big, too important*, for us kids ... and we shouldn't be leaving the house for that long!"

"Right, that's true, but that's just it; we only left for one second, you said so yourself! We walk in and out of the house all the time for longer than a second."

Tanner smiled; she was right. "But it sure seemed like much longer than that, perhaps days, and it was so wonderful!" He paused in deep thought. "Well, you're right. And, who *will* take care of all those guinea pigs?!"

They giggled again looking at each other with deep joy and excitement because they had "discovered" a whole new world together.

"Raaaa....! Got ya!" yelled Troy suddenly.

The twins turned quickly to see him. He had sneaked up on them to scare them. It had worked all too well. They sat staring at him, still shocked as if caught doing something wrong. Neither spoke. Troy knew something was up.

"Hey, what are you two up to?!" Troy demanded. Guinevere couldn't help herself from looking down at the opened box. Troy looked down too and noticed that the box was in two parts. Then he saw the rings sitting within the black material. Eyes meeting, Tanner scrambled quickly to put the halves back together again.

"Hey ... hey! You've broken it! And ... and ... you've found some rings inside.... I see 'em there!"

"No ... no!" Tanner denied, securing the box to its whole shape once again. "You must have seen this!" He handed him the flask next to Guinevere. It was a lie, and a very poor one at that. Tanner knew it, but he felt that he couldn't trust Troy in as bad as a mood as he had been in lately.

"*No ...* " Troy pushed aside the flask and yanked the box from Tanner who along with Guinevere began yelling at the top of their lungs. Troy immediately began twisting and prying at the box until Bonnie first, and then Paige, Thomas, and Archer ran in.

"Troy, what's going on here?!!" with raised voice Bonnie looking at the box. "Give the box back, you bully!"

He held it back. "I caught these two '*blockheads'* with the box broken open, and it had rings inside it, and then Tanner locked it back up again!!! Didn't you???" He stared at Tanner.

They all looked at the twins who looked almost innocent and distressed. Tanner was about to cry.

"Is that right?!" asked Thomas eying them carefully. "Troy, dad said that the box was empty, a Chinese 'trick' box carved out or something like that."

"No. I saw it in two pieces with lots of rings inside. Guinevere, you know it's true! *Tell them! ... Tell them!"* But she did not, shaking her head, weeping and rubbing her eyes. Troy grew more and more irate.

Guinevere and Tanner exchanged glances. Tanner ever so slightly shook his head 'no' to her. They both looked up and neither of them said a thing.

"Okay, speak up!" Bonnie commanded. "Troy, give the box to me before you break it."

He had continued working it over, twisting and pulling this way and that. When he gave it to Bonnie, she began to do the same and handed it to Thomas who also tried to open it. All waited a few moments watching.

Then Thomas said, "Troy, if this is some bad joke of yours, we'd like it if you'd stop right now; even if it's a joke, it isn't that funny anyway."

Troy turned red with frustration and trembled. He pushed past Thomas and stomped up the stairs, yelling back, "You guys are all a bunch of block-heads!"

A few minutes later Mrs. Mitchell yelled down. "Kids, enough playing down there. You've had enough; it's been a long day. Time for bed. Come get your teeth brushed. You can play in your rooms and read for a bit; lights out at 10:30."

The girls went up first. Guinevere hesitated slightly and looked at Tanner who shook his head and put his finger to his mouth.

Thomas and Archer lingered a bit on the stairs and saw this exchange. They then cornered Tanner as he made his way up the stairs. "Tanner, don't think we don't know your secret—*we do!*"

Tanner's eyes widened, believing Thomas who was only trying to get him to talk. Atop the stairs in the kitchen, Thomas placed the box on top of the fridge before turning to the second story stairway on his way up to his room. Out of the corner of his eye, Tanner saw where he placed it.

On the second floor, the girls shared a room as did the boys. Bonnie and Paige took no notice that Guinevere was not as talkative as she usually was. She had a book open on her bunk below them, but no pages were turning; she kept musing about her secret journey.

The boys' larger room across the hall held a hostile feeling. Troy, still seething, was not talking to anyone. Archer, who was more and more aware that Troy was angry with him, tried to joke around and even wrestle with him, but this was met with glares and withdrawn, standoffish pouting. Even armpit farts did not get a smile from him. Troy kept casting an evil eye at his little brother. Tanner avoided eye contact and stayed in his corner of the bed they shared. He closed his eyes, pretending to go to sleep. His mind was racing, however, pondering his momentous trip. Thomas and Archer read *Illustrated Classics* until it was "lights out."

At 2:13 AM Tanner found himself still wide awake. He wanted simply to hold the box again. Slipping out of bed, he crept down the creaky stairs leading into the kitchen. He paused intermittently and listened. From the stairs the moonlight shone on the box on the fridge. He climbed quietly onto the counter and beside the fridge. Just as he reached for the box, he sensed he was not alone.

"We've been waiting for you," said a whispering voice. A dull light dimmed on over the kitchen table. It was Bonnie, Paige, and Guinevere, who fidgeted and looked particularly worried. After getting over his initial shock, Tanner felt deeply betrayed.

Guinevere whispered, "Tanner, I just *had* to tell them. It's too *extraordinary* not to." She had just learned to spell the word *extraordinary* the week before.

"But *you promised!*" Tanner whispered back sorely. But rather than anger, he felt relief that Bonnie, whom he trusted, would help know what to do with the box. *"Besides,"* he had been thinking, *"this is the family's trinket box, not simply mine! All of us should eventually know about it; and perhaps my parents already did!"*

He knew what he needed to do next. He took the box over to the table, pulled apart both halves and with a "pop" the box opened once again. Removing the black material, Bonnie's and Paige's eyes lit up at the sight of the golden and greenish rings. Guinevere then explained in some good detail, with Tanner making additional comments, their journey to the place of guinea pigs and about the boulders, trees, and the pools. Paige and Bonnie kept glancing at one another with a glimmer in their eyes. The story had pleasantly entertained Bonnie and Paige. They, however, were ready to get their "hands on the goods." At one point, impatient with the story, Paige quickly reached in and picked up a green ring. However, she put it back when Tanner grabbed her hand and became very visibly distressed. "Put it down!" he said somewhat loudly.

At this, Bonnie said matronizingly, "This is a very, *very NICE story*, Guinevere. We're *sure* that you and Tanner had a great time *there*, wherever *there* really is and however you *really* got *there....*" She winked at Paige, "but we really want to look at these rings *right* now."

Then, Guinevere realized that all along the two older girls had *not believed* any part of the story, except for the fact that Tanner had indeed opened the box earlier with her in the basement. This crushed her spirit almost to the point of tears, which she held back with great effort with pouted lips, although tears began to squeeze out.

Bonnie pressed Tanner, "May we *please* now have a closer look at *these rings?!*"

"Yes," insisted Paige, "we just want to have a closer look!"

Before Tanner could firmly get a hold of the box to close it once again, Paige shoved her fingers inside it and pried the box from his grasp. The two older girls got up quickly and pattered down the stairs into the basement with opened box in hand.

Tanner and Guinevere got up to follow them. But Tanner stopped, reached out, and grabbed Guinevere's arm. "Shhhhh!" He pointed upstairs to the bedrooms. If their parents woke up, he knew they would get in "big trouble." They waited a few seconds still as statues. But the house remained quiet.

Tanner then nodded to Guinevere and whispered, "It's safe." She nodded back and the two tiptoed down into the basement without a creak.

At the bottom of the stairs Bonnie and Paige met them coming back up wide-eyed and brimming with smiles and giddy. Bonnie looked at them squarely with hand on each of their shoulders and apologized immediately. Paige was holding a pair of guinea pigs.

Chapter 10
The Giants' Pool of Emergence

In the end, Bonnie and Paige prevailed upon the younger children to go along with their plan. At the moment of "the exchange of rings" during the imaginary military wedding, Paige would put on the golden ring, while all of them held hands. Bonnie urged them, "The 'holding hands altogether' will be the hardest part."

Because the kids had been called to bed before the wedding ceremony the night before, the girls reasoned that the boys were still obliged to go along with it as planned on the previous day. This needed to take place before Mr. Edwards would pick up Paige and Archer at noon. Thomas didn't much care for the idea. But when they were promised that the ceremony would last only "a minute" and would simply involve the girls and Tanner walking down the aisle and putting on the rings and nothing more, he agreed. Archer didn't mind as long as the boys could be in uniform and girded with their weapons. Troy alone strongly protested. Yet his role as "pastor" was the most essential part. In the end, Bonnie promised to do his chores for the next week and he began to soften. At that, Thomas contested with a smile, "Now, wait a minute ... why did I agree so fast?!" But, to convince Troy, Bonnie wrote out a note and signed it before Thomas, Guinevere, and Tanner as witnesses. With the promissory in hand, Troy finally agreed.

"You'll not be disappointed," Bonnie reassured him, winking at Paige.

"Don't be such a blockhead, Bonnie!" Troy said in his typical foul manner of late.

Troy stood at the end of the room with his scabbard belt looped over his shoulder, looking very displeased. He casually held a Bible with his left hand while resting his right hand on the scabbard. He was the most unfriendly, even hostile, preacher the world had probably ever seen.

Thomas, as the groom, and Archer, as the groomsman, then walked in. Thomas set his watch to stopwatch mode. He reported, "10 seconds and counting." He was keeping the wedding to the promised one minute. Thomas had a rifle slung over his shoulder on a makeshift rope and Archer had around his body a working bow without any arrows as well as his canteen. The group looked more like mercenaries than a wedding party.

From around the corner at the signal of Guinevere, Bonnie came stumbling down the center of the room. She had dressed herself in a gaudy outfit of purple and pink and wore an old pair of heelless lady's dress shoes that actually fit her. At Thomas' announcement "20 seconds and counting," Bonnie sped up and began rolling her right hand at Guinevere and Tanner to hurry them down the imaginary aisle. Paige also pushed them from behind with a large satchel and some charcoal art supplies. Tanner held the trinket box, which was open, but somewhat hidden under the opened black packing material. He wore a large grin along with his backpack full of supplies including the curved flask on his hip. Guinevere carried her large purse packed full of apples, granola bars, and various other items including her mini snail terrarium.

At "30 seconds and counting" Paige came around the corner hurriedly and stopped abruptly across from Thomas. She was dressed in an old off-white cocktail dress, the closest she could find to a wedding dress. For shoes she wore a very odd pair of glass looking plastic slippers that didn't fit her well and kept "slipping off."

Thomas looked at his watch, "35 seconds and counting."

Paige said excitedly, "Okay ... so ... uh ... here we are gathered here today. Um ... now is when we need to hold hands as Thomas puts the golden ring on *my* finger."

"No ... no ... no!" protested Thomas. "That's not how it goes, Paige. People don't *all* hold hands at weddings!!!"

"Well, in this wedding they do!" Paige blurted. "And ... the bride is *always* right!"

"No way ... I'm not holdin' *anyone's* hand!" Troy interjected. Impatiently he said, "Thomas, just take a ring and put it on her finger, *okay?* Let's get this done with!"

"But I want to wear a ring, too," Thomas said jokingly. "Why do I get the ugly green one?!"

Troy was growing more impatient. "Let's just get this over with, Thomas. Take the ring from Tanner." Realization then struck him. "Hey ... hey!!!" Troy noticed the opened trinket box in Tanner's hands. "Hey, look, I ... *I told ya! I knew it!* I told you ... *LOOK!* He's busted it open again and it has rings in it!!!"

Thomas, dumbstruck, looked sternly at Tanner and Bonnie. "Tanner, *you little liar!* What's going on here, *Bonnie...?!"*

"Well ... let's not talk about that now," she said quickly. "Let's just have Thomas put the golden ring on ... Okay?! ... since he wants it so badly, and we'll talk about it after that. Okay?!"

Paige quickly took one golden ring, and counted out loud, "Ready! One, two, *THREE...!"* just as Troy yelled at Tanner, "You're a blockhead!!!"

At 10:34 AM on that Saturday morning in the basement of the Mitchell's home, that part of the room which just moments before had been occupied with seven earthen youth dressed up with assorted weapons and gear—one holding a Bible and scabbard, another a bouquet of fake flowers and a satchel, one with gun slung over a shoulder, another with bow and canteen, one with a purse, another dressed gaudily in pink and purple, and the last one with a hip flask, backpack, and open ring box—was now empty. Only one hard plastic slipper remained behind.

They all surfaced through the green water. Bonnie came up last with Troy. She had only just managed to grab his hand the instant before Paige shoved the golden ring onto Thomas' thumb at the count of "THREE." As had happened before, each climbed out and sat down on the bank, disoriented from the journey. The Crossroads had never seen such a wedding and war party arrive. Tanner instantly fell asleep on the shore and dreamt such real and contented dreams that he never wanted to awaken again. And then there were the guinea pigs. All colors and sizes were scurrying about. Some of the wedding party found a large tree to lean up against. Others of them gazed out dreamily over the beautifully serene landscape populated with boulders amidst pools and lonely trees here and there as far as the eye could see.

But slowly they began to remember who they were. With his hot temper of late, Troy was the first to remember as irate as he had become. His feelings were only amplified in this new place. Thomas, on the other hand, with his state of confusion before entering, was extremely perplexed and kept asking questions of everyone. Bonnie and Paige remained quite calm at first and grew increasingly excited. As during her first visit, Guinevere snatched up a guinea pig and held it, caressing its soft fur. She watched the older kids asking each other questions and talking to one another, all except Archer who sat blankly beside the sleeping Tanner running his right hand up and down the shaft of his bow.

Eventually, they all returned to the normal range of their former rationality. The full "presence" of the place weighed on them all.

"Okay," Thomas queried, "You don't know where we are, but let me get this straight. Bonnie and Paige, you made this happen? How did you do it?!! Are we *dead?* Did you poison us or, what?!" Thomas was stuck on this detail of how they arrived at this strange place by possibly dying, assuming that they were in some form of the afterlife.

"*No ... No ... No,* Thomas." Bonnie answered as assuredly as she could. "We are alive. We never died, at least I don't think so. The golden ring brought us here, and that's why we needed to hold hands so that we could all come together. You see, Tanner and Guinevere came yesterday, and then ... well ... Paige and I came last night, I mean, early this morning. But both of these visits were *accidents.* This trip, however, with the seven of us was our plan *on purpose*, mine and Paige's."

Troy was listening, too and was not impressed. "So, we have you two to thank for this?!" He eyed Paige and Bonnie angrily. "You brought us *unwillingly* here, wherever *here* is. And what is the deal with these guinea pigs anyway?!" He paused and became distracted. His demeanor lightened up when he beheld the little creatures scurrying here and there—he loved visiting pet stores. He looked happily at them and started to chuckle to himself. He was diverted momentarily and picked one up.

Bonnie, watching him, answered, "We don't know about these guinea pigs. But somehow, they just made the place seem safer." She took a deep breath. "So then, Tanner opened the box...."

Troy stopped her mid-sentence, "That's exactly right! See, I told you, Thomas ... and no one believed me, *no one*, especially you, Thomas!" His face turned red.

"Well," defended Thomas, "the box was closed when I looked at it. Who could *blame* Tanner for wanting to hide that he had broken it?! And look at him ... he's had quite a trip. All of this must have been quite difficult for him." They all looked at Tanner sleeping with a dreamy smile on his face.

"'Blame' Tanner, you say?!" Troy restarted his anger. "Blame the *spoiled brat* more like it! You guys always believe him and *never* me!"

"But look at all the wonderful guinea pigs!" Paige strategically broke in. She paused and then mused out loud, "If you ask me, I think the pools take us to other worlds." This flash of revelation evoked a strange momentary effect on them all. It had surprised Paige herself to say it.

"To *other worlds?!* That's silly!" replied Thomas.

"Not at all," retorted Bonnie. "Think of it—we arrived in *this* pool, and it is by this pool that we go back to our home—on *earth.*"

"*Anywhere* away from you all would be better than here," interjected Troy. "Or, better yet, maybe you could go somewhere *else*. I'll stay with these guinea pigs." His anger eased as he looked at them again.

But what Troy said in anger became their plan.

Tanner and Guinevere, and then Bonnie and Paige, then related how they had successfully arrived at the Crossroads and left through the earthen pool. The "Crossroads" was the name they had designated this place. They believed they understood how the gold and green rings worked. The golden rings sent people from earth to the Crossroads coming up through the pool that was the portal by which to go back to earth. Green rings brought them back to the world connected with the pool. Theoretically, they would use the green rings to travel out to other worlds, and the golden ones to always go back to pool for each world in the Crossroads. One question remained, however: Since the green rings brought them back to the very same spot of their original departure, where would a traveler enter into a new world? Bonnie ventured the guess that there might be a corresponding pool that visitors could use to enter into the other world. But it was only a guess.

It did not take long for the earthen youth to agree how best to try out the nearby pools. They would send Thomas, Archer, and Troy into a pool as the first explorers since it was their "turn" to go. Archer was very insistent that "fair was fair" and all the others had taken more trips than Thomas, Troy, and Archer. However, Troy declined to go with them. So then, Thomas and Archer agreed to pop into another world and come back immediately.

By now Tanner was fully awake. When he heard their idea of popping in and out of other worlds, he became terribly worried, and so he turned to doing something useful. As they talked, he pulled out the new notebook given to him that same morning by his mother, found a pencil from his backpack, and started drawing a map of the boulders and the pools. Guinevere watched him; she had forgotten to bring her own notebook along. Tanner showed them his map, and they all agreed to use the large tree near the earthen pool as a reference point. They tied a scarlet scarf from Bonnie's outfit around it with the knot demarcating one side. There were just enough trees around to make this a great idea. The boulders were scattered about and not all the same shape, size, and color. This allowed Tanner to make a reliable map of their immediate environs. So, Tanner was quite content to "stay back and chronicle things."

Bonnie wanted someone else to stay with Tanner. Since all (except Troy) were in a good mood and very eager to go exploring other worlds, they decided to have Troy stay behind with him. Thomas threatened Troy not to lay a finger on Tanner. Troy cared less.

Archer and Thomas got fully geared up for their first journey. They chose the pool to the right of the "earth pool" from the knot view of the large tree. With gold rings in hand, they put on a green ring and stepped in holding hands. They sunk down and popped out of sight. The others waited and waited. They soon became a bit impatient.

Paige began to doubt the decision, thinking to herself, "*What will mom and dad do if Archer doesn't come back home?! What will I do??!*" But the guinea pigs scampering about prevented her from worrying too much. They also gave her an idea.

Tanner had immediately begun counting and when he reached one thousand and sixty-four, Thomas and Archer surfaced from the pool again.

When he came up from the pool, Archer had enough presence of mind to shout out immediately, "A Jungle!!!" However, it then took a while for him to remember who he was and who the others were. As more time passed, he and Thomas explained more and more what they had seen, smelled, and even heard on their trip. Tanner was writing things down furiously using his coded shorthand with his own alphabet, grammar, and syntax. He had newly developed it, and his father had not yet decoded it, which was a game of theirs.

After this first expedition, all of them travelled together except for Tanner and Troy. With each successive journey in and out of the different worlds, Tanner imagined that the number of Guinea pigs was dwindling. At the same time, his own interest in going along increased.

Finally, after the fourth journey, Tanner spoke up, "I'd like to go on the next trip."

"I don't think it would be a good idea to leave Troy back alone," said Bonnie.

"I'm fine. Go without me," Troy said, although he was getting more than curious. He, however, remained still quite angry with them all.

"Troy, if Tanner is going to come with us, you *have* to come, too." Thomas stated.

"But what if I don't *want* to?!" Troy played this up a bit intentionally trying to be difficult. He was beginning to enjoy this a bit too much. He wondered *"How far can I push them before I agree to go, the blockheads?!"*

"Come on, Troy," said Archer. "It's fun! Just once. Come on, let's go! This is the last trip."

"Well, if I have to," Troy huffed, looking sharply as his little brother.

So, they marched over to the second pool past the Earth pool on the right from the perspective of the knotted scarf on the tree. They all stood in place along the bank and waited for Troy who reluctantly approached, playing his "bad mood" all the way to the end. He was muttering to himself and inveighing at them; his tongue increasingly was unloosed. He enjoyed the feeling of being free to say whatever he wanted with no parents around. He swaggered over to them standing in the pool, railing more and more at them. "I'll go ... I'll go. But, you *all* are a bunch of blockheads! Mark my word! Blockheads!" just as Thomas grabbed his hand as Bonnie put on a green ring. As they descended into the pool, Troy was unable to help himself from continuing his tirade, his words being the last to resound as they disappeared beneath the green waters.

The altitude was high, the atmosphere thin. A light breeze blew. The air held a chill. The deep blue sky began to lighten as the morning sun peaked above the vast mountainous horizon. Hues of orange and red combined to make a solid band across the eastern sky—a dawn of a new world.

Tanner was the last of them to walk out of the enormous terracotta pool. In front of them, the enormous scale of the surrounding landscape dwarfed them like some quarry of stone. Around them appeared to be piles of rock amassed against craggy slopes that overlooked the broad, expansive seemingly unending plane where they stood. Opposite the sunrise, this plane stretched many soccer fields before narrowing until they could no longer see any specific features but the open sky on the left and the massive rockface on the right.

Tanner noticed first that their party was minus one. "Hey, *where's Troy?"* he asked. Tanner saw the others in their silly wedding and military attire standing around and staring at a large black, shiny mass. The others looked bewildered. To his surprise, Tanner then saw the mass arise, take humanoid form, stumble forward, and proceed to utter, "Seriously??! *What* are you staring at, you blockheads?!"

Chapter 11

Salton-suhl Tukal, the Giant King

At first Troy was in denial of his condition. As he swayed and stumbled about, he kept rubbing his arms with his odd appendages to remove the slick, oily sludge.

"Who covered me with this mud?!!" he kept asking. "It's already starting to harden. Thomas, is this some joke?!"

Thomas attended him first. "Troy, the mud must have come from the water although no one else has it." It dawned on Thomas that this substance was not a mud coating; he was looking at an alien creature of some kind that was at the same time his little brother Troy. Confused, he didn't know what to say or how to help him.

They all saw that Troy's black face had three eyes in triangular arrangement. He also had a line of holes where human ears would have been but without an outer ear and encircling halfway around the backside of his head. That much could be clearly seen. Both features confirmed Troy's appearance was not accidental, nor simply mud stuck to his body.

Guinevere and Paige kept staring at Troy on the verge of terror. All the others felt sick to their stomachs; Bonnie felt it the worst and had a lump in her throat as if she were suffocating at the thought of Troy's transmutation. She felt she had swallowed a piece of glass. Somehow Troy's Bible, scabbard, and clothes had ended up on Archer's arms as he came through the pool. This was very odd, and Archer shook his head as feeling as if the others blamed him for Troy's appearance. Archer awkwardly gave these to Bonnie and stood there forlorn.

Tanner didn't know what to do, so he took his notebook out and busily worked his pencil to capture Troy's new form, especially his head.

Troyton's New Head, sketch by Tanner Mitchell

He paused briefly to note the time upon entering this new world. His watch was working once again, but it seemed to be advancing much more rapidly than at home. He stared at his watch as he pondered what this might mean. But while he was fiddling with it, Guinevere snuck up behind him and snatched his notebook. She walked to the other side of Bonnie and glared at Tanner. She began her own doodling. Tanner sighed and looked at his watch again. He felt disgusted with himself for letting her get his notebook so easily. It would be impossible to get it back by force because Guinevere was stronger than he and it was too embarrassing to ask the others for help. He'd just have wait and be as sneaky as she had been.

"What shall we do?!" Bonnie gasped in despair, finally able to say something.

"We've got to go back right away! It ... I mean ... Troy... will be changed back to normal, I would think," urged Paige, totally grossed out by his appearance.

Meanwhile, Troy was not as worried about his condition as the others were; he couldn't see himself. His new form felt quite fine and actually grew on him. He felt a brute strength in his limbs and a calculating mental acuity. His thoughts were laid out like some sort of mathematical grid in compartments, clear and organized. His exterior was growing firmer and graying a bit. His sense of sight and hearing were enhanced as if in 3D. He was unique; and he was toughening. He reached over and easily picked up Tanner by his backpack, lifting him clear off the ground with one hand before putting him back down somewhat shakily. He was still solidifying.

"Hey, stop it! Put me down!"

"Boy...," said Archer, "You look funny, Troy."

"Well," Troy replied instantly, "you've always looked funny to me, too. Now I guess we're even." Just then, he felt a strong pang of hunger unlike any he had ever known before. His inside felt completely empty and his energy waivered. "Oh ... Oh ... Do we have any food??? I'm starving!!!"

"Here," offered Guinevere, fumbling for it from her purse. "It's an apple ... ah ... from the farmers' market."

Troy picked it up, eyed it with a doubtful expression, put it in his mouth, mashed it about into something like applesauce that oozed out, before spitting it out completely, coughing. *"Peeeeuuuwwhh!* That's bad." He spat it out, spraying Archer and Guinevere with it.

"If you ask me," Paige repeated impatiently, "let's go back right away!"

But as she said this, the rising sun fully began to blaze on them over the peaks of the mountain range, flooding light into the whole barren concourse edged with rocky mounds now made visible surrounding the pool in the center. Without warning, a thunderous voice boomed out and echoed,

"The Conductor in good pleasure has brought us another watchling!!!"

The voice startled the wedding party who huddled around the transformed Troy. All looked for its source. Thomas first identified it. Behind them in the bright sunrise he noticed something like an amphitheater with a seat hewn from the mountainside with a massive figure blending in and seated upon it some forty feet tall. The massive size and posture of the rocky form sitting there reminded Thomas of Abraham Lincoln in his memorial which he had just recently seen on a family vacation. He pensively whispered to the others and pointed, "Over here! See!!!"

"Look at how new and soft he is—his blackened innards!" the giant said. "I always enjoy that, and how quickly they harden up!" The earthen travelers did not understand to whom he was speaking.

The giant's gaze shifted noticeably to them. "My goodness! And what *sort of creatures* are you?!" The voice echoed among the surrounding mounds. "Your silence *betrays* you are fearful. Be not afraid! You are not from our realm—that much is obvious. And yet, you softlings seem to know this soft stoneling beside you. Am I not *correct* in this? Speak up, now."

Stepping forward, Bonnie managed to mutter an answer past the lump in her throat, "Sirrrr ... Yes, we know him. He is my younger brother. I am Bonnie, and this is Thomas and Tanner and Guinevere and Paige and Archer." She pointed to each one, except for Troy inadvertently who did not look like Troy to her. "And you are right, sir, to observe that we are not from here. We are from another world we call 'earth,' er, ah ... if you might of heard of it. But we don't belong here; sorry for coming here. We didn't mean to disturb you."

"Yes," Paige continued Bonnie's line of thinking. "And we will be going back now. Thank you. Goodbye!" She began herding the others towards the pool.

"No, you shall not leave!!!" boomed the giant. "Given your elder age and care for this new stoneling, and in the absence of any other suitable giant watcher, you are by my authority hereby appointed as Watchers over ... over ... now, what is your name, Watchling?" he raised a shaky hand and pointed at Troy who reactively perked up and acknowledged his gaze, but said nothing. "Yes, you watchling, what is your name?"

"Mister," started Troy. "My name is Troy. And who are you?"

"Well, yes! Good question! You are a smart one! I am the Giant King, Salton-suhl Tukal of the Conductor, animated by His servant, the Great Mover." The king paused. Then, as if reciting an ancient formula, he continued, "You are named Troyton-suhl, Watchling of the one-thousandth Cycle of the High Season, governed by the Great Mover. May you never be overshadowed and removed from its light! Look, your watchers are there around you. Learn the way of the Conductor from them." His massive right hand swung open broadly, his eyes searching about, before bringing it to point at the earthen youth standing there. He narrowed his gaze upon them. "And now, Watchers," his left hand then swung forward sweeping and stopping at Troyton-suhl, "see to your watchling! Teach the way of the Conductor to Troyton-suhl."

"Well," Paige interrupted. "Thank you very much! This is, ah ..., this is very, *very* nice, and *so very kind of you!* Yes, indeed. But we really need to put this little gold ring on here ... and just jump back into the pool and be going...." She looked at the others, signaling ardently saying under her breath, "Let's go, let's go...."

"Stop!" The king quaked. He jolted up, towering above them, and stomped once, faltered, and teetered, slamming back down on his throne with a deafening force. A sweeping gush of dust rushed past the clan of seven at the side of the pool.

Guinevere, trembling, started tearing up. She had dropped her pencil and stopped writing. When she stooped down to pick it up, it had disappeared. She looked to her left, and then the loosely held notebook was snatched out of her unsuspecting right hand. She turned around to see

Tanner standing next to Thomas smiling as he scribbled something down.

The older youth worriedly looked at each other and at Troyton-suhl.

"There are reasons *three* for me to forbid you to leave. First, you are obliged to your watchling, Troyton-suhl. Since the slowdown of us all and the loss of Active and Moving Giants—in addition to the wayward departure of too many other sluggish Giants to the deep of the Northern Caverns and to the Far Eastern Borders—there has been a shortage of able elder Watcher Giants. But the Conductor has always provided one or more watchers by coordinating their visits to us elders *precisely* at the emergence of a new watchling from the pool ... *providentially.*" He stressed the last word. "*Precisely providential*, I say. So, on this one-thousandth cycle, it is evident that your clan was given for Troyton-suhl to be his watchers. He is your solemn charge now. I know he is not much to look at—soft, black, and all—but his appearance will quickly change to match our handsome, glorious giant features."

He stopped speaking as suddenly as he had started, slowly holding out his arms and extended his hands and digits looking rather pleased with himself as if he were a specimen of the giant's race. The youth looked at each other and waited several moments, afraid to say anything that might possibly anger the giant. Thomas wondered what a "cycle" was. Tanner was busy sketching and writing. Guinevere darted mean looks at him, but he didn't notice.

Archer finally dared to speak up, "But that is only *one* reason."

The Giant King was taken out of his reverie and started up again, "Ah, yes. My neural pathways, pardon me, are *slowing.* You are gifted at math, I see. Zero and one is *only one.* Yes, well, the second reason is quite irrelevant compared to the first: If that ring is *truly* gold, then it is forbidden in the Pool of Emergence. Gold in this pool is the reason there are no other active watchers. The pool has been tainted and has prevented us from perpetual motion; we have slowed down and stopped ever since it was introduced." Evidently, the topic troubled the King, and he began his odd, distracted gaze once again.

Another deep and massive voice began speaking to the left of the king, "See our example." A nearby knoll spoke up; it was in fact another giant. "Yes. You must be watchers for watchling Troyton-suhl and you cannot place that gold ring into the Pool of Emergence. It is forbidden; we will not allow it!"

"Yes!" another voice chimed in from beside the other. "And watch wisely, learn the One Way, and walk in it!"

The youth looked closer at the various mounds of rock amassed against the craggy slopes around the perimeter encircling them. Now they could see that these were a row of nearly motionless giants. Disturbingly, only their heads swiveled and their mouths moved. Otherwise, they appeared "frozen."

"We are the Elders whose motion has ceased. By the mercy of the Conductor we speak. We wait for the beginning of the Restoration by the flow of heavenly dew to come at the rescue of the One Gem. Let there be praise to the Conductor for His great wisdom!"

Guinevere turned her gaze once again to the Giant King. She was renewed in her courage and was curious to learn more. "But, what is the third reason, King Salton-suhl?" Her higher pitched, crisp and clear, piercing voice carried well over the stony terrain and contrasted with the booming voices of the stone Elders.

"Oh, another math-statistician! Yes, the third is the most important reason," the Giant King said solemnly. He stretched out his massive arms towards them. "You seven have a word from the Conductor, a commission, if you will, a mountain to mold, a quarry to excavate, a valley to find, a trove to traverse, a dome to divide, *even a gilded giant to defeat* ... or whatever this may mean. I have just dreamt of it. Listen to the Word:

To feed the hungry is for you to succeed
to gather the sustenance of their every need;
Evil is spreading to souls down below,
but enter you must the lands that are low;
Help those who there reject evil plots
to rescue the sole one left with the spots;
Though a death it meets when twin giants give leap
but awaken it will by the Conductor's great keep.
Dew from on high will then sprinkle the sky,
to mend the moving of those who once did die.
One watching the watchers will need to take hold
to rid the lowland of that one gild of gold.
Stay true to the One who now bids you to go,
but return you will through the waters' green glow.

At that Word, Troyton-suhl leaped up and skipped like a calf let loose. He danced about greatly enjoying the Word, just as King Salton had. But his enjoyment was short-lived under the duress of his severe hunger pangs. He bellowed, "I am starving! Feed me! I need something to eat right now!" He looked painfully down at the hollow of his middle cavity, sunken and empty.

"But what can you eat?" Thomas asked.

Troyton-suhl only repeated himself again louder.

Thomas looked at the Giant King Salton-suhl and redirected the question to him, "What does he eat? Please, tell us, King Salton-suhl."

Troyton started searching around and about the group, faltered, and fell dramatically whimpering, "Feed me! Feed me! I need ... to ... eat!!!"

"What are you waiting for, Watchers?!" the King asked. "Fetch him some granite stone from yonder quarry. There is but one 'good' helping left in two portions that is pure. That quarry has fed *all* the watchlings from the beginning of our time. But alas, this is the last meal of this age from it. You will need to attend his "Course of Growing" along the Great Skyway and find suitable rock at its restways. May the Conductor give provision!"

The King then addressed Troyton, "Now, go to the Western Sea Tides! This is your first task and journey. As for its distance, this rhyme will assist you: 'Only nine-thousand strides to the Western Sea Tides; twenty-nine more to the Golden Isle Shore; if eastward-borne, only eleven-thousand paces to the highest places, and ninety thousand more to the Golden Shore.'"

Archer and Thomas went immediately to retrieve the granite piece. They struggled back to the group, shuffling together with a cinder block sized piece of granite held between them. They lowered it in front of Troyton-suhl, careful not to crush one of their fingers while setting it down. Then, with one hand outstretched, Troyton-suhl kneeled before it and paused; he strategically placed his hands on the granite piece. He concentrated, it quivered, and then it suddenly fractured, crumbling into mouth-sized pieces. Smiling, he began popping the shards into his mouth. The others watched stunned. When he righted himself, his frame gesticulated and convulsed somewhat, and one could hear scraping sounds emanating deep from within his gullet that sounded at times like fingernails on a chalkboard. Thomas held his hand over her ears, cringing. He hated that sound.

Bonnie alone struggled to carry the other rectangular piece of rock over, smaller that then first. She asked the Giant King, "How is this normally served, King Salton-suhl?"

"Garnished with gem; the less color the better, typically," he answered.

Thomas perked up, "With Jewels?"

Archer asked, "Are these jewels plentiful, Sire? Would we be able to fetch any?" Despite the implication, he was not interested in sharing any.

"No," replied the King sadly. "They are not plentiful any more around here. But they are still to be found with careful excavation here and there;

a keen giant can sense them, especially embedded in solid rock. Otherwise, one must search for one of the known troves or find a new stash. Certain giants, and let me say *evil ones*, have hoarded them only to stop moving before ingesting them. The Fools! The gems prolong our motion, you know. The largest trove in the Western Expanse lies just past Therndon's Peak, protected by the Watcher Anton-duhl Meer, if he still moves! Beware of him, for he is wily. To my knowledge, no one has been able to match his wit."

"Yes, a very important trove with the One Gem," added one elder Giant, with the others agreeing.

The King paused to look at them sternly, and they grew quiet once again. "Patience, Elders. What we hope for may not yet be now. Patience. Let the Conductor direct Troyton-suhl."

After some awkward silence, one of the Elders boomed out, "And ... don't forget Lodeton's Trove facing the blackened Kliffs of Kalm to the northeast!"

"Yes, yes... if they should go east at some time," the King agreed. "In any case, these troves may be of use to your watchling; but beware, they are dangerous places with snares and what not. But you are good at math—zero, one, two, three—and should have no problem disarming them." He smiled giantly.

Suddenly, Troyton-suhl cried out with a most terrible whine, "I'm thirsty, give me something to drink!" He could not help but to blurt it out. To himself he thought, "*How demanding I am!*" He then loped over to the Pool of Emergence and dropped his head in the water. He did not surface for nearly three minutes. Thomas kept track after the first minute, very worriedly indeed!

Meanwhile, Bonnie had noticed the King's keen interest as Troyton-suhl ate and his nodding while he was drinking. Overcoming her fear more and more, she dared to ask him, "King Salton-suhl, may I get *you* something to eat and drink?"

"Bless you! Bless *you*! Yes, please and thank you. There is that small stone there by you. It has been just beyond my reach for many a Mover's passing, and I have longed for it. It is not much of a stone, but I would eat it still. Thank you." The King's mouth quivered.

Bonnie ventured to ask, thrilled to be serving a king, "Sire, since there is no gem to garnish this morsel, may I suggest dipping it in this pool?"

"Splendid! Just splendid! Yes, softling Bonnie, that would be perfect. I am quite dried out and my acidity might be improved with some of that water."

Very pleased with herself, Bonnie enrolled the help of Paige. Together the two of them picked up the stone, dipped it in the pool, and then just managed to lift it to within King Salton's reach. He picked it up and ingested the tiny morsel with much relish and facial gesticulation. No scraping sounds were heard, as when Troyton-suhl ate. Bonnie delighted in her culinary success.

As Troyton-suhl drank on and on, Tanner thought that he could see his blackened body grow rougher, greyer, and larger with each passing minute. In fact, his graphite interior was excreting and converting the freshly consumed rock, with the aid of water, into his hardened exterior form made up of minute, interlocking shell-like material. At the same time, unseen to anyone, his innards elongated while publishing and integrating fresh mineral networks within his giant nervous system.

Troyton-suhl slowly stood up taller than before, "Ah, that's better. But I'm itchy!" He began to scratch himself so that even little chips of himself flew off. The scraping made a terrible grating sound. He would occasionally push his fist into his arms and thighs here and there. He marveled that his exterior was hardening.

"Now, what is the way to the Western Sea Tides, my King?" Troyton-suhl asked, as he bowed in homage to Salton-suhl. It was always the custom to ask the Giant King for such instructions before setting out on the long journey.

The King pointed, "That is the true way westward. Do not depart from the Holy Path. Follow the Great Mover westward until you reach the Sea Tides."

That being said, immediately Troyton-suhl turned, placing his right foot back at the pool's edge, and began striding with a steady pace westward along the ancient Giants' Skyway.

"Hey, stop, Troy! What are you doing?!" yelled Archer.

"I'm hungry!" was all that he yelled back at his watchers. He showed no sign of slowing.

And with that, Troyton's clan of watchers had no other choice but to follow along after him as he paced steadily westward. Paige periodically let out a yelp as she went because she had on only one plastic slipper.

Part III

Providential Encounters

Chapter 12

The Path Downwards

As if watching a marathon race a mile in, the wedding party spread further and further apart along the massive Giants' Skyway.

The meticulously constructed inter-mountain highway bridged the western and eastern coasts and spanned the southern region of the Giants' domain along the wide mountain range. The Skyway was bordered to the south with ridges and occasional overlooks that served as slurry stops. To the north, more variation existed; stark cliffs would give way to gradual jagged slopes, but occasionally to an inviting overlook to a massive valley or a slightly more elevated plateau.

The ancient Skyway was in need of some repair. Cracks had developed as the large subterranean plates shifted ever so slightly. This left rather sizable fault lines difficult for humans to jump over. Also, for the miniature human travelers the otherwise insignificant pieces of stone debris for giants were much larger than gravel strewn across a sidewalk, requiring constant side-stepping to navigate around.

On and on Troyton-suhl instinctively strided westward to find food and complete his journey. Behind him trailed his watchers distributed like ants along a scent trail. They varied greatly in their speed and endurance to keep up. Thomas was closest behind Troyton-suhl. Behind Thomas were Bonnie and Archer. Bonnie had stopped twice to look back and wave the others on to pick up the pace. Tanner and Guinevere lagged further and further behind Bonnie. Even so, Tanner was still striding evenly along while Guinevere was skipping and stopping now and then to take in the magnificent mountain views illuminated by the bright sun overhead. Behind them a distance Paige hobbled along, periodically shouting, "Oww! Ooh! That hurts! What was I thinking?!! My shoes, I miss my tennis shoes!" She carried her only glass slipper.

The jogging continued for what seemed like hours to Bonnie; she kept hoping that she could catch up with Troyton-suhl and Thomas. Bonnie realized that she had not seen Paige in a quite a while and could no longer see Tanner and Guinevere around the occasional broad bends along the Skyway. Since she was in the center of the string of travelers, she had to make a decision—the party was spread too thin and it was only going to worsen. Since Archer was closest to her and Thomas, Bonnie's plan was to send Archer ahead to keep pace with Thomas and Troyton-suhl. She would fall back and collect the others to stay together. Two groups were better than several. After talking it over with Archer amidst strides, Bonnie stopped at one of the large bends and caught her breath. She watched Troyton-suhl, then Thomas, and finally Archer continuing on the huge roadway up and over a distant crest and out of sight. Looking back, Bonnie could see Tanner and Guinevere now making their way around the previous bend, still over a half mile back. Their colorful little outfits contrasted with the ashen stony alien world. But Paige was nowhere to be seen.

"What was I thinking?!" Bonnie said aloud, kicking at the ground. She plopped down with her hands over her face sobbing. *"Oh, God, help us!"* Fatigue and self-criticism pressed upon her. Tears flooded over her and she was overcome with feelings of despair. Her thoughts raced. Too many questions remained unanswered. She had not anticipated such bad things happening. She recalled her mother's statement in the kitchen, "Things will go amuck. Welcome to the real world." But this was no kitchen, and this was not her world. What they had played with, as if it were some game, had turned quickly to bite them in the butt, and hard. Their lives were in danger, and she and the others had had no time to think of what to do. No, that wasn't true; Paige had been right—*they should have immediately left.* And yet, the Giant King was so certain that things were "supposed" to be this way *providentially.* What did that mean in this situation? To him, what happened was *on purpose.* But did that make his view of things the *right* view? He had mentioned a "Conductor"—who was that? What part had the Conductor played in what had happened, if any? Was he good or bad? Was the Conductor like the God that she had learned so much about at home and at church? Was He God the Father? She reasoned further, "*Was God to blame for this terrible situation? No. That couldn't be. God was supposed to be good and not let bad things happen to good people.*" There was no one to blame, except perhaps for the maker of the rings, whoever that was. *Dangerous things these were indeed!* But then it was all of them—no, she had to admit—really it was *she*, the 'I' of Bonnie herself, who had trifled with the rings. She had been thinking only of herself and her own sense of adventure. She had been bored of her life and always the one responsible for the others. Bonnie had come to realize, when thinking about grammatical person, that speaking in second or third person could too often protect the "I" and the "we" of the first person. The third person effectively distanced the singular first person, absolving that one of responsibility. But she—the first person, the 'great' I—was responsible for dabbling in something beyond her, beyond them all, beyond their world, in fact. She pondered, "*Was this now beyond God, too? Was God merely an earthen god or God of the entire universe, of even this place?*" She then confessed out loud, "Oh, Lord, I have risked the lives, and perhaps even the eternal fate, of others—sisters, friends, and brothers, and especially Troy. Poor Troy!!! Forgive me!!! Can Troy be turned back into his normal human self?! Please, help us, dear Lord!" She sobbed.

Rubbing her eyes and looking back again, Bonnie saw the twins approaching her. They were striding and skipping gaily, holding hands now. Each was eating a granola bar. Bonnie's heart lightened at the thought of them—how their coming into her world had been a wondrous marvel! Both had wriggled their way into her heart and her family's life. She smiled at them but immediately felt a heartfelt pang for poor Troy and Thomas going off in the opposite direction further away.

"Here. You must be hungry—we've been walking quite a while." Guinevere held out a granola bar to Bonnie. "Where are the others? Why aren't they here?!" she asked with a surprised look.

"We couldn't all keep up with 'Troyton,' and so Thomas and Archer went along with him." Bonnie took a bite of her bar and thought it best not to say too much. "We'll meet up with them later," mustering as much calm and assurance as she could. "Have you seen Paige?"

"She's back a ways behind us," answered Tanner. "We hear her now and then calling us."

"Oh, I see her rounding the bend now." Bonnie was relieved. The granola bar was helping her spirits considerably.

Putting Bonnie between himself and Guinevere, Tanner proceeded once again to pull out his notepad and made a few entries, saying out loud, "Nine-thousand and two hundred and fifty-three," and then scribbled some more.

"Nine-thousand two hundred and fifty-three what?" Bonnie asked.

"Steps."

"Steps where?"

"About how many strides I've taken since we left the Pool of Emergence this morning." After a few more seconds, he had finished his calculation. "Shucks, that's not good; we've gone only about three and a half miles. It's taken us five hours and thirteen minutes on my watch—not a fast pace. That can't be right. I think my watch is off. Oh well. It will take us a while to get there. Let me see...."

"What will? Get where?" Bonnie asked.

"The Giant King said it would take nine-thousand strides to arrive at the Western Sea Tides," Tanner explained. "It would have been nice if 'this distance' had been given to us based upon *our little* strides. But since I counted over nine thousand of *my* strides and since there is no sea in sight, the King must have meant a giant's stride." He sighed. *"Of course it would have been,"* he thought to himself.

Paige finally limped up to them, flushed and worn out, looking back behind her. She feared that something was going to sneak up behind her. Guinevere held out a granola bar.

"Hi, Paige. Are you okay?" Tanner said curtly with a smile. "Now, help me out here, Bonnie. When the Giant King stood up, he was about ten feet shorter than our sixty-foot maple tree. Right? That would put him at about fifty feet tall. His giant body, from what I saw of it, appeared proportional to ours; legs in the same place and about the same length. We must remember that one's stride is generally proportional to one's height." He got out a measuring tape from his backpack and asked both Guinevere and Bonnie to walk naturally past him. He took measurements, wrote down the figures. He then measured their heights, wrote down more figures, and developed a ratio. "Yep," he satisfied himself. "While walking, the ratio of stride length to one's height is about point forty-five; that means a fifty-foot giant walking would travel about twenty-two and half feet per stride. Multiply that number by nine-thousand and that's how many feet we needed to go to reach the Western Sea Tides where Troy is heading. That's two hundred and two thousand and five hundred feet, give or take, depending on how accurate my stride calculation is. Since a mile is 5,280 feet—let's see—that's about 38 and a half miles total—but we need to subtract the three and a half miles which we traveled already, and that leaves us with 35 miles to go." Tanner worked out some more figures. "At our current pace ... let's see ... that would take us 53 hours."

The gals stood quietly while Tanner wrote all his calculations down more neatly. They were impressed with his calculations.

"Well, that's just about like walking a marathon and a half," Bonnie said, doing her own math.

"Not me," Paige said with finality. "I'm *not* gonna do it unless someone carries me. Any volunteers?" She nervously looked around them and up the northern slope.

"I don't think we'll make it that far either," Bonnie agreed. "But I think the boys might just be able to keep up with Troy."

"I could too, if I tried. I'm a boy!" Tanner replied quickly. The older girls smiled.

"Boys tend to like math more than girls, so you obviously are a boy," Paige said. "Not that girls can't do math ... we can." She paused. "Tanner, would you help me with my math when we get back home? I teach you charcoal art." She figured this might take his mind off their predicament.

Tanner felt better even though his mother had told him girls could be just as good at math as boys. Wanting to show off a bit more, however, he dropped his notebook and gear, pulled out his compass, and began studying it. "Just as I thought," he mused. "We are heading due west based upon the sun's rise—those bends were a little tricky, though. So that's east, that's north, and that's south." He pointed in each direction, "Got it?"

"Yep," replied Guinevere. "I got it." She held out his notebook and pencil with a smile and walked over to Bonnie. Tanner stuck out his tongue. Bonnie remained unaware of their quarrel.

Now it just happened that where Bonnie had waited for them was a pit stop for the Trioptic Giants. It was a slurry slope, one of several rest stops for travelling Giants heading westward. The overlook gave them an ample view of the southern lowlands.

Paige had noticed this southern outlook with some anticipation when she had approached them. She also had the eerie feeling that they were being watched from above. It unnerved her. This feeling was only made worse as she was last in the wedding train; she had struggled not to panic.

The painful pebbles underfoot and rocks along the path prevented her from running in a full sprint. Her feet were cut up and starting to bleed a bit as it was, but the others hadn't noticed. With the young children present, she didn't want to openly discuss her thoughts with Bonnie. So, she anxiously walked to the outcropping and looked over the edge. Below trees sprinkled the slope cascading into a verdant sea of forest. To the right a valley cut deeper than the slope before joining the flat bottom further below. Paige didn't know its name at the time, but she was looking at the Valley of Turnus, a place that would have ultimate significance in that world, as you will soon learn, dear reader.

Paige wanted badly to descend to the softer sylvan landscape where she figured the soil would be gentler on her aching, burning feet than the Skyway with its rubble. So, she asked, "What was the message from the Conductor guy that the King spoke to us about?" She looked back at them pensively and then above and around them. "That was a weird rhyming riddle, wasn't it?!" She turned back again to look down, and continued, "Was that like *funny*, or what? They obviously enjoy rhymes here—did you see Troy's response? I suppose that's how the Conductor speaks to them. Yeah, it said something about the *lowlands*. Do you think it might be something we should consider?" She looked back at Guinevere drawing in the notebook.

"Yes." said Bonnie. "Troy actually made me think of King David dancing naked before the Lord." This sounded awkward. "I mean ... not so much him being naked ... but his ... uh ... dancing so freely ... umm ... but to the point, I think my dad would say that this *rhyming* speech is 'contextual' for them. What that means is meeting people where they *are* in order to speak with them in a way that they can understand and appreciate." She continued, "God became a person to speak directly to us so that we would understand clearly that God cares deeply for us and wants us to live a life of deeply caring for others. It's God's way to show love and speak clearly to people in ways that they can understand and want to follow." Bonnie found comfort speaking somewhat philosophically about this; thinking of her father also gave some relief from their current bad situation. In this way, she was regaining her presence of mind.

"But what does *that* have to do *with us?!"* Paige was growing impatient with no plan.

"Well, this way of *speaking* makes it easier for the original *audiences* to understand at that time, *back then*—like thousands of years ago—but it also makes it harder for us to understand *right now*. This is why the Bible is so misunderstood by us *today* because it was *originally* written to people in languages and situations *different* from our own."

Paige interrupted her again, "Okay. Certainly, we're in a different situation. *How* are we ever going to understand what the heck to do? And how is it that *we understand* the giants' language???"

"Yes, I've wondered this too. I'm guessing it's providential somehow ... a gift to be able to understand and speak to each other. It's like hearing and watching a Shakespeare play, right, set in Elizabethan times quite different than our own. If you keep *listening* and *trying* to make sense of the meaning of the words and the situation, a *sense* comes to you eventually, especially when you begin more and more to understand the flow and context of the story—its main characters, their motivations, and relationships. This happened to me once watching the 'The Tempest' with my cousins. It was very odd!" She paused and continued. "Well, that's how dad describes studying the Bible, too. It's a story with a series of connected scenes, you know, that actually fit together once you see how."

"Well, I'm not seeing it."

"Me neither, to be honest!"

"So, what are we *gonna do?"* Paige pressed the point. "What about the Conductor's *riddles* spoken through the giant king? What exactly *did* he say? Didn't he mention the '*lowlands*'? Shouldn't we be looking for *them?"*

She pointed down below into the valley longingly.

Bonnie looked at Tanner.

He frowned and pointed to Guinevere, saying, "I wrote it down ... it *seemed* important. Guinevere, may I *please* have my notebook back now? You've had a good turn with it."

She looked sheepishly at Bonnie, shrugging as if to say "*Okay*," and with great intention deliberately and slowly handed it back to him.

Tanner was indeed disappointed with himself that he needed Bonnie's help to get it back. Nevertheless, he received the notebook and flipped through it. He found the spot and read: "To feed the hungry is for you to succeed, to gather the substance of their every need."

"That's not right," interrupted Paige. "Not 'substance,' but 'sustenance'."

"Okay. Well, what's *that?* I'm only eight!" He made the correction.

"Please don't remind me." Paige smiled. "I guess I'll give you vocabulary lessons while you help me with my math. 'Sustenance' is *food* ... so ... I think we all know that this refers to helping 'Troyton-*sal'*—isn't that his name here?—Find something to eat. Come to think of it, I'm pretty hungry myself."

"No, Troyton-*suhl"* Tanner corrected.

Nevertheless, they all agreed with Paige's interpretation. Guinevere passed her the last of the apples she had brought. She too joined Paige looking out anxiously over the steep southern slope.

"What's next?" asked Bonnie.

Tanner continued, "Evil is spreading to souls down below, but enter you must the lands that are low."

"*There*! There it is!" Paige interrupted him.

Guinevere agreed, "Yes." She walked nearer to the edge and looked down. "That's low, *isn't it?* And...." She trailed off.

Just then a gigantic rodent quickly popped in and out of sight behind a large craggy rock on the slope not more than forty feet away at what appeared to be the start of a path. She blinked, and it was gone. Guinevere questioned whether she had imagined it. But she blinked again and it stood there in plain sight and quickly hopped back out of sight. She looked at the others, but no one else had seen. Its bear size didn't alarm her because its demeanor and features were such that she could only imagine it was friendly. The creature was agile and fidgety. Its eyes were masked white like a ground squirrel's, and race stripes streaked its sides.

Bouley Scurry of Verthana, Caelestepedia 48.376/455.23433

This animal was, in fact, a Bouley—creatures that regularly traveled up and down the slopes, alone or in scurries, to roam among the forests feeding on the fruit of its trees and leaving well-worn trails just the right size for earthen folk.

"And what?" asked Bonnie.

"Well," Guinevere continued excitedly, *"Look!* There's a way down! I think we should go." She studied the slope for further signs of the creature.

"Let's go, then," urged Paige.

Bonnie nodded in agreement. "Anywhere has got to be better than up here! That sun is beating down on us!"

Paige looked around one last time and stared up at the slopes behind them. She was quite certain now that they were being watched from above, so she eagerly led the way quickly down, not wanting to be last in the train while the others followed, hurrying to keep pace with her.

Chapter 13
A Bouley's Gift

Troyton-suhl had sustained his pace straight through on into the mid-afternoon. The sun energized his stony frame, warming and animating the motions of his graphite infused limbs. Lagging behind him, and quite unbeknownst to him, was Thomas, and farther behind still, Archer. Finally, Troyton-suhl, feeling again the pangs of hunger and recognizing edible rock, stopped at a roadside pool that was nearly dried up as in a drought. Nearby, a sizeable granite slab had been placed and eaten away, not by erosion, but by previous watchlings. The wayside rest stop had been well-appointed for a giant, one of dozens of areas erected by them and supplied with nutritious red granite all along the Skyway east to west. Considered sacred for a new watchling's journey, other giants did not pillage them. And so Troyton-suhl quickly set to work; placing a hand on the stone, he focused and fractured out morsels that he began ingesting.

Thomas arrived next, greatly relieved finally to catch a breather. He didn't mind running but surprised himself that he could maintain such a pace. Hands on his knees, he glanced at his watch which seemed to be running quickly. *"Time goes faster here,"* he thought. The sun had peaked and began to descend giving way to the evening sky. Throughout the run, he had seen no clouds. *"Odd,"* he thought.

Shortly thereafter, Archer came jogging up and sighed in relief, "Oh thank God!" He had finally caught up with the other two.

"Way to go, Archer!" Thomas cheered him in. "Awesome! Glad to see you!"

"*Whew!* ... What a jog! ... I'm so thirsty. I couldn't go much further. My legs are numb and I've got cramps." Archer was catching his breath.

"Me, too."

"What on earth is Troy doing?"

"Eating. He's so busy eating he hasn't even noticed me yet, the little pig—or should I said 'big' pig—he's taller than me now, I'm sure of it." Thomas was growing very concerned about his brother and how, and if, they ever would get him back home. "Archer, did you see the others? I can't see them coming yet. They're all coming still, aren't they?"

"That's just it," Archer answered back huffing. "Bonnie *had* to stop. We talked it over. Paige was way, way behind ... *geeez* ... even behind Guinevere and Tanner! So, a good way back, Bonnie figured they would *not* be able to keep up with us."

"What??! You're kidding me, right?!" Thomas was sick to his stomach.

"No, they're back, *way* back." Archer pointed and shook his head. "This *sucks.*"

This came as a hard blow to Thomas. The two friends sat there lost in their thoughts. Thomas then asked, "You didn't happen to get any food from Bonnie, did you?"

"Well, no. Remember Guinevere had the food.... *Crap!!!*" Neither said anything for a moment pondering their predicament. Archer spoke up again, "What the heck were those *sisters of ours* thinking to bring us here without *hardly* any food?!!!"

"Well, we should have gone back right away after we went into the Crossroads," Thomas commented calmly. "But ... we went along with it. There's nothing we can do now. At least Guinevere had some sense to bring some food."

"But she's with *them,*" whined Archer.

"True ... okay ... let's think about this. We've got to take stock of our situation. In a movie I saw once, the people stranded on an island did two things right away. First, they figured out what stuff they had. So, let's start there."

This task was manageable and gave Archer something constructive to think about. He started, "I have my bow with string—but no arrows. If I could make some, we could hunt with it. Also, I have this canteen with water in it. Dang, I forgot I had it!" He took a deep drink and handed it to Thomas.

"Oh, that's good!"

"Also, I should still have that lighter I found at the playground; let me see...," Archer placed the bow in front of him and rummaged out the lighter from his pocket and tested it. A flame flicked up and stayed on until it started to burn his thumb. "That's all I have other than my cowboy hat, leather vest, and the rest of my clothes." He stopped momentarily before adding, "Oh yes, and I have one piece of gum." He smiled.

Thomas nodded, "Good, then. We have weapons, a canteen, and fire! That's something at least." Then Thomas put down his useless heavy gun next to the arrowless bow and took his turn. "Alright, I have this gun, missing its pin, with the rope strap, my Swiss Army knife—thank God for Aunt Betty!—and this change ... thirty-seven cents; and my watch, of course. It still works, although it's busted, I think. That's it, besides my hunter's hat, camouflage jacket, and what I'm wearing."

While the two were sizing up the situation, Troyton-suhl had made a couple trips between the diminishing pool of water and the granite slab. Even as unappetizing as this was to watch and listen to, Thomas and Archer watched his noisy eating and began acutely to feel the pangs of their own hunger. Then without saying anything, Troyton-suhl laid down under a slight outcropping, appeared to fall asleep, and remained completely motionless.

Thomas pointed this out to Archer and put his finger to his mouth, "Shhhh...." Then he continued in a whisper, "Okay, the second thing they did in this movie was to figure out what needs they had. Then, they worked to meet those needs with what they had and what else they could find or make."

"Well, that's fairly obvious," Archer said quickly. "Food—we ain't got none unless the gum counts."

"Right. No food. That's the first thing we should work on."

"Oh, speaking of food and ... um ... I'm so hungry I was thinking of saying 'grace'...," Archer said. "And, that gets me thinking that we have one other thing, God. We're reading the Book of Esther as a family and God's not even mentioned at all in it! But my dad said God is *the* main character of the story, somehow arranging things that happen, and when they happen. And God gave the Israelites food when they needed it. So, God is a real resource for us, too."

"True. Let's pray then before we look for any food. But ... I wonder ... do you think that 'God' is here, too? I mean, this is a different world." Thomas had pondered this question.

Archer paused. "Well, I hadn't thought of it—but isn't God *everywhere?* Even on other worlds? My pastor says God is *everywhere*."

"Yeah, I think so. That's right." Thomas nodded in agreement. "And that means that the Conductor the giant king mentioned, if He is truly *good*, is very possibly the same as our God or somehow related to Him—maybe an angel or something. So, God might even have had—I mean, probably *must have had*—a hand in what's happening to us now." Inside Thomas, the feelings that this conclusion evoked were mixed; comforted certainly but also foreboding since he had teased Troy for being a jerk—now Troy-ton-suhl. He thought, *"Was Troy now being punished for my own failures and faults?!"* This was not pleasant for him to consider.

"Well, let's pray then," Archer said.

They bowed their heads not knowing *who* would pray nor exactly *what* to say. They sat there silently and prayed. After a few moments, a bouley popped up above the southern ridge and trotted over to the pool not more than thirty feet from them. It didn't seem to notice the three visitors. It carried a large, melon-like fruit—reddish and succulent. This was the creature's regular feeding time. The bouley proceeded to perform its cleaning and eating rituals, first washing its front paws and mouth with circular motions in the water and then dipping and washing the fruit and smelling it occasionally. Archer saw it first. Thomas noticed Archer's frozen gaze and turned to see the creature. The bouley then froze and stared at them in return. It fidgeted with his fore paws. It had never seen a human before, nor had it yet caught their scent. It enjoyed no predators in its world.

After some uncomfortable moments for the boys, who slowly reached for their useless weapons, the bouley turned and hopped away back down the ridge. But it had left the fruit behind. After several minutes, the two boys cautiously went over to pick it up. It's delicious, sweet smell drew out Thomas' Swiss Army knife, and he cut through its rind and into its pink flesh. The boys ate half of it. Nothing in their world had ever tasted so good! It tasted a bit like watermelon and strawberry, but with more robust flavor then these. It felt much more satisfying in their stomachs. They wrapped the other half in Archer's vest to eat later. Feeling sleepy, the two agreed that a little "shut eye" would do them both good while Troyton-suhl continued to lay motionless. Once he awoke, they would need to keep pace with him once again. So, they went over and laid down near to him, supposing that when he would awake, they would be woken up, too. Well fed, the two friends quickly fell fast asleep next to the growing, stony Troyton-suhl. They slept hard.

However, Thomas and Archer were mistaken. Awaking with only one hour of daylight remaining before nightfall, Troyton-suhl stepped over them (fortunately for them) and continued strided westward as the two young earthen boys slumbered on.

Chapter 14

Hilasdem, the Last Silver Snail

Guinevere continued to catch glimpses of the bouley all the way down the mountain slope. The path kept the travelers veering eastward away from the valley but ever down into a sylvan land filled with wondrous sweet and fruity fragrances. Further down along the path, each one of the four had picked up fallen fruit from one of the various kinds of trees. The fruit smelled "fantastic" according to Guinevere. However, she did not tell the older girls about the creature she kept seeing because she thought it might scare them, who then might decide to go back up the mountain to "safety." Besides, Guinevere had felt very good about descending into the woods. Before long, she let Tanner in on her secret, and the two whispered back and forth about the mysterious bouley as they journeyed downward to the lowlands. They began to imagine what sort of creature it was and what it would be like to ride on one.

Tanner pulled out his notebook once again and added several new pages of drawings and symbols. He and Guinevere agreed to a truce and shared the notebook from that point on.

As the earthen youth traveled downward, the trail leveled. In fact, they entered the northern region of a massive plateau known as Sylvanwood. The trees grew denser and varied more in kind. The underbrush was plentiful but somewhat dried up. It hid smaller rabbit-like and squirrel-like creatures that scurried about as well as rather large insects.

Paige was startled each time by these and would blurt out, "Did you see *that?!*" or "Look there! Didn't you *see* it?!"

The Mitchells, following Bonnie's lead, made a game of this by *denying* they had seen anything. "No. *Where*, Paige? *Where?!*" Then they pretended to be angry, "Paige, are you playing *games with us?!*"

Paige eventually caught onto their joke and began saying things like, "There's *nothing* interesting moving over *there*. Don't bother *looking*." Or, "Don't look at *that* fascinating creature by the white tree!" Her strategy worked because the others turned their glances, eager as they were to see some new animal or insect, and she caught them looking and smiled.

Once they spotted several large lady bugs clustered on leaves munching away. "Why, they're as *big* as a lamb!" exclaimed Paige. She wondered to herself, *"If ladybugs get this big, what about other bugs ... or spiders!"* She didn't verbalize this scary thought.

At the bottom of the trail laid a pine forest with upthrust rocks and an occasional rivulet trickling out from the rocks. Parts of it reminded Paige of the Canadian Shield she had travelled through once. Night was quickly falling and it grew suddenly rather dark. All were feeling the fatigue of the journey.

"There's a nice boulder to sleep next to over there," pointed out Bonnie. "Perhaps we can put some branches over the top like a lean-to."

"I wonder how cold it's gonna get tonight," Paige worried. "But it's comfortable enough now." She had found a newly broken off branch and was pulling it over. "I haven't seen a cloud in the sky today ... *isn't that odd, Bonnie?"*

"Oh. I hadn't noticed."

"Come here and try this!" Guinevere blurted out. While Bonnie and Paige were readying their make-shift shelter, the twins had split open one of the large almond shaped fruit they had found. "It's delicious." The two older girls stopped their work and ran over.

"Stop! What are you doing? It might be poisonous! You shouldn't be eating that until we know it's safe!" Bonnie chided them.

"It smells sweet. Besides, how are we going to test it?!" Guinevere stated matter-of-factly. She offered a piece to Bonnie, "Here, try some. I saw one of the animals eating one earlier." To their surprise, it was quite edible. Feeling no ill effects, together the party finished eating a whole fruit.

"Time for sleep!" Bonnie announced as if at home playing the role of her mother. But Tanner had already fallen asleep snugged up beside the boulder. Seeing him, Bonnie dubbed their sorry lean-to "good enough," and they all snuggled in next to him.

Humin Melon Fruit, charcoal by Paige Edwards

After lying down for a short time while drifting off to sleep, the ground beneath them began to vibrate. Then, the boulder started inching away from them, accompanied by distinct, little, wet smacking and suction sounds.

"What's *that*?!" Paige sat up fast. "Did you *feel* that??! *Shhh, listen!*" The others woke up with a start.

All at once their tiny canopy fell on them. As they remained huddled among the fallen branches in the dusky night, they watched mystified as the boulder rolled away. The problem was, however, that it was not "rolling"; it rather glided away. More alarming to them, however, was the sight of three humanoid creatures running alongside the boulder and then jumping agilely on top of it.

Tanner, fully awake now and wanting to act bravely, stood up and yelled, "Hey there! That's *our* boulder!"

Bonnie quickly pulled him down and shoved her hand over his mouth, smothering him temporarily, hoping the creatures had not heard. But the boulder stopped. One creature jumped down and began walking directly over to them.

"Is that you, Orín? It's me, Na'al. Come out. *Orín? ... Orín?*" It waited. "Sedgénu ... Sedgénu. Okay, I've *said* it. Now come *out!*"

Another creature popped out of hiding to the other creature's right. "Sedgénu, to you, too, Na'al. See, isn't that helpful?" Orín had developed a secret password 'system' that Na'al thought unnecessary.

"But I thought you were hiding over *there.*" Na'al pointed to the party's fallen lean-to. "Did you bring others?"

"No!"

At that the two hunched down, tense and still. Looking at each other and nodding, they began walking stealthily towards the fallen branches.

"It may be a bouley," Na'al whispered. "I smell humin fruit."

"Or, perhaps some wily yunts with their tricks," said Orín.

Bonnie and the others ducked as low as they could into the limbs in a futile attempt to hide. Their brightly colored wedding garments, even in the dark, would give them away.

Na'al clearly saw them then cowering. She stood and yelled back to some others, "Gnurl, Ranít, Hilasdem ... would you mind coming over here? We have a problem. Something *new* is here, I mean, like *really new.* And I think they're sentient with speech, too."

"*New?* Are you sure?" said a deep throbbing voice.

Bonnie had hoped that by remaining still and waiting it out, these creatures would leave them alone. She contemplated acting dangerously, jumping out at them and baring her teeth or something like that, but then thought the better of it. She feigned rather to play possum. From their brief conversations, she counted four of one kind of creature and one of another kind, which when it spoke, produced deep vibrations that pulsated inside her chest ... it was truly frightful.

The conversation that ensued confirmed Bonnie's count. The four earthen youth overheard bits and pieces from the whispered and urgent conversation of these strange creatures.

"Ranit, yes, *new?* ... Are you sure?! ... If they are something new, then we must beware."

"The Conductor foretold...." another said.

"But Hilasdem is *the* last Silver Snail!" said another.

"I know.... We must *go* to the *Narrows....*"

"Wheldon-olt's whereabouts are still unknown...."

"Bydelus has eyes everywhere ... he captured the others and is going to *harm* them."

"Harm them? They plan to put them to *death!"*

"Time is of the essence. We can't delay," throbbed the deep voice.

Finally, Paige snapped; she could take it *no longer*. She stood up and yelled out in a flurry of words in one long breath, *"Okay! We give up!* Please make it quick and painless and be sure to somehow let our parents know! You *know* what to do, right? Or *maybe* you don't? You have to go back up the mountain, turn right, go until you reach the pool, and when you get out of the first pool up there it's the pool closest to the Tree with the scarlet scarf on it. The green ring takes you back all the way!" Paige stopped to catch her breath trying not to panic.

Slowly the rest of the party stood up; Guinevere and Tanner slid their hands up into the air in full surrender.

The Musselkin stepped back wide-eyed.

To the earthen youth, these humanoids were quite petite, had long pointed ears, and looked quit child-like, yet were quite intelligent, even 'mature' sounding. They wore light, elegant garments made with warm colors. Two were clearly females with longer hair and jumpers and the other two were certainly males, slightly stockier. To Paige, the jumpers were more like pinafores.

But then a long tube like a white limb of a sycamore tree extended towards the earthen youth. From this next two knobby-ended smooth branches protruded still further out towards them. Slowly and then persistently a pulsating sensation started deep inside their bellies and the waves attuned themselves and pitched into audible sound, "Greetings, in the name of the Conductor, newlings. Please forgive our startling of you ... you, too, have startled our weary souls. But we intend no harm. I am Hilasdem."

"Yes, greetings," Na'al said anxiously, putting her hands up in the air as she looked at Tanner and Guinevere. She nudged Orín to do the same. Orín obliged her with what he thought was a greeting.

"Greetings! I am Orín. This is Na'al, Gnurl, and Ranít." He glanced at each nodding. Gnurl and Ranít put up their arms too. "We are Musselkin of the Silver Snails ... I mean, of *the last* Silver Snail ... *uuuff!"* Na'al jabbed Orín sharply.

"Yes," Na'al continued. "What Orín means to say is that we have urgent business and need to know which *side* you are *on*? And what is *your business* here?"

Bonnie and Paige also raised their hands in surrender until all stood about with arms held high.

When it appeared to Tanner that these new creatures had indeed *surrendered* in turn to them, it seemed safe for him, and then for Guinevere, to lower their hands. Then all the others followed suite. "Hi," he said.

Bonnie cleared her throat and introduced them, "Um, ... *this* is Paige, who surrendered us to you," she smiled at Paige. "*These two* are my sister and brother, Guinevere and Tanner. And *I* am Bonnie. We are from another world. You asked which 'side we're on.' Well, we're *on our own side.* We know of no other sides. We came into your world accidentally...." She paused and corrected herself, "Well, we came *on purpose* ... from a pool located somewhere above in the mountain. But our only purpose now is to help my giant brother become one of us *humans* again and go home back to our world."

The Musselkin's eyes widened at her last sentence. Bonnie realized that she may have divulged too much about their own situation.

"You have spoken truthfully, Bonnie," the large snail spoke again. "Even a yearling like myself can see this. You may entrust yourself to us. We are servants of the Conductor. Did you say there are others of your kind in our world *right now*?"

"Yes." Tanner eagerly spoke up. "There are three others of us up there, but one of them was turned into a giant ... *uuufff.*" Paige elbowed and glared at him, who took the blow, stepped forward, and pleaded rapidly, "We need your help! Our brother, Troy—now Troyton-suhl the new giant—is running to the Western Sea Tides up on the mountain Skyway, and we came down here. But the Conductor has given us a word through Salton-suhl, the Giant King, and we followed the big creature with long floppy ears down here...."

"What?!!" Bonnie interrupted him. "Tanner, what's this? What creature are you talking about?! You didn't tell us about this!!!"

"It's all my fault!" Guinevere chimed in. "I didn't tell you about the creature—it hopped and had long ears with black around its eyes like a racoon. It's cute. We've named him Bungy."

Gnurl entered the conversation, "That sounds like a bouley, actually—a wonderful animal of our world, used by the Conductor to bless and guide us. I smell, too, that you have eaten of humin, the bouley fruit."

Hilasdem vibrated startlingly, "Did you say, Salton-suhl the Giant King gave a Word from the Conductor? What is this Word? Please, tell me."

Tanner looked at Bonnie, who nodded. So, he picked up his backpack and pulled out his notebook, "I wrote it down in here." He rifled through his backpack some more and pulled out a flashlight. He clicked it on—the Musselkin stepped back in awe—and Tanner continued, "Okay, I think I wrote it out correctly, right Paige?" Their eyes met and they shared a smile. He blushed, but no one saw. "Um, okay, right here is what it said,

To feed the hungry is for you to succeed
to gather the sustenance of their every need;
Evil is spreading to souls down below,
but enter you must the lands that are low;
Help there those who reject evil plots
to rescue the sole one left with the spots;
Though a death It meets when twin giants give leap
but awaken it will by the Conductor's great keep.
Dew from on high will then sprinkle the sky,
to mend the moving of those who once did die.
One watching the watchers will need to take hold
to rid the lowland of that one gild of gold.
Stay true to the One who bids you to go,
but return you will through the water's green glow.

That's it." Tanner ended and looked bright-eyed at his new friends.

"Well," started the musselwoman Ranít, "if that's not as plain as the drummels of a derbel's hive. They're not with Bydelus, that's for sure. They've been sent here to help us!" The Musselkin all readily agreed.

"We must be quickly on our way, far far away from the Valley of Turnus!" Na'al urged. "The twin giants are working its southern slopes and we must protect Hilasdem, *the Last One*. We have lost precious time. Would you please come with us?"

"Well," responded Bonnie, speaking on behalf of them all. "Thank you for the offer ... but we must consider this together privately, please. Give us a moment." She turned to look at her party discerning any dissenting view. Guinevere and Tanner each wore eager looks; Paige grimaced slightly and shrugged her uncertainty, but then slowly nodded.

Bonnie turned back to the Musselkin and the last Silver Snail, "Okay, we'll go with you."

Little Guinevere tugged at Bonnie's dress and asked, "How much farther will we have to walk, Bonnie? I'm *so* tired."

"Not a problem," vibrated Hilasdem. "Hop on top, you two little ones can sleep a bit. But I have some questions for you; we have much to discuss tonight."

Chapter 15
The Yunt Pack

The stars twinkled dimly overhead as if veiled behind a sheath of water. Archer stirred and was the first to awaken. He was unsure exactly where he was. Then he remembered, *"I'm at the Mitchell's house ... sleeping over."* What a dream he had had! He then looked up and noticed the stars and

Archer stargazing along the Giants' Skyway, Gimp art by Archer Edwards

gazed studiously at them; they in turn gazed serendipitously back at him saying, "*This is not the Mitchell's house.*" He instinctively began to search for the familiar star constellations. When he couldn't see the Big Dipper, Orion, or any of the many other "normal" constellations, nor in fact the

Milky Way, the strange stars announced to him, *"Neither is this your world, nor even your galaxy...."*

Suddenly, Thomas snorted and startled Archer.

He woke him with a quick shove, "Thomas, Thomas! Wake up! Get up!" Archer looked about; no one else was there! He urged him again panicking, "Wake up! Troy's gone! We got to go to follow him!"

Thomas shot up then. He had been dreaming and had forgotten all about their burden. *"Oh my!* It's dark ... it's very late! Let's go! Maybe we can catch up with him yet tonight!"

Gathering their meager belongings, they set off immediately to follow Troyton-suhl along the ancient Giant Skyway heading westward, illuminated only by the alien starlight.

After walking around the next bend, Archer soberly said, "Boy, I can't believe this is happening."

"Me either."

"Surreal."

"Unbelievable, really."

"Well, it's *kinda* like camping, though. Remember the Sleeping Bear Dunes last year?"

"That was a *great* trip. But this trip sucks! These mountains are quite *a bit taller*, don't you think?"

"Are you joking?! These are *huge*, more like the Rockies!" He laughed. He started jogging and Archer matched his pace.

"At least this broad road is easy enough to follow with the stars out."

"Do you see the moon anywhere?" Thomas asked Archer, knowing that he liked astronomy.

"No. There may be no moon for this world. There's also no Milky Way."

"No candy bars?! Haha. You hungry?" asked Thomas. He didn't understand.

"No. We're in a different galaxy."

Thomas stopped and the two friends looked at each other and then laughed, for to cry would not have been manly.

"Well," said Thomas, "this is *way* better than the Sleeping Bear Dunes." Archer didn't think so, nor did Thomas really. They jogged on quietly for a while.

"Hey, that reminds me, Archer. Did you get any of the rings from Bonnie?"

"No. I suppose that Tanner still has them. If anything happens to him, I suppose we're stuck here in this world."

"Well, let's hope not. The others wouldn't leave without us, *would they?*" asked Thomas.

"No," replied Archer with some conviction. "Paige would get in *big* trouble." He laughed nervously. "But *somehow* we got to meet back up with them."

They were silent again. Their fun had turned sour so quickly.

"Okay, let's pretend we're marooned here," Thomas continued.

"We *are* marooned here," Archer stated.

"Never mind that. That only makes this more urgent." Thomas wanted to have some sport with the younger, more fearful Archer. "Let's talk survival again. We've figured out what we have—we still have that half piece of fruit, right? We already talked about what we need. To review, we need to follow Troyton-suhl, keep eating to stay alive, and we must add—*obviously*—meeting back up with the others and getting back to our world in *our own* galaxy." He finished this dramatically.

"Yep. That about sums it up."

"But, Archer, there's one other thing that I've learned from the movies. We need to think carefully about what *dangerous things* lurk around in *this* world—like bad guys, man-eating animals, aliens, and stuff like that. I've noticed often movie characters don't ever consider this last thing at all, and then ... *they* ... *GET KILLED!!!*"

"*Shut up*!" Archer said impatiently. "Don't be *stupid!* You're not scaring me!"

"Then they *GET EATEN!!!!*" The words echoed along the Skyway in the enclosed corridor they had just entered.

At this, however, Archer shuddered and ran a little faster. Thomas was rather pleased with himself, having pulled off his joke quite well. In fact, it was a little *too* well done, for he himself gripped his useless rifle tighter and picked up his pace with Archer and looked behind him anxiously.

"Okay ... so ... what if you're right?" Archer pretended not to be bothered, keeping pace with Thomas. "We had better talk about that now." He renewed his grasp on his arrowless bow. His other hand groped and patted the outside of his front pocket for the lighter should they need to make a fire to scare away any animals.

As the two boys ran and talked nervously along the ancient Skyway, a pack of ape-like creatures followed them eagerly, excited by the strange creatures that had just begun to run.

"Did you *see* them?!" Archer, looking back, had caught a glimpse of the creatures.

"*What??* You're joking, *right?!*" demanded Thomas.

Archer answered by running faster with all his might, leaving Thomas behind.

"Right??! *You're joking?* You're just getting me back...." Thomas tried to catch him, looking behind him.

"*No*, I'm not! There's at least *five* of them!" Archer yelled out. "*Run! They're after us!!!*"

In fact, the scent of the split humin fruit had attracted a pack of foraging yunts, curious, fun-loving animals, although Thomas and Archer, of course, did not know this. The yunts loped merrily after these new creatures with some delight. They weaved in and out amongst themselves, at times mimicking the boys' running style looking between one another as if in some competition to outdo each other in this. In their excitement, the yunts squealed a bit like pigs and even at times yelped like beagles—a strange and terrifying cacophony to Thomas and Archer.

So, needless to say, the boys ran as fast as they could, looking back periodically to see if the animals were 'gaining' on them, which they were not. Rounding a bend, barely visible now at night, the boys redoubled their desperate pace to get away. They kept a good running pace up until, at one point when both had looked back simultaneously, they tripped head over heels on a rock wall laying across the middle of the skyway, nearly invisible in the starlit night. The boys, momentarily disoriented and confused, righted themselves and scrambled to put their backs against the short wall. They fumbled with their weapons and peaked back over, peering sharply about the road for the alien creatures. Nothing moved and all was quiet. The creatures disappeared.

After some moments, Thomas whispered, "We've lost them."

"I *doubt* it," Archer replied. "Why were they chasing us? Did you notice when they ran upright, like *us*?"

"Maybe they want something ... um, that fruit! Give it to me."

Archer did so and Thomas threw it back over the wall. They sat down again taking big breaths, calming down. But they soon heard padded steps, sniffling sounds, and smacking of lips. The friends looked back over and Archer let out a whimper at the sight of the five creatures taking bites out of their humin fruit. Archer got his lighter out. The yunts finished eating, sat down, and looked at the two earthen boys peaking at them over the top. With a couple of clicks, Archer lit up a small circle of light around them and pushed his hand towards the pack. This allowed the two finally to get a good look at the yunts.

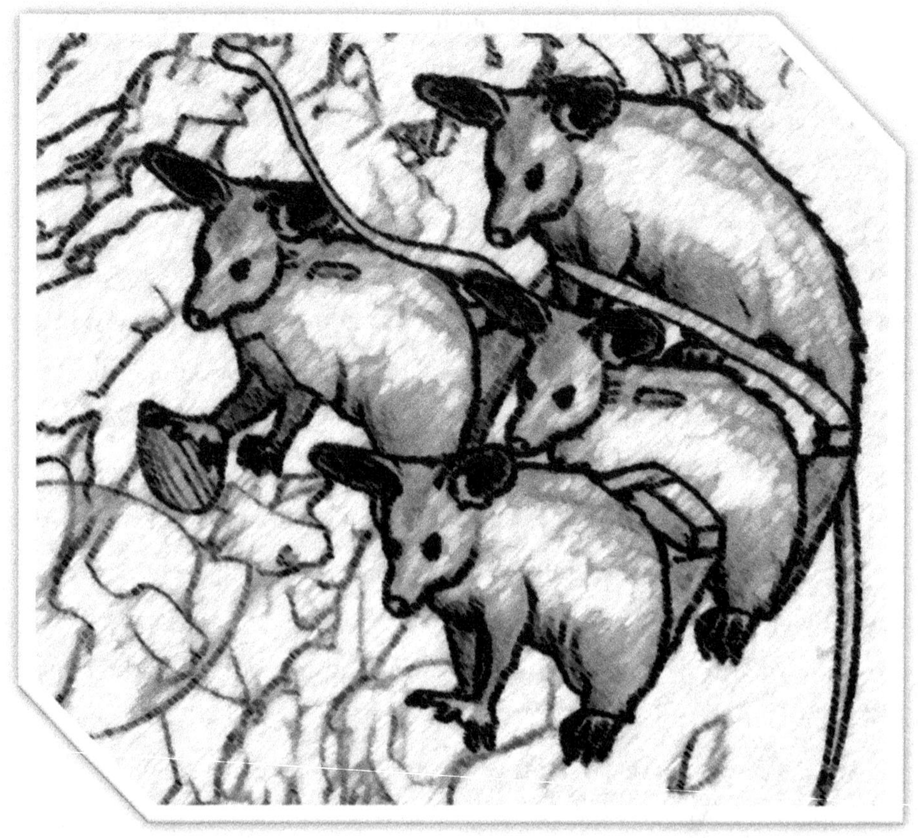

Yunt Pack as related by Archer Edwards and Thomas Mitchell, charcoal by Paige Edwards

Thomas first thought of them as skinny brown bears with rabbit-like heads, large ears, and coarse hair. But as they debated later about the incident, Archer rightly pointed out that they were not nearly fat enough to be bears and had large fruit bat-like ears, long tails, and beady black eyes like opossums. They moved more like monkeys, mostly on all four feet but also were able to stand upright on their back feet.

The lighter did not bother the yunts one bit, however. After taking turns taking bites of the fruit, they sat and stared at the two earthen boys huddled together with useless weapons, who had to take turns holding the lighter because it burned their thumbs. The passing of the lighter between them was at first somewhat frantic, because it would get so hot that they had to blow and spit on it to cool it down before the other would fire it back up. All the while, the ever-watching yunts, amused by their antics, would lean in closer with awful, large grinning teeth to see and imitate what the boys were doing.

All was quiet except for a periodic "Ouch," spitting sounds, and then clicks. Eventually, the two earthen lads stopped with the lighter since they figured the creatures meant them no harm. So, instead they grabbed and pointed their weapons firmly at the yunts, and eventually slouched down against the wall, weapons pointed up, and fell asleep in a ready position.

Unbeknown to the sleeping boys, after an hour when they were fast asleep, the yunts hopped upon the wall and one even dared touch Thomas's head. This yunt entered into Thomas's fitful dream awareness and felt what he was then feeling; it learned much about these new creatures. Another yunt placed its forepaw on Archer's shoulder and guided his dreaming a bit to show him more about the Skyway environs. While this occurred, another yunt slowly pulled Archer's bow from his grasp and another placed a branch of equal size with a large leathery leaf at one end; it was, in fact, an uneven trade since the leaf would later provide helpful daytime shade and nighttime warmth for the boys. The yunt pack then corporately defecated nearby in a communal pile as was their custom—their final offering to the strangers—and went on their way foraging throughout the night.

Chapter 16
The Conductor

Bonnie and Paige took in the alien world with their new alien friends. The journey during the night was truly magical. The two older girls had come to have no reservations about going with the Musselkin and their snail, as they thought of Hilasdem. They were convinced that Na'al and Orín and the others were on the *right* side. Guinevere and Tanner had quickly fallen asleep with the gentle swaying atop the huge snail. As the twins slept, Bonnie and Paige walked along and listened as their Musselkin companions eagerly and trustingly related the many terrible events of the previous year. Hilasdem rarely spoke and focused instead on finding the correct trail and the right food, stopping on occasion to devour some succulent fern frond or large leaves of various shrubs that were made sparser due to the drought of the past year.

During the night Bonnie and Paige learned about the boundaries of Sylvanwood, its divisions and governance by the Musselkin, which had turned corrupt and corrupted in turn the majority of the Musselkin who had grown lazy and complacent in their responsibilities in the lowlands, which upon learning disturbed Paige and Bonnie. This story made the dark of the night even darker. The Musselkin had recently preferred, rather than working together, to rival each other in their artisanship and creative designs. They competed with one another to attain to higher levels of social status through game play and other amusements, which Bydelus, his wife, Harpís, and their only son, Creyvyn, had initiated. This "first" family also had introduced many *new* words that nurtured longings and wants and fostered ideas which then formed actions and behaviors and habits inside and among the Musselkin. Na'al, Orín, Gnurl, and Ranít took turns relating and explaining all these matters, weeping intermittently as they did so because the story also involved the dying of many Musselkin and nearly all of the snails.

Thus, too, Bonnie and Paige learned of the drought and plight of the Silver Snails by the hand of the three Trioptic Giants—Wheldon-olt, Bryton-duhl, and Nimbrik-al. The girls were aghast that such slaughter could happen, especially in a world made by the Conductor, presumably God of "all things." And, yet, in their very own world of earth, they almost daily heard news reports of murders, bombings, wars and worse no less by the hands of humans against humans made in the image of God. Bonnie thought that one might readily expect "scary" giants to do such things because in "Jack and the Bean Stalk" and other such stories, giants always seemed to be "grinding kid's bones to make their bread." She was definitely glad that Tanner and Guinevere were sleeping as they talked of these horrors. However, while this was true, her thoughts went out to Thomas and Archer, fearing what they might be facing with Troy up in the giants' land.

The severity of the situation in Sylvanwood worsened, in the estimation of both Bonnie and Paige, when their Musselkin companions gave special attention to narrating the dreadful rise of Governor Bydelus. His rise, it became clear to them, had been responsible for many of the evils that had begun to plague the Musselkin—*"bad done on purpose."*

"This is '*damnable*'," the earthen girls agreed.

"What does *damnable* mean?" Na'al didn't understand.

"It's when what someone does is *so* bad, *so* evil, that *this* deserves severe punishment," Bonnie explained. "It's an official pronouncement—God's judgment—that something is indeed so evil and so utterly to be avoided that it's shunned *forever*."

This notion the Musselkin understood as being "estranged," foretold and explained to them by the Silver Snail Decordem, but to its *uttermost* extreme.

The earthen youth were then told that it was at Bydelus's hand in the making of the gold giant effigy that the first ever Musselkin death had occurred to one of Bydelus's own friends, Governor Kataloas. Paige and Bonnie then realized that death had *never* occurred in Sylvanwood prior to this tragedy, either to snail or Musselkin.

Paige was curious, having admired the Musselkin's lovely skin, "So, ... if you don't mind me asking ... how *'old'* are each of you? I mean, your hair and your skin are *beautiful.*"

"Old?" The Musselkin looked at each other and chuckled. Na'al spoke for them, "We're not sure what you mean."

Bonnie grew more curious still, "You know, 'new' verses 'old' as in been around a long time, like by counting days, months, and years old."

"These are things we *don't* count," offered Orín.

"But, don't you *know when* you were born, when you started to exist?" Paige was flabbergasted.

"Well ... *when* is not as important as *that we have come to* exist—*that's* what matters," explained Na'al.

"So," asked Bonnie, "Don't you have an *age*, as in ... like ... how many *years* since you were born?!"

"No," flatly responded Ranít.

"What a *silly* notion!" Gnurl laughed with Ranít at the thought of this.

"Why," concluded Paige, "I guess that makes you ... *age-less!"* She laughed with Bonnie at the thought of that.

As they continued in the night, some Musselkin, it was explained, blamed Bydelus, too, for the ever-growing drought in which the spring fed streams and morning mists were diminishing. At this suggestion, Hilasdem spoke up that, although there was a connection, it would be mistaken to blame Bydelus specifically for that. But the snail offered nothing else about the specific origins of the drought.

The conversation continued that, in view of growing public concerns that Bydelus's rise to power had somehow correlated, or even caused the drought, Bydelus himself maintained and prevailed upon the masses rather that the drought was "a celestial sign" that what had befallen the snails by the hand of the three Trioptic Giants was due to "Providence" since the drought prevented the rearing of the young snails anyway. "It was obviously time for the snails to 'fend for themselves' rather than burden the Musselkin," he insisted. Indeed, Bydelus explained that Wheldon-olt, Nimbrik-al, and Bryton-duhl were sent from the Conductor above, who had brought the giants to them for their enlightenment and advancement through the wonders of their public works. And this claim to speak for the Conductor and to explain away the evil murder of snails due to the plan of the Conductor, Bonnie then surmised, was in fact the worst and indeed the most damnable of Bydelus's actions. It was, indeed, "devilish" to claim that blatant *evil* was God's doing.

Further details of the "Bydelus narrative," that Bonnie and Paige heard, are worth relating here for you, dear reader. Bydelus, as you may remember, was the governor of the second city of Nimbyn in the Central District of Sylvanwood. Upon the completion of his one-year term, Nimbyn would alternate to become the first city. The selection of all the governors was by divine appointment, in which the Conductor would communicate through any achenes filled sedge shrine who was selected as governor for the next year. By divine law, this selection must be confirmed by two or three witnesses. Never had a governor been chosen twice in succession. Yet, this is what Bydelus had laid claim to, with not two nor three, but with *four* "witnesses." And, with the alternation of the first and second cities, he thus became governor of the first city of the Central District, and so also Chief Governor of the Musselkin for the year.

The populace of his city of Nimbyn, which he elevated to the status of "nobility" (a new word), was enraptured with his manner of speech and progressive thinking. He gathered around him the "best" of the citizens—the "elite" class (another *new* word)—and garnered wider influence even among the other districts. Six of the other nine governors soon supported him, and the other three were removed from any influence, two through "accidental" deaths and one through exile, Sir Dernal of the second city of Kerr, Na'al's father, who had formed an underground coalition faithful to the Conductor. Orín, Gnurl, and Ranít were among the seven hundred still faithful to Hilasdem, the Last Silver Snail.

When the slaughter of the snails began in earnest, the giants were relentless and ruthless. Some Musselkin supporters of Bydelus aided the giants in their capture, which was not easy, since the adult snails traveled broadly. The snails' journeying at night while the Giants slumbered, made it that much more difficult to track them down when they fled. Moreover, the snails travelled far abroad through the salty Silver Sea and out east across the sweet inland sea. When in Sylvanwood, the Musselkin had always, as stewards of the snails, kept a basic accounting of the whereabouts of each one of the snails. But, fatefully, as it was well-known, it was time for the snails to return to Sylvanwood, some after decade-long journeys, for breeding and rearing of the newly born snails. These young snails were nurtured by the Musselkin and remained below the mountain slurry ridge for their first six months eating voraciously and growing at a pace to match. Both mature adults and these newly hatched young snails were wiped out almost entirely by the three giants within the first month of their descent into the sylvan lowlands. At six months, the young snails would have traveled westward across the Silver Seas to undergo their furtivement, a rite of passage in which the snails would grow in their knowledge and relationship with the Conductor. The exact nature of the journey remained a mystery to the Musselkin, and since they themselves were quite unmotivated to journey over rushing river or broad sea (being the land lovers that they were), they never imagined even asking the snails about it, content as they had been with what relationship the snails offered them in relation to the Conductor within Sylvanwood. To the Musselkin, the boundary of knowledge was accepted within the constraints of divine mystery—any further inquiry would have been considered sacrosanct.

The previous year's yearling snails, returning from their furtivement, were also snatched up and devoured by the giants to the dismay of many, but sadly to the ignorance of most. Instead, Chief Governor Bydelus filled and occupied the minds of the Musselkin with other ventures and pursuits for the "betterment" (another *new* word) of their surroundings and the realization of hitherto never even conceived imaginations of possessions and glory. Among the masses of the Musselkin, the giants' labors and marvelous works arranged by Bydelus began to satisfy their lust for more, for ease and for glory, and so excused the giants' murderous violation of the second law of the universe.

This dark, depressing Bydelus narrative took up the better part of the night's journey. At its end, at the deepest darkness of its depths, the eastern sky began to lighten. Spirits lightened, too, and an excitement grew mysteriously among the Musselkin friends. The snail stopped at the end of a foggy clearing, growingly illuminated by the sunrise. The Silver Snail's shell started to shine gloriously, radiating iridescent colors in gentle reflecting prism bands.

The Conductor's Green Flame on Sedge Achene, photograph (edited) by Bonnie Mitchell

Bonnie pointed to a sedge clump nearby whose fruited achenes were each glowing with a flickering green flame.

"Wake up, Guinevere! Wake up, Tanner!"

Bonnie urged the little ones. The Musselkin were now very excited and anxious-like, but not anxious in the way humans too often are, but truly worshipfully expectant. They possessed an underlying joy in their feeling. Tanner and Guinevere rubbing their eyes sat up at the first song of the morning throbbing through them from the snail upon whom they sat:

"Praise to the One who warms the night and shines upon our drowsing;
Praise to the One who fills the morning and enlightens us in our rising;
The Conductor is his Name, the One whose wisdom created us all,
Snail, Kin, and Giant, the Conductor sustains despite the fall!
Accept our praise, most glorious One, who loves us eternally,
Receive our thanks for Your provision granted not sparingly.
Praise, Praise to the Name, the Conductor, the One and the Same.
May it ever be!"

The Musselkin and the snail worshiped together by the sedge as the green flickers glowed richer and deeper. Then the human twins jumped off Hilasdem as another song began. Paige was the first to notice that the Musselkin had taken off their shoes; she fit right in. Pointing this out to the others, the others took off their shoes, too.

After nearly an hour, as the mists were completely dispersed with the fully risen sun, a hush fell upon them all. The whole sedge now blazed brightly in emerald green and a voice spoke clearly and warmly from it shimmering brilliantly: "Acceptable in my presence is your praise, faithful Musselkin. Blessed are you in my praise! You have acted with wisdom and prudence in these troubled times to have received my sent ones."

The voice paused as heads turned and eyes gazed upon Bonnie, Paige, Tanner, and Guinevere with wonder.

"Welcome, Bonnie, Guinevere, and Tanner of the Mitchell Family, and Paige of the Edwards Family. Your coming into this world was not by accident, as you have already discerned. Nor was it by your own design, but it was by my will for the benefit of *all*. Of your part to play, I have already spoken, through Salton-suhl, my servant on the mountain ranges. You can be assured that your brothers are well and Troyton-suhl is growing by strides and bounds. After their mission and yours is completed, you will all reunite after the start of my Restoration.

"But now, my faithful Musselkin, you must be careful to carryout out your part. You must travel with haste to finish your journey to the Narrows across from the Kliffs of Kalm. Do not worry what befalls you there. But do as Hilasdem counsels you, turning neither to the left nor to the right. Follow his word. Watch to learn my Wisdom that dwells fully in him for your benefit and even for the sake of the wayward giants.

"And now, behold, here is my Last One, Hilasdem, my Beloved One. Listen to him in all that he says. Peace be with you!"

The green shimmer flashed brightly at these last words and then dulled, leaving the sedge bush unharmed. The sun seemed suddenly to make the woods brighter and full of life.

Eyes of surprise turned to Hilasdem, whose tubular eyes gazed back gloriously at them standing around—the silver shell emanated the green glow that did not fade. A throbbing penetrated their bodies, "I must not travel anymore in the sun today. Our one group must go now in two parties but still acting as one. Na'al, Orín, Gnurl, and Ranít—my faithful ones—Remember all my words to you." The snail's neck protruded fully, and eyes were extended to the utmost and full of earnest. "My time to leave you has come. But you four must go ahead to the Narrows. Be watchful, but fear not what will befall you there. I will soon come with the others during the night."

Despite looks of confusion and some alarm at these words, Hilasdem's confident gaze and presence quieted the Musselkin's anxious spirits and questions arising out of doubt that they considered asking right then. And, so, the two parties split—the Musselkin continued their journey eastward during the heat of the day while the earthen youth stayed in the shade with Hilasdem. Unknown to the four eastward travelers, the giant Wheldon-olt was constructing a bridgeway across the narrowing of the Great River connecting Sylvanwood with the Land of Kalm. The four Musselkin journeyed directly to that very location.

Chapter 17
Tipton-tyne Baer

At the crack of dawn, Troyton-suhl woke up. The Great Mover's warm rays filled him with optimism and motion. His thoughts were fresh and well-organized; his limbs sturdy and able. He was still himself—Troy, a boy from earth. His dreams had confirmed in his self-awareness that he was still "human" inside his soul. But he also was something else in his flesh. He felt torn between this new composition of his flesh and his own will and thoughts. These converged in his longings and wants. This convergence was the battleground. Not long upon waking, he had realized this. His behavior towards the others, his family and friends, had been detestable, and yet he had been "powerless" to do otherwise—or so he had thought. He had been immature, acting like a baby. He had wrestled with this "excuse of powerlessness" throughout the night as he slept. He sat up now alert and ready for the challenge of the new day.

"*Whoa ... Ahhhhh!!!*" Troyton heard someone scream. "*Move, move, move ... It's an avalanche!!!*"

Troyton-suhl turned and was relieved to see Thomas and Archer scurrying away from under him as he stood towering above them. He smiled. He enjoyed being so big and strong. He belted out, "It's me, guys! Don't worry! It's me, Troy!"

Thomas and Archer turned and shielded their eyes from the rising sun to gaze at the now eighteen-foot tall Troyton-suhl. They then looked down; they were standing in fresh dung. "Yuck ... Shit!!!" They laughed to say it "Shit!!!"—back on earth they would have gotten their mouths washed out with soap.

"Geez," Archer groaned. They stepped out of the scat carefully and looked up at Troy.

"Oh, my God!!! Troy, or Troy-*ton, you are a giant indeed!*" Thomas said relieved. "We lost you last night and came running and then these five scary creatures chased us, surrounded us, and were going to eat us, and ... then crapped over here *apparently*. I can't believe my eyes! We *found* you! Here you are!"

Troyton-suhl replied, "No one will eat you if *I* have anything to do with it! Guys," he continued, "I've ... well ... I've got to ... um. I treated you bad, real badly—I was so hungry and I ran to eat!—and I ... I ... knew it was wrong ... but I left you two lying there last night ... but my stomach ... and ... my body," he looked down and rubbed his belly, "it just kept running and aching and I needed to keep striding until it was dark and then I just laid down here until I woke up." He looked up at the sun. "I dreamt and thought about it all night long! Lord willing, I *will not* run off without you again. Please ... forgive me, will you??!"

"Well...." began Thomas, who was surprised and couldn't even fathom what to make of this confession from his rock-hardened little brother. "I'm surprised to hear you apologize. Yes, I am ... relieved even because if you were still mad at us ... I wasn't sure, you know ... we'd be in a lot of trouble, you being a giant and all. Just look at your arms!" Troy smiled and looked as he flexed his arms.

Archer chimed up, "Yeah ... please don't run away from us anymore. I mean ... we've had quite a time of it. We had to split up from the others, we're hungry, and we've been chased by a pack of ugly bears and nearly burnt our fingers off just to scare them *off.*" As proof, he and Thoams raised their burnt fingers for his inspection.

Troyton was suddenly overcome by remorse. He let a let out a deep sigh and his eyes flooded with dark carbon fluid resulting in large dark teardrops that rolled down his cheeks. He was still just a boy inside the giant exterior. The others noticed. But suddenly a strange look fell upon Troyton-suhl and he doubled over.

"Ohhhhh ... My belly hurts right *here*," Troyton-suhl said, pointing to a bulging line along his mid-section, an oozing seam.

Thomas wanted to offer to help him, "Well, let me see, maybe you have a cut here ... or something is stuck ... in right *here*. It looks like your *bleeding*," he poked at the spot. "Kneel down," he urged. The giant tentatively lowered himself but this made the spot even more uncomfortable.

Both Archer and Thomas looked at the seam. Thomas saw grey milky dribbling from the crease. "Do you *bleed* at all?" he asked.

"Not that I know of... *Oowwww ... ouch!!!* This's worse than a cramp!!!"

"It looks like ... you may have a sliver or something in *here*. There's something sticking out, like a broken plate or something. Kinda *gross* ... um ... Archer, help me pull on *this ... here...,*" he pointed, "to see if I can grab something out of it. If it hurts, just let us know. One ... Two ... Three...."

Troyton's flap opened, and a fluid wave sloshed out all over them. The two were soaked in a gooey Trioptic Giant slurry mess.

"Ooooooh ... Yuck!!!" the two shouted, completely covered with grey slurry. They stood frozen arms out from their sides in shock. "What the hell?! Oh... it smells!!! Are you ... okay? Are you bleeding to death or something?!" asked Thomas.

"Aaaahhhh ... no ... that feels *so much* better. Thanks!" Troyton-suhl said. "Whew! I was hurtin' bad. No. I'm not bleeding. See, there ... it's just stopped. I just need ..." he looked around, "some toilet paper or something."

"Did you just ... just ... *eeewww* ... I don't even want to say it ... did you just *crap* on us?!" Archer was utterly disgusted.

"At least it doesn't smell *that* bad ... it's *like* clay," Thomas said, trying to smear it off his arms, belly, and legs and slinging it to the ground.

"*Phew!* ... it stinks to me, and bad!" remarked Troyton. "Let's get out of here *fast!*" He straitened up and stepped away. "To make it up to you—*even as smelly as you are!*—I'll carry you. Climb up!" He reached down with both arms and the two scrambled up to sit on each shoulder. This was a small consolation to them for having been shat upon by a Trioptic Giant.

Nevertheless, the copper-colored giant with the two slurried grey clan members were soon striding across the giant skyway with the rising sun at their back. Troyton-suhl, despite their smell (which was not terribly bad for Archer and Thomas, we assure you, dear reader), kept reflecting out loud with them about his experience inside his rocky shell of a body. Noticeable to Archer and Thomas was that Troyton spoke using words 'at home' with the physical sciences, and often specifically with math and physics. He discussed momentum, inertia, gravity, trajectories, friction, density, and angles. As they walked, he calculated stride rates and distances. They made games of timing using Thomas's watch and guessing the number of strides Troyton-suhl would need to reach certain waypoints; or, how long it would take to reach the next bend in the distance. Troyton's calculating mental acuity was truly astounding. He finally figured about himself and shared with them, "I have my own inner self and will, but the mind and body of a giant with purpose, trajectory, and inertia."

After several hours the boys happened upon another wayside pool, equally drought-ridden, but full enough for a swim. Troyton strode right to its edge and stopped promptly. "Let me *first* get a drink—is all I ask—before you *must* take a bath," urged Troyton-suhl. He bent over and drank for nearly ten minutes. He then surfaced and strode over to the granite deposit to eat his fill of the rose-colored granite. The two other boys entered the pool and began swimming and splashing about. Thomas was able to dunk Archer once, evoking a "Your, jerk!" and laughing; but he couldn't do it again.

From the far end of the quarry, a gruff, giant voice startled Troyton-suhl, "*Pssst*. Over here ... would you spare me a morsel?" Troyton-suhl was surprised and looked about him inspecting every nook and cranny.

"*Here* ... over *here*. I'm on the edge. Yes, here," he urged him on. "Youngling, could you spare me a morsel? I'm an old-timer who's slowed down to a stop."

Troyton-suhl saw that the giant had eaten all the granite in a circle around it. It was pitiful to think of his condition, abandoned and forlorn. "Of course, sure," he said. It was the right thing to do. "Here, you can have the first piece." He strode a few steps over and surrendered up the fragment. "What's your name, old-timer?"

"Tipton-tyne Baer is my name, from the Cobelstoyne Clan watched by Anton-duhl Meer of the gems," he replied. "Rather, of the *One* Gem."

Hearing "gems," Troyton-suhl began something akin to drooling even though he had never tasted one. "Oh, isn't *that* interesting? My name is Troyton-suhl of the ... of the ... Mitchell clan, of the world Earth, born here in the one-thousandth Cycle of the High Season."

"*Say* ... that's *exotic*! Did you say one-thousandth cycle?! Hmmm ... I've *lost* count. I haven't seen a watchling in quite some time—by the size of you—I'd guess 23 hours old?"

"Precisely. I came out of the Pool of Emergence yesterday morning."

"And Mitch-*ell* is your watcher? I've never heard of Mitch-*ell*."

"Well, yes, *kinda*. To speak more precisely, on earth I'm a *Mitchell*. But my watchers include these two softlings," he pointed to Thomas and Archer who, very unimpressively, were splashing in the pool, laughing and horsing around. They looked at Troyton a moment as Thomas dove hard to dunk Archer and they laughed hard again.

"Yeah, times are tough *for sure...*" Tipton-tyne said shaking his head. "Probably no other suitable watchers are around. They're not scrawny yunts, are they? No ... can't be. What sort of softlings are they? I've never seen their exact kind on our world."

"Well, believe it or not, under my stony exterior I'm one of them, too.

We're from a planet we call 'earth.' We're humans, created by God and redeemed by God's Son, Jesus, and awaiting His return and a New Heaven and a New Earth." Saying this surprised Troyton-suhl, but their cosmic relevance he rightly figured bore *even* upon the current condition of this falling world.

"*Really???* That's what we're awaiting! Welcome to *Verthana*!"

"So, *that's* where we are. Never heard of it." Troyton continued, "King Salton-suhl said that he believed that the Conductor had brought us here for a purpose. Even in my present form, I have calculated the possibilities based on all that I know, and my only conclusion is that your Conductor represents what is All-Powerful and All-Good and must be the same as our God on earth."

"The Conductor, you say? Hmmm ... I wonder. One-thousandth cycle? Naahhh .... Well, never mind. But I am glad that Salton-suhl is still a movin'." He sighed and paused still musing on the matter.

"Wonder what?"

"Oh, nothing ... *really*. Well ... it's really quite something, once you've seen it. I always thought it was meant for the restoration of us all, but Anton-duhl *just would not listen* to me!" He broke off as if recalculating a distant conversation.

"Here is some more rock," Troyton-suhl passed it to Tipton-tyne as the other giant chomped and thought.

"Yes ... Yes. It *must* be. It all figures together. Listen! I must tell you about Anton-duhl and his trove." Tipton-tyne grew hopeful and eager to relate these and other details to help Troyton-suhl, and hopefully his own world. "Listen carefully to what I say. The treasure trove exists just beside this here Skyway towards the Western Sea Tides, where you're heading. You can enter the trove on the *right* through the Corridor of Time and after passing through the market galleries. The trove is just beyond this and has a mosaic floor that is *booby-trapped!* But, don't worry, I helped to make it!

One avoids the traps by stepping *properly* on the tiles laid out in a grid. Start on *the left*! They are *nasty* traps, well-advertised to scare away any giant wanting to dare brave the trove. The traps guard Anton's treasures, which contain among many other gems, *one white gem that dwarfs them all*—the *One* Gem of the Giants!"

Troyton-suhl interrupted, "Why are you telling me these things?"

"Because *you*," he paused and said more quietly, *"you must rescue that One Gem!"*

Hearing this, Troyton's graphite constitution craved that *this* was a diamond gem. In fact, it was a huge carbon-chained rock unlike any diamond on earth. We can tell you now, reader, that it was the largest gem of its kind in Verthana, the size of an earthen stove.

As their journey continued, the three boys enjoyed each other's company more and more. Although the encounter with Tipton-tyne, a frozen giant, was eerie for Thomas and Archer, their journey had nevertheless turned into a treasure hunt. He had told them the exact location of the trove. He had drawn it out in the debris around about him, like a map. It was one-hundred twenty-one strides of a mature giant past Therndon's Peak and set off of the main skyway on the right through a narrow but visible corridor through the wall face.

The trove itself was not meant to be "hidden" since it was a place of trading valuable stones for giants to prolong their otherwise slowing motion. At the one end would be, as Tipton-tyne had drawn and explained, the treasure room. It had a tiled floor with mosaic overlaid patterns and showcased the One Gem. It could be seen and approached from the open gallery. However, it could not *safely* be reached unless one entered by a hidden door from a certain internal cavern, which Tipton-tyne strongly urged them not to try to find, since Anton-duhl fashioned it himself and it was strictly off limits even to his closest clan members. So, the only way to reach the gem was by carefully navigating the massive, jimmy-rigged tiled floor, which Tipton-tyne himself had conceived and co-created with Anton-duhl. Tipton-tyne had gone into much detail about its mechanics in the cavernous sub-flooring and sidewalls. But—and this is a big but—Anton-duhl had always sent Tipton-tyne on "errands" when "activating" the floor tiles of the trap so that even Tipton-tyne did not know which tiles were in fact booby-trapped and which ones were not. All Tipton-tyne knew was that the mosaic itself, with all of its attractive formulas and sophisticated mimicry, was a diversion.

The pedestal where the One Gem itself sat was also booby-trapped, but Tipton-tyne secretly had observed completely how this feature worked (not indeed truly going on "the errand"), which he related in detail to Troyton-suhl. When it came down to it, the actual bare necessities of rescuing the gem consisted in knowing the formula for correctly passing over the floor tiles to reach it and then to make a calculated exit understanding the bobby-trap on the gem pedestal itself. In other words, it was definitely "doable."

So then, Troyton's westward Course of Growing continued as Thomas and Archer were carried happily along while all were eagerly looking ahead for Therndon's Peak since, just past this, a treasure trove awaited them.

"What are you going to do with the diamond, Troyton?" asked Thomas. "What did Tipton-tyne tell you to do?"

"He said I should finish my course to the Western Sea Tides, and that I would know once I was there. He also said that I should not eat it, no matter how great the temptation would be, and that I should await further instructions for the gem's placement and use."

"By whom?" asked Archer.

"Well, Tipton-tyne did not make that clear, but I'd figure he meant the *Conductor*, by his look."

"There it is! Look! Therndon's Peak!" Thomas had seen it first, although his position on Troyton's head had given him an advantage. "We've *made* it ... *we've made it!*"

Part IV

The Drama of Verthana

Chapter 18
Bydelus's Administration

Bydelus was growing weary of the weekly ritual, and yet he understood the importance of this "encounter" with the Conductor for the majority of the Musselkin. How easily tricked they were! They were under *his* control which compelled Bydelus to conceive even more ambitious plans. However, what once had been exciting now was dull routine. The fire rock's appeal to him had weakened with time, and he was eager for the big day of revelation two days hence. The afternoon would be spent perfecting the pyrotechnic effects at the remote quarry dug out by the industrious giants. This thought got him out of bed in time to see the first glimmers of the sun. He had not slept well, once again, but was used to this.

Bydelus scampered to the eatery and grabbed pieces of bread and dried fruit from the larder. He loved his new limestone home; it was a fantastic marvel. It was what he had longed for. The protection and security it provided him were beyond words. Many of the Musselkin elite also enjoyed such habitations. The giants had made them so quickly—and, *at what price*? Gems and their praise! That's all! Bydelus only wished he had built more residences for himself as getaways in the more remote parts of Sylvanwood—in the northeast overlooking the Kliffs of Kalm or southeast in Collynwood. It was a small consolation that he had arranged the construction of one such home, his Dome House, at Dome Rock along the western shores of the Silver Sea overlooking Roetin's Bay.

As Bydelus got himself dressed, he reviewed what the three giants had accomplished. The only cost to Bydelus was that he had to steadily supply their palates with gems which they were only too eager to eat. In addition to this motivation, the Musselkin's enthusiasm for the giants and their endeavors drove them to great feats of accomplishment.

First, they had all but exterminated the meddlesome Silver Snails who manipulated the Musselkin. Whenever these were spotted, the giants hunted them with great resolve—so tasty were they.

Second, Bydelus had the giants work on the most public and immediately beneficial projects. The choices were easy. In order to draw attention away from the Silver Snail slaughters, Bydelus had the giants deforest massive quadrants of the Central District to increase production of their main crops—barley, wheat, and okras of various kinds—that increased their food stores. These excesses he proudly purported were "to have plenty to give to the needy" who were displaced by the giants' movements and projects. At the same time, this clearing made available tens of thousands of linear feet of lumber—trees like earthen basswood, cherry, hickory, walnut, mahogany, and butternut—for carvings, statues, and in-laid decorations of all kinds. Large stores of kiln dried wood were amassed for fast production and free distribution to all Musselkin to occupy and impress themselves with their own artistic work. Competitions, unlike any hitherto entertained, were held with prizes consisting of the use of a giant for a day or the construction of a new residence, which had become quite fashionable.

Third, the giants added critical infrastructure with public works consisting of roadways to connect the various districts—"all roads leading to Nimbyn"—which Bydelus had pronounced "Principal City in Perpetuity." The roads took considerable effort but made transportation and communications between districts much faster and more controllable.

Fourth, the giants were employed variously to those who could afford them—wells were dug, houses built, conclave centers erected, shrines fabricated, and even statues raised. But, the crowning building projects were kept as surprises for the Musselkin. Bydelus timed them with the annual

Harvest Festival held in the Northern Central District at Nimbyn. He split the giants up to work on two monumental projects. Bydelus sent Wheldon-olt, because of, he maintained, his "greater experience" (but really because of his increasingly uncooperative and questioning ways of late), to build a bridge to cross the Great River at the Narrows near the black Kliffs of Kalm. This would mark the next stage of the evolution of the Musselkin nation. Since the Silver Snails had thoroughly explored and traveled across the Silver Sea westward, now Bydelus planned for the Musselkin to explore the regions eastward. These "talking points" would be delivered at a momentous speech at the new Central Coliseum, which was the second secret project. At the Valley of Turnus Nimbrik-al and Bryton-duhl (his true favorites) would construct the Central Coliseum—an amphitheater that could seat the entire Musselkin nation, minus those "rebels and unfaithful snail lovers." Wheldon-olt had discovered this location at the south reach of the Valley of Turnus; its natural contoured shape could easily be supplemented with quarried limestone to form the rows and rows and rows of ascending seats. It would stand over one hundred and fifty feet tall—*this* would truly be *his* crowning, colossal creation.

The timing for the creation of this coliseum was indeed "fortuitous." Bydelus had received reports from his informants that the northern regions below the giants' mountains had been abandoned by the Musselkin, as had been expected, who traveled south to the two-day Harvest Festival. Project updates also indicated that the two projects would be completed in a timely manner. In fact, the Central Coliseum would be completed first, thus allowing the two younger giants to arrive at the end of the festival then to pull the leading noblekin on a massive rolling platform in a parade along the northward highway leading to the Central Coliseum, at which place and time Bydelus would offer his inaugural speech as "Chief Governor in Perpetuity," while simultaneously announcing the completion of the Bridge of Narrows. This glorious evening would then be brought to its climactic close with the skylight display of the fire rock, but only if he could get the timing perfected in this afternoon's trials.

The Bridge over the Narrows, photograph by Bonnie Mitchell

At the door of his personal quarters, Bydelus was met with "Greetings, Lord Bydelus. The masses are at the Shrine. We must be on our way." His escort had arrived.

"Yes ... yes! Let's be on our way," replied Bydelus curtly. They walked hurriedly out and onto the newly paved walkway. He asked, "Are all the arrangements made for this morning?"

"Yes, as usual, Lord. However, all the local sacred sedge grasses have been burnt up, so we needed to use limbs from the bouley ferns."

"Well, I doubt the people will take much notice of that—it's the fire that excites them, and we have plenty of that."

The two walked hurriedly until they reached a misty, excavated, paved clearing. An open-styled, peripteral sanctuary had been built in the center, around which several hundred Musselkin stood with anticipation to view the central altar upon which the fern fronds had been placed. The sun was just rising; the crowd's mood was expectant.

Bydelus advanced to the center platform and began the ceremony. "Oh, what a lovely morning this has become with you all here, and on the eve of the Harvest Festival! The *Conductor* is obviously well-pleased with us!"

But, a lone contrary voice objected. "The Conductor is not pleased! You must all change your hearts before you fall prey to Bydelus'...." and the voice was silenced. Those nearest observed several Musselkin dragging away a single individual.

Bydelus ignored this interruption and continued the ceremony. "And the Conductor overlooks our differences and the obstinacy of the few. Now behold, the Conductor speaks to us...."

Music and drumming started softly. The altar beside Bydelus turned red and yellow burning the large green fronds. A hush fell upon the crowd. The musical instruments increased their fervor and the drums their beat. In a final eruptive flare of fire and smoke, the moment was over and left the burnt remains of crisp pieces of fern on the altar with a puff of a terrible smelling odor.

As the smoke cleared, someone shouted out on queue, "What was the *word*, Lord Bydelus?!"

Another shouted out, "Yes! Speak for the Conductor to us!"

Feigning coming in and out of a trance dramatically leaning left then right, Bydelus initially showed a scowl, which brought terror to many, but slowly recontoured his mouth into a large, gaping smile to the relief and pleasure of all. He spoke slowly, "The ... Conductor ... is very, very ... pleased with us all ... and will not punish us ... despite ... the few wicked ones among us who interrupt His ceremonies!" He sped up, "*This* is the Conductor's message for us today: 'Have *fun* at the festival; there awaits a *giant* surprise at its end!'"

Cheers erupted at the mention of a "*giant* surprise" because the Musselkin were quite enraptured with anything associated with the giants.

Bydelus believed he had pulled off the event very well, despite the annoying interruption. His anxious thoughts turned immediately, however, to find out which miscreant musselman had attempted to subterfuge the ceremony. Making his way through the crowds gathered to shake his hands or simply touch him, an official appeared and motioned for Bydelus to come quickly. An interrogation was underway of the offender at the home of a nearby noblekin. Bydelus abruptly excused himself from the crowds to hurry to the interrogation room. He entered this meeting but needed to work immediately to compose himself. He knew the "troublemaker" all too well.

"So, Dernal," he said condescendingly. "You have blundered for the last time! What were you hoping to accomplish by showing up at this morning's ceremony?" The question was not answered. Bydelus continued, "Your Musselkin alliance is *faltering*. Yes, indeed, it is. We have captured several pockets of your resistance groups, and you shan't be hearing from them ever again. *Ever!*"

Dernal knew what that meant but calmly said defiantly, "There are many others that you know nothing of. Your days are marked, like your thoughts and actions. These are like botched carving in the etching for all to see. The Conductor will deal with you soon. He has told me even this morning that at the end of Harvest *you will reap what you have sown.*"

Bydelus recoiled at this word. "*How did Dernal know my plans?!*" he thought while struggling to regain his composure.

A nearby assistant stepped forward and slapped Dernal awkwardly, as others held his arms. With this, Bydelus regained his composure and resumed his interrogation. "So *you* say."

"No. The *Conductor* does." Dernal turned and was slapped again.

"Oh, Yes. I see—these are idle claims of a troublemaker to frighten us. They are the remnants of snail *stupor*-stition—utter buffoonery! Enough! I will learn from you *more* about these '*others*' you have mentioned. Where are they?" Bydelus shouted. "Speak up!"

The guards plied pressure to the ribs of Dernal with something like a yawara stick. He flinched momentarily before saying, "You will learn nothing more from me. End my life, if you please, but as for me and my kin, we stand firm with the Conductor."

Nodding to the noblekin applying the pressure, Bydelus continued, "So, you admit it is *your* family—Na'al, your daughter, no doubt, and her band of 'brigands.' You should know we're hot on their *snail trail*—they're the *last* of your bands." Dernal then fainted from the thought of "harm" or even "death" coming to his daughter, so unaccustomed was he (or any of the Musselkin) to such violence. It was more than he could handle emotionally.

From this interview, Bydelus had learned more than he had hoped. *"So, it was Na'al!"* his mind raced. *"We must find her! She's probably with that last, nasty snail—Hallisden or Hilusdem or whatever its stupid name is."*

In the end, after brooding over the fate of his prisoner, Bydelus finally figured that Dernal would still better serve him alive than dead. If needed, he would be executed along with other traitors—his wife, Darsá, along with Praktor and several other former leaders who had rejected Bydelus's headship—as a public spectacle at his new Central Coliseum.

So, Bydelus turned next to consider other matters of his plan. He had already sent messengers to check on Wheldon-olt's progress on the bridge and to continue the search for Na'al's party and the last snail. The plan was to find these in time for his "epiphany as Chief Governor in Perpetuity." He thought smugly, *"Yes, they will be caught in my trap and bear the wrath of Bydelus Chief Governor of all of Sylvanwood."*

Chapter 19
The Corridor of Time

Troyton-suhl took firm hold of Thomas and Archer and began thunderously running through the echoing valleys and corridors until he reached the peak towering above him with a giant-sized stairway circling upwards and around its exterior.

"This was a residence at one time," commented Troyton-suhl. He marveled at the workmanship rubbing his hand up and down admiring it. He then naturally and quite instinctively leaned into the wall face extending his hands far apart while planting the nub of his "nose" also touching the wall. Concentrating, his mind reached into the rock face and found an intelligible grammar imposed within it atomically. He did not have to learn this grammar; he just knew it. Electron valencies circuiting around their protons and neutrons had been ever so delicately adjusted to communicate notions. After some moments, these clarified as distinct words combined into ideas and altogether coherent discourse. He began reading the history of Therndon's Peak, its design, its construction, its layout, and even signatures of its former inhabitants; and so, he left his own and "signing in" also Thomas and Archer.

Archer just watched somehow understanding how normal this was, but Thomas grew concerned.

"Troy ... Troyton!" he shouted. "Troyton, what's *wrong?* What are you *doing*? Are you okay??"

Troyton dropped his arms and released himself from the hand rune. His head turned to Thomas. "Yes, all's good. This wall is like a book, a welcome book of the clan who once lived here."

"A book??? How is it a book?"

"It's hard to explain. I was just reading it from within."

"What? On the other side of the wall? There's a book you read?" Thomas was confused.

"No, from *within* the stone, its atoms. I see or *rather sense* tiny light particles spinning, layered but ever spinning, circling their cores. I can't explain it well. But these pathways have been adjusted and I can *read* them. Let's see ... you've studied chemistry, right?"

"A bit."

"Okay—well, *I haven't* ... but I've heard Paige *bragging* about it at dinnertime—electrons, protons, and neutrons, I'd guess. I think the electrons are spinning in adjustable and comprehensible ways."

Archer chimed in. "Anything important for us to know?"

"Well, no and yes. This peak belonged the Tumbel-duhl Clan of the Smytstoyne Watchers. Therndon-al Byrl was its most recent watcher; and his watcher was Lohrdeb-fuhr Dehl, and Lohrdeb-fuhr's was Heydon-ohr Buhr, and on and on. There have been one hundred twenty-seven watchers here. But, interestingly, Therndon-al watched over not three but a clan of four—very odd; Wheldon-olt Maar and two unusually formed twins, Nimbrik-al Pedul and Bryton-duhl Nadar."

"Why unusual?" Archer asked.

"Well, they emerged from the pool of Emergence—you know, where we entered—as *twins*. This had never happened before."

"Hmmm...." Thomas spoke up. "On earth that's not so odd—we have Tanner and Guinevere, who, it's true, however are odd!" He chuckled.

Archer returned them to the topic. "Okay. So, what about the *'yes'*? None of this seems important."

"Well, these last three's signatures are not so old and their contributions are *sloppy*—at one point this whole welcome book began to show signs of deterioration, and then recently it's a downhill dive. These last three giants were abandoned—at least that's what Wheldon-olt wrote. I have an uneasy feeling about these latest watchlings. I wouldn't want to run into them. I don't trust them. I suspect they're still lumbering about."

At that thought, Thomas hurried them up. "Well, okay, then. Let's get going and be on our way. We'll leave this Therndon's Peak to them!"

"Yes, yes." Troyton agreed. "But, we must go *past* Therndon's Peak one-hundred twenty-one strides of a *mature giant*, as Tipton-tyne directed. I'm only 25 feet tall now. So given that a full-grown giant is 50 feet tall ..." he slowed his speech, "... the number of my strides should be just more than doubled. Yes, that's right. Follow me!"

He began pacing his strides until he had reached 240. But there was nothing there—no narrow corridor to the right as Tipton-tyne had explained.

"Well, maybe Tipton-tyne had the number of strides wrong," mused Thomas.

"No. You must remember that we Trioptic Giants are quite calculating and Tipton-tyne is still sharp as quartz. He knows where this corridor is. Look over here," Troyton-suhl pointed out, "It appears that these slim set of sheared rockfaces have been used to fill in a gap here." The others came over.

Then Archer pointed something out, "Look, some markings were scraped off on the side here." He was right; but nothing was said in reply.

Troyton-suhl looked up and figured that he could scale the skyway wall to see what was on the other side. Thomas and Archer, figuring his intention, stepped away for fear of falling rock. They watched Troyton-suhl adeptly climb up and rumble out of sight. Shortly, he returned peaking over the top and boomed down, "The filled corridor continues over here, just as I figured. Perhaps a rockslide filled it in." Archer doubted this explanation very much.

Troyton-suhl returned and repeated the climb effortless with Thomas and Archer hanging onto his neck on his back. Atop the higher northern wall, the clan observed just how expansive the highland mountain range truly was, extending far across to the north beyond what they had previously been able to see. Thomas noticed a series of dark spots a long way off, which were actually cave openings. In fact, they were the nearest entrances to the mineshafts of Rhuinnmall.

From atop the wall, it was easy to climb down into the corridor on the other side, for there where what appeared to be giant steps downward in a narrow crevasse. Archer pointed this out; but the others ignored him.

Once in the opening on the other side, Troyton-suhl thought it best to put Thomas and Archer down. Immediately, his attention was drawn to various colorful imprints, scrawls, equations, and formulas that were scribbled all about the corridor walls on both sides. These markings, although interesting enough, were quite faint and foreign to Thomas and Archer, who remembered them differently. But to Troyton-suhl they were mesmerizing; he alone could calculate their meanings and soon became lost in their contemplation.

Laid outstretched fully in figurations and calculations along both sides of the stoney corridor before them etched here deeply, there faintly, sometimes in hues of blue, red, purple, and green with many stains of shades in between was presented the entire history of the giants. In

Corridor of Time Rockface 1,
Canva Thomas Mitchell and Archer Edwards

short, the etchings and designs told their story.

Taking it all in, Troyton-suhl became sullen and distracted, gazing and turning his head here and there.

Intentionally, such was the desired effect on a giant. In this way, the story functioned simultaneously as an advertisement for the need for gems and the proper mixture of rocks and colored jewels and mineral substances. This "Corridor of Time" had been perfectly placed along the western skyway for growing giants—to divert them—and in years past had been a trading hub of the giants' realm. Giants would travel for tens of thousands of strides to trade jewel and gem, and to sell recipes and whatever other discoveries they could barter with, or, on rarer occasions, to offer mercifully in goodwill to other slower giants begging for help. Many a thundering argument and dispute had erupted here, often with terrible brawls that sometimes ended with body trawls extracting precious, private data.

Corridor of Time Rockface 2,
Canva Archer Edwards and Thomas Mitchell

Troyton-suhl was truly fixated with the story and stopped listening to Thomas' and Archer's repeated requests to tell them what it meant. As Troyton-suhl 'read' the wall, he meandered along the corridor, taking in both sides in swaying back and forth, as the colorful pictograms and figurations wrapped back and forth with the interweaving of the story. The narrative was indeed a complex tapestry of giant proportions. Occasionally, Troyton-suhl would begin sobbing; at other times he would burst into expressions of joy and hope. His two earthen companions were truly foreigners there.

Finally, after reaching the far end of the corridor before the entrance to the main gallery, Troyton-suhl began sobbing uncontrollably and then trotted back to the beginning of the corridor from which end they had climbed down. He began tearing at the fallen rock fill and sheared stone walls, some thirty feet thick, which blocked the corridor's entrance from the skyway. He was trying to unearth and view the pictures and stories, which, he had come to realize, told of the very beginning of the world of Verthana and of the giants' fall from perpetual motion to their complete stoppage.

Thomas and Archer followed him and stopped, keeping well back as stones and rubble were thrown behind him. It was indeed a pitiful sight to see the half-sized giant, shaking and sobbing, tearing at rock, dwarfed by the height of the blocked off corridor that interrupted the colorfully etched walls. Thomas and Archer each felt as if they had a rock lodged in their throats watching him. Eventually, after some time, Troyton-suhl slumped down in the corner, shaded there, as it was, from the descending sun. He fell asleep since it was time for his mid-afternoon nap.

With Troyton-suhl sleeping, the boys took the opportunity to explore the gallery at the other end, which in scale reminded Thomas of a convention center where he had once seen a Home and Garden show. Tunneled ceiling shafts, some with mirrors, channeled the sun's rays to spill into the gallery. The center featured a massive fountain area. Water gurgled sparsely up from the middle; it was only an eighth full. Barren, blackened shelves surrounded this in the room's periphery, and what looked like massive marble display cases and bookshelves were knocked over and splayed all about. The two could see that the gallery had been laid waste and looted some long time ago from the amount of dust that had settled.

"Look!" Archer picked up a small emerald. "Wow! What do you think it is? Is it *valuable?*" He had never held such a costly thing in all of his life.

Thomas inspected it. "Gee, I guess so. I think it's an emerald." Archer pocketed it. The two boys rummaged around with earnest. Thomas flipped over a broken black slab and perked up, "Look! Here's a red one," from some debris Thomas lifted a quarter-sized garnet for their inspection. He surmised, "These were left behind; perhaps they're too small to be of any benefit. But, Troyton-suhl might get some; he's still growing." Thomas was surprised at how used to thinking of Troy as "Troyton-suhl," his little giant brother, he had become.

Like mice in a deserted kitchen, the two earthen boys rummaged through the wreckage. At first, periodically they stopped to listen, "Shhhh! ... Did you hear that?" But since they never heard anything, they more and more rummaged with reckless abandon. Each of their minds raced more and more from the thought of feeding Troyton-suhl to considering how to sneak their treasures past the Giant King on the event of their departure from this world and whether the precious gems would somehow make it home in their pockets through the pools. But their dreams ended abruptly when a giant figure appeared at the corridor's doorway and stared at them. The sunlight was giving way to night in the late afternoon and backlit the giant's massive frame.

"*What are you doing?! I hear you!*" the giant boomed.

Thomas and Archer twirled around only to see a giant taller than Troyton-suhl standing at the door. They said nothing and froze motionless, hoping like a rabbit at dusk, not to be seen.

Chapter 20
Anton's One Gem

"What are you doing, you sawed off runts??!!" the voice boomed with greater force than the first time.

Thomas offered a feeble reply stammering slightly, "We ... ah... We ... are finding gems in here. Look, there's plenty—even for you—*here.*" He lifted the front of his shirt full of multi-colored gems and jewels of various sizes including one opaque piece of quartz the size of a baseball. He stood in an offering gesture. Archer imitated Thomas, and the two stood awkwardly, extending their bulging shirts forward towards the giant.

The giant approached cautiously amidst the rubble and debris. It stopped under a light tunnel with a grin. Thomas and Archer returned his wry smile.

"You *bully!*" Archer shouted, "You big, big, giant *bully!* What gives you the *right?!* You can't have these gems; over *my dead body* you'll even see 'em!!!"

"Is *that* what it will take? Then, so be it!" The giant grabbed Archer and lifted him up one-handed. Thomas was helpless to stop it. Using a digit from the other hand, the giant deftly prodded the struggling Archer's t-shirt full of gems that poured out onto his massive palm cupped underneath. "Ah ... these morsels are small but they look *tasty.*"

"Give 'em back!" Archer protested, "They're *mine, all mine! I found 'em* ... they're my *PRECIOUS—oh so PRECIOUS*—stones!!!" Archer started laughing, of course, because Troyton held him. Archer had recognized the ever growing giant.

Troyton-suhl now stood thirty-six feet tall. While napping, he had continued to grow and was consequently very hungry. "Mmmm," he mumbled as he tasted the delicacies in his hand.

Archer watched in wonder with just a little sadness at his loss.

Reluctantly, Thomas offered up his stones, "Here, try mine. This big one looks like quartz to me."

"Mmmmm....Yes ... quartzite included with the right amount of titanium."

The three friends spent the next half-hour searching for morsels for Troyton-suhl to try. He was able to lift fallen display cases and rock slabs to expedite their searching. Troyton's excited manner of consuming the gems with lots of "mmmm-ing" and detailed descriptions of their varied contents and flavors greatly increased Thomas and Archer's hunt, which resulted in many great and sizable finds. Troyton-suhl learned that he actually had the innate ability to discern the value of nutrition and benefit of a gem or stone. Several he outright rejected, and gave back to the boys, "Too much calcite in these," or "There's an imbalance of magnesium and titanium—save that one for later." One horrified him completely—"Gold! That's included with a gold vein—See!—Get that away! Please throw it in the corner and don't take it. I must not touch gold or it could end the motion of me!"

Soon only one hour of daylight remained. With the new angle of the setting sun, a glimmering brilliance grew more and more from the far end of the gallery across a magnificent, tiled floor. The clan of three stopped their rummaging and followed the source to the dazzling One Gem.

Troyton-suhl looked around and quickly conceived of the gallery's configuration. "See how the Great Mover's shafts have been so constructed for it to shine on the One Gem at the first hour of daylight, then at midday, and then at one hour left of daylight." He felt a pang of desire rising. "It's time to get the *big* one. Here," he continued, "you guys must sit on *this—don't leave it*. You can watch me. You'll know when to turn and hold on." After calculating some figures in his head glancing at the One Gem and then at the entrance to the gallery, he propped up a bookcase at a sixty-three-degree angle to the left of the central fountain on top of two other rock pieces so that that bookshelf was suspended off of the gallery floor. He lifted Thomas and Archer in. He then turned to face the tiled floor leading to the One Gem.

Pausing and taking in a deep breath, Troyton-suhl kept thinking out loud to Thomas and Archer. "I see that the tiled floors are arranged in a pattern of fourteen rows and nine columns."

Archer figured, "That's one-hundred and twenty-six tiles then."

"Wrong." Troyton-suhl replied. "There are one-hundred and twenty-seven tiles—one is under the gem pedestal itself, hardly visible. Remember that was how many watcher's Therndon's Peak had. I've been thinking about this since then. One-hundred and twenty-seven is a prime number—so prime numbers must be the key. Some giants would have figured that much out, however. But they *obviously* didn't know what else to do, for the gem is still here." He paused dramatically. "What else *is* there *to observe?!*" he asked himself, looking at the dizzying mosaic floor, whose tiles were imprinted all over with elaborate equations.

Thomas asked anxiously, "But don't you know what to do?!"

"Ummm ... well ... Yes ... I do. That's it. It's just come to me now." He paused momentarily and then continued, "Figuring all the prime numbers in sequence along this nine by fourteen grid results in three paths of 'safe steppingstones' that one *could* take. This leaves the last fateful row being completely empty of safe steps by making use of the largest gap—fourteen— between prime numbers from what I can take time now to figure! Ingenious! And yet that would be *too* easy; well, too *easy*, in fact, to *believe*. But that must be it! So, one should be able to step on any of the prime numbered tiles. Troyton-suhl paused, But ... *which side* to start counting *from?*"

He instinctively thought to start from the left moving to the right and repeating this sequentially for each row. But he wondered whether this was the natural thinking of an earthen boy or the default calculation of a Trioptic Giant.

He decided out loud, "I will start from the left according to these best calculations. Any doubting giant would walk this trek perilously because of these distracting mosaic patterns on the floor—which are, in fact, elaborate and absorbing mathematical equations, if you haven't noticed, as if they would guide one to the One Gem, *BUT*—and this is a big *BUT*—which actually have nothing to do with traversing the floor! Ha!!!" He continued excitedly, "Also, too, I see these wonderfully edible stones in the niches of the side walls. See 'em? These would likely cause an especially hungry and desirous giant—which I am *NOT*—to lose track of where one is. But not me ... *No!* I'm goin' in, starting on the left!" he finished by recalling Tipton's advice to him. Troyton-suhl took one hop onto the second tile and another one landing on the eleventh tile. There Troyton-suhl looked at the empty niche shaking his head. He then hopped to the nineteenth tile, snatched up a reddish gem of enormous caret weight, ate it, and proceeded to jump to the twentieth-ninth and thirty-seventh tiles. He snatched up a huge blue sapphire in a niche and ground it down his gullet. During his hopping, he gobbled down other large stones niched in the walls. He then backtracked to the twenty-ninth tile and hopped over to the thirty-first tile and up to the forty-first and to the right over to the forty-third. All these numbers were, of course, prime.

Thomas was worrying. "Hey, I thought you weren't going fall for these niche stones!" From his perspective he could not keep track of rows of prime numbers with Troyton's hopping about.

"No, I didn't say *that*. I warned of losing track of the prime numbered tiles."

But Archer pressed him further, "Troyton-suhl, what will happen if you—I mean ... I'm not saying that you are going to—but if *you* should step on a wrong tile?"

"I'm sorry. Yes, I should have warned you two. Should that happen, you should duck because gyro-propelled columns from behind these side walls will come out smashing me to smithereens. But they won't. I am quite sure of it now." Troyton-suhl then hopped to the fifty-third, sixty-first, seventy-first, seventy-ninth, eighty-ninth, ninety-seventh, and one-hundred-seventh tiles—it was a 'column' ascending the right side to the One Gem. "Okay. I got to make one last big jump here. Shhhhh!!! I'm almost there!" Troyton-suhl calculated carefully for a moment and then leaped. In midair, Thomas observed that Troyton-suhl glanced right and attempted to make an adjustment to the left. He landed at an angle and his head turned and eyes fixated on a large rubble pile to the right of the One Gem. Troyton-suhl teetered there precariously on the ledge of the platform, arms wheeling for balance. Archer, not able to bear looking, ducked and braced himself.

Suddenly, a gigantic hand reached out from the rubble and seized Troyton's right hand tightly, "Who dares to cross my gallery to take my gem, *my One Gem*?" The voice echoed emptily. Troyton-suhl still struggled to stabilize himself pushing then pulling against the arm, which precariously countered him perfectly and kept him literally on edge, on the verge of falling backwards onto the booby-trapped floor. "Well, well! Who has calculated the puzzle to approach the Gem??" The half-frozen giant eyed the gem longingly. "Speak up, or I will let you fall—and you would not fare well, youngling."

"Troyton ... *uh* ... *Troyton-suhl* is my name. I'm of the Mitchell Clan, a youngling of the ... of the ... new Cycle of the High Season." He purposely left out which *number* that prodigious season was.

"Is that *soooo?* That is your name, you say, but *why* are you here? *How* did you find your way in and calculate the solution to my tiles?" the giant asked peevishly.

"I was sent to the Western Sea Tides by King Salton-suhl." Troyton-suhl stopped. He did not want to mention Tipton-tyne.

"Okay, that is *why* you are here along the skyway—you clearly don't want to tell me *'how'* you've come here and solved the floor. I blocked the outer corridor, so someone must have told you how to find this gallery." His grip tightened on Troyton-suhl, whose new giant growth was no match, however, for this much older adversary. The giant continued: "Well now, I'm no newly cooled lava rock, you know. Look at me in this state, frozen solid all but for my able arms ... if only I could reach my own, priceless Gem I might but move again!" The giant greedily eyed the diamond.

Troyton-suhl said nothing.

The other continued, "You know *too* much, youngling Troyton-suhl, and you are talking *too* little. Now, for the last time, tell me *how* you found this place and *who* helped you decipher my code."

Troyton-suhl felt the determination of his foe. "Yes, I know much. This much is true. I met Tipton-tyne along the...."

"Ohhh, that *awful betrayer* of a watchling! That slurry faced scum of a scoundrel, born and fed of a pebble! *You* must be from his clan, I bet. I've never heard of a *Mitch-ell!* Aren't you?! Well, you know very well then who I am—Anton-duhl Meer of the One Gem—and I'll reduce you to rubble and teach ol' Tipton-tyne Baer not to meddle in *my* affairs again!"

"No, wait! Wait! I can help you ... I have been sent here with a purpose from the Conductor! It's the one-thousandth Cycle of the High Season and it's time for the Restoration to begin!"

At that, Anton-duhl erupted, "It's *mine*, all *mine!*" and cursed all manner of obscenities only full appreciated by *mature* giants which Troyton-suhl could only partially understand being unaccustomed to such vulgarity. Anton-duhl also shook Troyton-suhl violently back and forth along the edge and his nervous system began fracturing, synapses breaking, at this assault.

Now was Troyton's last opportunity. Reckoning his reach, he grabbed the One Gem when pulled back and forth close enough, and tossed it upwards, shouting, "Well, here! Take it, if it's that valuable to *you*." Antonduhl released him and flung out his flailing arm in a useless attempt to catch the gem. Troyton-suhl calculated his jump away from his grasp perfectly turning back to face the entryway with limbs spread out to catch the coming wave.

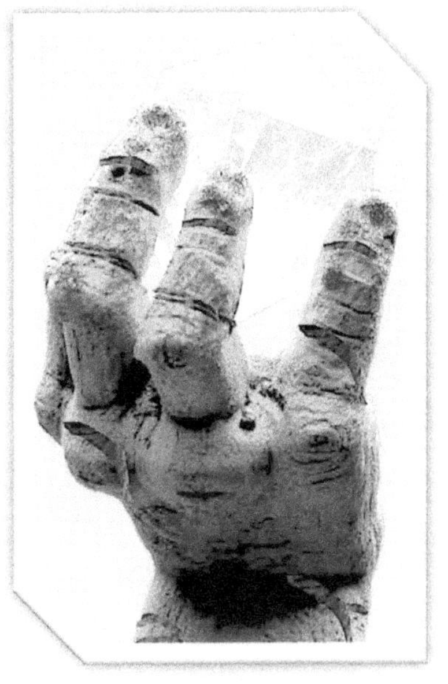

The One Gem held by Troyton, Canva and Gimp edited, by Thomas Mitchell

"No, No, *No!!!! You pebble-brained fool!!!*" were the last words of Antonduhl that Troyton heard. Triggered by the lifting up of the One Gem, a horrendous crashing white wave swept down on them instantly, propelling the airborne Troyton-suhl over and across the mosaic floor to the gallery in a dusting, blinding white cloud. Thomas and Archer had ducked just then and braced themselves before the wave of talcum powder hit them. The wave lifted their bookcase aloft and surfed it out towards the entrance of the gallery. With a final blasting rush through the narrower cave opening, Troyton-suhl and the bookshelf board came spilling out into the vast corridor with a great "whooooossshhh," sallow dust covering everything.

"Whoa! I calculated that just right!" shouted Troyton-suhl lifting up his head half-buried in the white powder. Thomas' and Archer's coughing turned to laughter as they climbed out of the bookcase unscathed by the white tide. They had only received a good dusting. Joining Troyton-suhl, they began hollering, whooping, and cheering.

Suddenly, Troyton-suhl stood up and performed a giant jig. The earthen boys continued laughing. Troyton-suhl did not join them; instead, he then ran up and down the corridor flapping his arms and slapping himself trying to rid himself of the alkaline powder. The calcium carbonate in the chalk reacted with his acidic features to produce a salt of calcium chloride and carbonic acid. This reaction could be seen foaming at his mouth, ear holes, eyes, joints, and points of laceration. The carbonic acid was further reacting to release water and carbon dioxide, which produced the foaming. The painful chemistry looked like this: $2\ HCl + CaCO_3 \rightarrow CaCl_2 + H_2CO_3$ // $H_2CO_3 \rightarrow H_2O + CO_2$.

"This talcum is a kind of poison to me! Ouch ... ouch ... ouch! It's affecting my joints and motion! I need water quickly before I won't be able to see or talk anymore!" He eventually laid down away from the spilled-out powder. Thomas and Archer ran immediately to him as they fumbled to open their one canteen and began pouring little sloshes of water on his eyes and mouth.

Troyton-suhl pushed himself up jerkily and pointed to his leg joints. "Pour here and here, too.... Thanks! Oh, you're almost out?!! I'll need a bath ASAP." He looked up. "Ah ... the Great Mover is almost setting. I'm getting sleepy already. Here, climb up!" He offered the two his arm. They scrambled up it and onto his shoulders as the giant righted himself and headed back up out the corridor, limping jerkily.

Archer was shocked but still had some sense to ask, "Where's the gem??! *That's* what we came for—*to rescue the gem.* You aren't going to leave it here after all this effort??!"

Troyton-suhl raised up is fisted right hand and opened it. "Right *here* it is," with obvious disdain and disinterest. And right there was, in fact, the monstrously beautiful diamond. "Now hurry up. I'm stiffening quickly and I need to be rid of this awful debilitating powder. I must ascend back into the sunlight! Hold on!"

Chapter 21
The Escape from the Narrows

"Na'al, Orín, Gnurl, and Ranít, you must go ahead to the Narrows" were the precise words of the Last One, and so the Musselkin companions were slightly sad to leave behind Hilasdem and their new earthen friends. All were tired from the night's trek but understood that the Conductor was orchestrating events. Especially fascinating to them was the arrival of the fancily dressed members from the wedding party.

The trails were flat and easy as the faithful Musselkin journeyed to the beautiful, and relatively uninhabited northeastern regions of Sylvanwood which ended in the place called the Narrows. Here, the Great River narrowed and constricted the river into a fierce, rushing force that was terrifying to any sensible Musselkin. From the Narrows one could also get a close up look at the strange land of Kalm, bordered beautifully with the sheer palisade walls which banked the eastern side of the Great River. No known Musselkin had every traversed to that land, nor was anything known of its probable inhabitants.

The Musselkin walked towards the sun rising higher and higher in the sylvan skyline as the morning mists evaporated. The vaporous mists were soothing to them, sprinkled with beams of sunlight breaking through the green covering above. The sun comforted their thoughts; it would accompany them until after they reached their eastern destination far from the center of Nimbyn and its tyrannical new leader, Bydelus.

Na'al worried for her father, Dernal, and the rebels who faithfully tried to confront and undermine Bydelus and his crew by convincing the masses of Musselkin of the truth. Ultimately, what was at stake was the deliverance of all Musselkin from their designs; already all but one Silver Snail in Sylvanwood had perished so mercilessly. *"And for what gain? And by the cruel hand of the giants!"* The thoughts revolted her and inside of her grew a resolute thought, *"No! Dernal, Praktor, and the remaining faithful Musselkin must put an end to the madness by the help of the Conductor and the Last Silver Snail!"* These faithful followers' sole task consisted in warning and mobilizing other Musselkin and letting them know that Hilasdem still remained alive with them, whose friendship brought the Conductor's presence and who would direct the Musselkin even yet, if possible, back to the way of the Conductor. Na'al's occasional feelings of despair were relieved with hopeful thoughts of the wisdom and forethought of Hilasdem and the Conductor.

Meanwhile, under the protection of a shaded hollow, Hilasdem and the four earthen youth lounged and conversed throughout the morning and early afternoon. In the daylight, the youth first noticed the "painted" blotches on the snail, which Na'al's party had put on it as camouflage. However, despite this, even then Hilasdem and the party were being watched by another from afar.

During their time together, the curiosity of the youth naturally turned the conversation to the nature of the snails themselves. They were like any earthen youth, who love slugs and snails, and so they were all ears. Bonnie, too, captured some wonderful pictures of the Silver Snail with the others and the sylvan glen in which they lounged and conversed. Hilasdem answered all their questions, about the Silver Snails and even more about their travels through the Silver Sea than even the Musselkin cared to know.

The Musselkin had never asked, in part because they were fearful of large bodies of water. Bonnie, Paige, Tanner, and Guinevere learned that the snails traveled under water, the depth of which was only sixty feet in the deepest parts. The snails breathed air that they caught in their shells while taking in enough water with a special valve took to sink them to the sea floor upon which they moved and foraged. Food was plentiful for them, delicious sea grasses, kelps, seaweeds, and algae. When the snails needed fresh air, they expelled the water ballast and floated to the surface, rolled, took in the salty air, and sink back down again. They would repeat this as often as was necessary to reach the Golden Isle—a paradise beyond even the beauty and serenity of Sylvanwood about which Hilasdem did not elaborate. Only this point was stressed, that the Conductor's presence was there *in fullness*—pure joy to know and a wonder and glory beyond delight.

Na'al holding Flower Bread, photograph by Bonnie Mitchell

The better part of the afternoon they spent learning about what plants, fruits, and roots were suitable food for the Silver Snails, most of which were also tasty and nutritious for earthen youth.

At one point Na'al offered them something quite unique. "Here," she offered. "We call this 'flower bread.' It's quite good and filling."

They each took one, and it was quite tasty.

They gathered ferns and leaves and even colorful roots for Hilasdem, who then dozed intermittently in the later afternoon. Bonnie and Paige also napped, since they had spent the night walking and talking with their strange new little alien friends. Tanner and Guinevere drew various pictures of the things related to them by Hilasdem. They also began to draw up a brief catalogue of plants and animals that they had seen. Throughout the day, when they were able, each of them drank deeply of the wisdom poured out to them from the Conductor through Hilasdem.

In the east, Na'al, Orín, Gnurl, and Ranít had reached the end of the grassy plateau, which turned wooded above the Narrows where it also began sloping downward looking out to the dark foreboding cliffs to the right. Only Gnurl and Ranít had been that far northeast in Sylvanwood before. It was for all both a terrifying and a beautiful sight—dark, sheer, palisade walls foregrounded by the mighty and swift Great River.

Gnurl reflectively said, "Our families came here during the low seasons, remember, Ranít? Those times seem so long ago. So much has happened."

"Of course ... yes," replied Ranít, who continued their shared reverie. "It was during these trips that I remember my first communing with the Conductor at the sedge bushes near Willowbough."

"That's one of my favorite stopover spots," said Gnurl. "Bouley scurries are plentiful there."

The party kept walking straight east down the green slopes—the river and cliffs coming in and out of sight through the dense tree foliage. The party patted along steadily down the worn bouley and long-necked deer trails. The pounding waters of the falls grew increasingly louder. The smell of the river flooded their senses and increased their excitement but also anxiety. These Musselkin younglings were, in fact, braving the immediate wash of the mighty falls!

"Look," Gnurl yelled out to Na'al and Orín over the din of the plummeting water. "The origin of the Great River is none other than the Great Mountains. Look up there!" She pointed. "You can see Color Falls starting from the highest peak in the mountains. Only, it's flow is half of what it's normally been."

Color Falls at the Narrows, photograph by Bonnie Mitchell

Soon they came upon an expansive rocky shorewash with sharp edged fallen boulders upon which they crossed carefully hopping here and there like frogs. Captivating to them, looking behind them, was the falls.

Sun began to flood the area. "What is *that?*" Orín asked.

Despite the drought, mists washed over the algae covered rocks, catching the setting sun's rays and splintering them into a tiny bow of subtle colors. Stunned at this unusual sight of a colors bowing over the mist, they paused several minutes.

Ranít and Gnurl said in tandem, *"The Colors!"* They looked at each other and laughed.

"Truly amazing," Ranít continued. "We'd watch these mists for *hours.*"

Gnurl looked south long and hard. "We must now go *south* to the *right.* The river bends and continues...." He stopped jaw dropped. All stared at a newly constructed massive structure spanning the high river bluffs.

Na'al was the first to speak, "What *is* it, Gnurl? *How can this be?*"

"*Why* ... *Why* ... it bridges *over* to the Kliffs of Kalm!" said Orín first.

"It's the work of one of the giants!" Gnurl realized. "*We must warn the others!*"

Just then, two enormous walls came slamming down beside them from behind. A voice thundered down at them, "Now, what *have* we here? Musselkin messengers to see *my* handiwork?"

Na'al was quick to reply, "We're sent here to see it and to report back." This was entirely true; the Conductor had indeed sent them, and it was reasonable to think that it was precisely to tell others of what had happened at the Narrows. All of them began shaking terribly; never had they been so close to one of the giants.

"*Who* sent you, then?" Wheldon-olt asked.

"The most *powerful One* in Sylvanwood, Who is in control, and directs *all* the goings on here. *He* sent us."

"Well, then ... is it time for us to meet him at Turnus in the Coliseum?"

Na'al paused—she knew nothing of a coliseum.

Her delay instantly revealed to Wheldon-olt that she was very possibly sent by someone *other than* Bydelus. So, he pressed on to ask another question, "You must have brought the gems for me ... *where are they?*"

"Our game *is up!*" thought Na'al.

But Orín dared to offer the giant an answer, "You will have plenty *when* you return. Your work is certainly worthy of it." His voice trailed off.

"Alright, then." The giant responded back. *"It figures! But,* I'll not be able to return tonight; the Great Mover is nearly set. We'll need to settle down for the night. *Come with me!"* Wheldon-olt, not knowing what else to do, decided then and there to keep them and carry them back to Bydelus at the morning's first light.

So, with the sun ducking below the western horizon, on the plateau of Sylvanwood Wheldon set to work excavating a pit to keep these Musselkin in. Then, as the sun of Verthana finally dipped below the Silver Sea and darkness fell, Wheldon-olt rolled over onto his back, sighed, and slumbered. Na'al, Orín, Gnurl, and Ranít, helpless in the pit, huddled together, prayed, and sang their favorite songs.

At the very same moment, Hilasdem and the earthen youth, Guinevere and Tanner, set out for the Narrows. The snail was even more deliberate than the previous night in its consumption of vegetation. A plant with leaves resembling those of rubber trees were the snail's prime choice. The youth slumped tightly together atop the snail, sleeping intermittently through the first part of the night awakening with the frequent foraging stops. Throughout the night, Hilasdem grew quite contemplative and did not speech much. But as the night grew deepest dark, the snail was eager for the encouraging attentiveness of the earthen ones. And so, as they journeyed ever eastward into the deepest dark, at one point he told them the following story.

"A certain kinsfolk once tended a forest. And in this forest were all kinds of trees; some stretched tall and some grew short and stout. Some had needles and others broad leaves. But one unique kind of tree produced the sweetest fruit from which the kinsfolk ate. Its shade was most comforting; its flowers the most fragrant; its roots the most soothing—so, it was the most cherished of trees."

The Silver Snail continued, "The kinsfolk tended and cared for such trees as these. Some collected its seeds and planted more and more of the trees. Others tended the new shoots and transplanted them into more and more favorable locations. They made merry and loved the trees and the trees loved them likewise."

Hilasdem paused briefly before continuing, "Now it happened that one kinsman found the trees to be good for carving. He felled a single tree and from that one tree produced the most exquisite figures and effigies. He took the branches and fashioned wreathes and festoons. He wore them proudly as garlands. All his work became renown among his people. His fame grew and grew. Quite expectedly, others began to follow his example. Tree after tree was felled, and the kinsfolk harvested the land of the unique trees in a frenzy of fervor. Fragrant garlands were worn by many, and more kinsfolk were eager to find their own. Even the young sprigs were all harvested. Eventually, there remained only one unique fruit-bearing tree, which was hidden for a time. But, when that time is up, it too will be felled."

"But *why?*" interjected Guinevere.

"This tree is me. But a cutting will be left to keep, which will root into all who have *good* soil."

A melody at that very moment interrupted them in the night.

Hilasdem halted before a wall of rock. "Quickly," the snail said. "Find some long vines and get the others out! I have work to do."

Bonnie, Paige, Guinevere, and Tanner dismounted quickly and set out to find some vines. They did so, but it was hard to cut through it. While the older girls were doing so, Guinevere and Tanner ran over to look down into the pit from which the melody ascended.

"Hey, it's us. Up here! We'll get you out." Tanner said.

"Ohhhh! Thanks be to the Conductor for your arrival!" Orín responded

"Is Hilasdem *with you?*" asked Na'al, who continued urgently, "We must *leave* at once! Quickly, get us *out!*"

"Yes, Bonnie and Paige are cutting vines to get you out. Hilasdem is doing *something* around this rock wall up here." Guinevere said.

"That's *not* a rock! It's Wheldon-olt, one of the rotten giants! He's asleep! We *must* leave and hide before he awakes at the rising sun."

Just then the eastern sky lightened into a pale-yellow glow.

Na'al and the others were beside themselves, jumping up and down. *"Hurry, Hurry, Hurry!!!"* they shouted excitedly.

Bonnie and Paige rushed over and peered down at them. "Here!" They threw a vine down, wrapping their end around a nearby tree.

With elvish agility, the Musselkin each scurried up and ran over to Hilasdem.

The snail, however, did not mind them, but was oddly gliding tightly around the ground and the form of Wheldon-olt. It was evident where the snail had begun because a thick residue was left behind. Hilasdem finished with Wheldon-olt's right side, which faced the nearly risen sun, and was turning along his head to continue along his left side.

"Hilasdem! Hilasdem! *What* are you doing? We *must leave* before the giant wakes up!" Na'al pleaded urgently.

"Don't yet bother me! I have to bind him up and *converse with him* before the others arrive."

"What others? What are you doing? I don't understand! We *must* escape *now!*"

"Na'al, my child, there is *no* escape for me. My time has come just as I have foretold you. The others will arrive, and I will be taken to the Valley of Turnus. You will *flee* now. Disturb me no longer. I must finish this task and talk alone with Wheldon-olt. Please, prepare yourselves for what you must do. I will speak to you again after I have left you for a time. Remember my words. Go! *All will be well!*"

Chapter 22
The Journey to Central Coliseum

To say that the Musselkin companions were terribly shaken by Hilasdem's words "There is no escape for me" would be an understatement. *They* were supposed to protect Hilasdem; but now *he* was protecting *them*. They had failed. So, there was nothing to do but obey. They took along with them Bonnie, Paige, Guinevere, and Tanner as they fled.

Paige naturally had lots of questions, "*Where* are we going *now?* Didn't we just *come* from this direction? *What* about *Hilasdem?!* Weren't you *helping* this *last snail?!*"

Na'al answered curtly, "Now we must go back to the Valley of Turnus. Something will happen there tonight. *I don't know what*, but we must warn the others. We must travel there with haste. Gnurl knows how to do so." Na'al directed the conversation to him.

"Yes, we must run to Willowbough, and from there, I think, we can catch a ride."

Tanner had been taking all this in. The sight of the massive giant, even while slumbering, had greatly impressed his imagination. He knew other giants were lumbering about Sylvanwood. As the party fled, he kept having the clear sense that they were under the watch of a giant *behind* them. But he didn't tell anyone because he didn't want to frighten them any more than they already were. Yet, he kept looking back behind them.

Hilasdem had just finished speaking with Wheldon-olt, a "captive audience." The snail slime that Hilasdem applied around his exterior held him fast. However, as the day continued, it would eventually crumble and break with the heat of the sun. Also, the slime could not withstand the giant's strength once fully animated by the Great Mover's full blaze.

Currently, a band of Musselkin messengers pulling a wagon approached the lying Wheldon-olt, not at first seeing the camouflaged Hilasdem.

"What's *this*? Lying *down* on the job?! You *lazy* brute! Wake up from your slumber, O sleeper! The sunlight has already shown on you!" Creyvyn, the sole son of Bydelus, rudely addressed the giant.

"I have just awakened and have seen the Light," replied Wheldon-olt. With some slight effort, Wheldon-olt broke free and rolled towards the Musselkins. They jumped out of the way, nearly crushed by his bulking mass. "I see you brought me more gems. *Keep 'em!* I no longer want them." Wheldon-olt stood to his full height, towering high above them.

A strange sensation grew inside the Musselkin as Hilasdem began to throb and peaked with audible sounds of speech, saying, "You, Creyvyn, do the work of *your* father *all too well*! Too bad it's for naught!" The Musselkins, stunned, were riveted as Hilasdem continued, "You must fulfill your *perfidious* role and take me. Wheldon-olt will allow it. Do it now!"

Immediately, Creyvyn ordered Wheldon-olt to pick up the snail. He did so gently. Then Creyvyn commanded the giant to pull the Musselkins on the wagon behind him, which he did slowly or it would have risked overturning the wagon and its passengers. Their journey would lead them to the newly built Central Coliseum. "*My father will enjoy this very much!*" Creyvyn thought. "*The last of the snails will be gone, and our family's dynasty will begin.*"

Gnurl and Ranít quickly led the way to Willowbough. Once they had arrived, immediately they gathered vines and began tying them together while the rest of the party waited and rested. Then they picked and cut open a dozen humin fruit, serving to all a traditional humin plate and placing the remainder out beyond the gentle grove in the glade.

"Paige, hold it *still* for Pete's sake! I've hardly taken any pictures!" Bonnie quickly snapped a shot and put her small camera away.

Paige Edwards holding Traditional Musselkin Humin Plate, photograph by Bonnie Mitchell

It worked perfectly. Eight entered the clearing and began eating the humin. Ranít and Gnurl approached the scurry (for that is what they are in a group) and gently placed bridals made of vine around two of them. They whispered soothing words as they did so. Then Gnurl and Ranít motioned for two others to come over with another set of vine bridals. This procedure continued until the whole band was readied for riding. With a hop here and a push off of a stump there, the party of travelers mounted.

Ranít and Gnurl directed their steeds to the Valley of Turnus, and the others followed.

The bouleys moved with great agility and efficiency, choosing the paths and stopping very infrequently at hidden spring pools for a drink. The Musselkin and earthen travelers dismounted at these times since the bouleys did not fear them enough to run away.

When they came upon the opening at the start of the Valley of Turnus, the riders dismounted to gaze at the massive construction feat—a wide district roadway leading into the Central Coliseum.

"What's this for?" asked Orín the others. "I've *never ever* seen anything like this. It's completely new to me!" The other Musselkin were likewise stumped.

"It's an amphitheater," remarked Tanner. "We have many of them on earth where we're from. They were often very bad places and lots of people and animals 'died' there."

"*Amfit*-eater?" asked Gnurl who focused on this new word. "We don't have any 'amfits' to eat. Are *those* animals?"

"*Amfi*-teeter?" asked Ranít. "Is this a sort of a *game?*"

"No. *Am-phi-thea-ter.*" Paige answered. "A round about place for spectacles." She had learned some Latin after all, *"Or, was this Greek?"* she questioned herself. "What I mean is it's a big place to sit in to watch something."

"Watch *what*, did you say?" Orín asked disturbed. "'*Died'* ... so, watching animals and kinsfolk *dying?* How would that be worth watching? That sounds utterly *evil* to me! Pardon me, but your world sounds awfully bad on purpose."

Paige sighed. "It *is* ... I mean, it *can be* .... it's confusing because it's *good* and *bad* at the same time just like people are good and bad ... but, yeah ... sometimes very *evil.*" She became quiet lost in dark thoughts. *"Clearly ... this amphitheater will be put to bad use* at a massive scale—I hope not '*dying!*' See the rows and rows of benches all around the sides ... and, at the far end, there's room for a huge stage."

"But, we have no such *big events* for so many to watch—I mean, our whole nation could fit inside there!" Ranít surmised.

"Well," Na'al added quickly, "we do have the Pojo and Crumkit games that Bydelus started. And who knows what he'll do next to get more control over our nation." Shaking her head she continued, "I *don't* like the looks of this ... this *amphi-teeter*, or whatever it's called. It's been made *in secret* along with Wheldon-olt's bridge over the Narrows. I fear Bydelus is up to something *very bad on purpose*. It's *evil!* He's timed all this to correspond with the Harvest Festival that ends today!"

"Look too!" Gnurl pointed out. "This new roadway leads directly to Nimbyn! That's *where* the festival is this year!"

"Right!" Orín said decisively. "So, we need to go there and warn the Musselkin about Bydelus's designs—*whatever* they are! Let's hurry! Time is of the essence! It maybe that we can reach the festival before the kinsfolk leave!"

"The bouleys will take us yet further, I think," added Gnurl. They all looked to Na'al and Ranít, who bobbed their heads in agreement.

Na'al said excitedly, "Having you earthen kinfolk along *may* convince many of our Musselkin to turn away from Bydelus once they learn that the Conductor has sent you to us!" She and the other companions eagerly looked at their earthen friends who met their gaze pensively in return.

Bonnie, looking at Guinevere and Tanner, proffered an objection shaking her head slowly, "I don't know about this. It seems we're heading right into the middle of things, Bydelus and all."

"You're right, of course," Na'al said ashamedly, meeting Bonnie's eyes and glancing downward. She had been too hasty. "*Going* is more dangerous than staying. We're likely to be 'arrested' ... yes, we *will* be ... I think so." She sighed, twitching her nose pensively, as Musselkin do.

This thought gave them all pause.

"Hey, I have an idea," Paige surprised herself. "Would you consider *splitting up?* Four of us will go and four will stay. I volunteer to go with Bonnie along with Orín and Na'al."

Bonnie sighed and looked at Tanner and Guinevere who were both shaking their heads up and down indicating *"Yes."*

"That will work, I think." Orín affirmed. "A very good idea, Paige." She stretched out her neck a bit and glanced away from Orín, attempting to hide a blush.

Ranít chimed in, "I am *saddened* not to go at this critical moment. But ... I will stay with Gnurl and protect these bright younglings." Turning to them she asked, "Would you please tell us again the Conductor's Word to you through the Giant King, Salton-suhl?"

"Tanner," asked Bonnie, "What did the King tell us?" By now Tanner had memorized the poem. He recited it slowly and quietly as Paige leaned in closely to hear.

"To feed the hungry is for you to succeed
to gather the sustenance of their every need;
Evil is spreading to souls down below,
but enter you must the lands that are low;
Help there those who reject evil plots
to rescue the sole one left with the spots."

"Stop there." Bonnie interrupted. "It seems clear that this much has happened already! Does this fit your thinking, too, Musselkin friends?"

"Yes," said Orín who was particularly adept at understanding the rhyming oracles of the Conductor, "although the first line, while I might take to mean feeding the snails, I believe I've heard enough of your story to know that this is Troyton-suhl. Right? The rest is about our present plight in Sylvanwood and our attempts to hide Hilasdem. Is that *all?* What does it say next?!" he eagerly asked.

And so Tanner continued,

"Though a death it meets when twin giants give leap
but awaken it will by the Conductor's great keep.
Dew from on high will then sprinkle the sky,
to mend the moving of those who once did die.
One watching the watchers will need to take hold
to rid the lowland of that one gilded of gold.
Stay true to the One who bids you to go,
but return you will through the water's green glow."

"Well," said Orín frankly. "I think I might understand the first line of that ... '*though a death it meets*' ... 'it' being the one 'with the spots,' Hilasdem ... but I refuse this meaning. It must be *wrong* or mean something *else*." The Musselkin companions looked at each other shaking their heads. Orín then said, "No ... I ... I take that back. I don't understand it *at all* actually. These verses must be speaking about the giants or something else we don't understand. Something *else* must be the 'one left with the spots.' These words are as *open* to me as a bracken thicket."

"'Clear as mud,' we would say," said Bonnie sadly. "This word *is* confusing and I don't understand it either. Honestly, I don't yet *feel* like we've fulfilled our part yet, *either*. Yes, we have helped you and Hilasdem but is there anything else we *should* do or even *can* do? I'm willing to go with Paige, but I would prefer Guinevere and Tanner to remain here where it is safer although ..." she paused, "I don't think *anywhere* is safe anymore."

"As much as I would prefer to go," started Ranít, "I will stay here. I would actually like to learn more about 'earth' from these younglings." She stopped and started again looking at her companions, "Remember the topmost cave on this side of the valley? That's where we'll take 'em. We should have a good safe view of things from up there. Gnurl, please, will you stay with me? Na'al and Orín, if you need help or need to send for us, use the signal—'Sedgénu'. Okay?"

Na'al laughed, "Yes! We will." Orín nodded in agreement.

And it was so agreed. With gentle pats Gnurl, Ranít, Tanner, and Guinevere said goodbye to the bouleys which instinctively knew that their task was done.

With baritone cheeps back and forth to the bouleys remaining, the four released bouleys trotted away.

Gnurl on Bouley, charcoal by Paige Edwards

Chapter 23

Bydelus, Highest Priest, Chief Governor Supreme in Perpetuity

As Na'al and Orín with Bonnie and Paige galloped along the paved roadway out of the cover of the woods, the bouleys grew more nervous and fidgety. Strange smells filled the breezes that wafted from the south—the wind was blowing northward from Nimbyn. Soon, two towers were seen in the distance. A din of cheering and crooning then became audible to the riders.

As they continued to near the spectacle, Paige cried out with incredulity, "What in this world is *that?!*" She gasped loudly. The group observed two monstrous giants pulling a massive platform upon wheels. Atop were hundreds of Musselkin. Behind, they saw a colorful wave of motion, a parade of many thousands following on foot. The bouleys, wide-eyed, stamped their feet; they could take it no longer. With multi-pitched urgent chirps and deep grunts, they stomped one rear leg and each reared up, throwing their riders, and fled before the approaching monstrous procession.

Dusting herself off, Na'al helped Paige up, and Orín the same for Bonnie.

Na'al looked and pointed, "I see Bydelus's banners, and some of the others of his 'nobility.' *By my Conductor* ... it looks as if the *whole* of the Musselkin nation is following them! This is worse than I thought!" Her observation was off by one third. In fact, just over two-thirds of the race marched behind the towering twin giants.

The enormity of their task now was evident to the companions: *They must try to warn as many of the Musselkin who would listen about Bydelus's ambitions and schemes*. So, they quickly discussed strategies.

Orín immediately took Bonnie and ran along the right side of the road while Na'al grabbed Paige, who began yelping "Oh ... owww. *My feet! My feet!*" But she hobbled along keeping pace with her as they went to the left.

As the two parties approached the marching hoard, the giants appeared to take no notice of them, straining on the tremendous harnesses attached to the platform. The two parties stopped as the massive giants passed between them, fearful they might be stepped on. Then, not losing a moment, Na'al with Paige and Orín with Bonnie ran along side of the platform of noblekin. Only a few heads leaned over the edge to look down at them; the two new "human" forms attired with wedding costumes attracted the interest of some.

After the platform passed, both parties spliced through the crowds each offering admonitions and shouting, "Bydelus *has* betrayed you*!*" and, "There is *still* one Last Silver Snail!" and, "We are *MUSSEL*-KIN! Return to the *Conductor's* Path!" and, "Put Bydelus *behind* you!" and, "Here is *one sent* by the Conductor to warn you—*listen* to her! See her *strange attire!* She is from the Conductor!" Some glared at them but kept walking; others hesitated but then continued. Some walked by in their own Harvest costumes, who nodded at the earthen girls in apparent approval of their own imaginative, fanciful costumes, but then moved on. But a few Musselkin stopped to join them and listened until there was a sizable company.

Like two opposing, clashing rivers, the two currents pushed against each other. As the parading mob filed along, more and more stopped and listened. *Orín's and Na'al's plan was working!* The new and oddly clad earthen girls, Bonnie and Paige, were turning more and more heads and attracting curious ears.

But despite the seeming success of their warnings, Bydelus had been prepared for any possible disturbance from the rebels that might arise from any quarter. So, two groups of guards and regulators were sent down immediately and broke through the two huddles and grabbed Orín with Bonnie and Na'al with Paige at virtually the same moment.

The regulators shouted out, "These are *outlaws!* Continue on ... nothing to see!" and "Just a costume to deceive! Don't believe a word from 'em!"

The platform then stopped and so the masses behind it. The guards dragged the two pairs forward to the rear of the platform, and they were quickly hoisted up with vines, bound, and brought before Bydelus. He awaited them eagerly.

"Aha! Na'al, the *snail lover*, and her friend, Orín, the *shifty one!"* Bydelus's beady eyes scowled at them. "But ..." his face lightened with curiosity, "what are *these* beauties? Disguises, no doubt?! No! Apparently not!" Bydelus had pinched and tugged at Paige's cheek.

"Ouch! Quit pinching my face!" protested Paige in a rage.

"And, apparently, they're intelligent, feisty ones, too! Can you explain these *ugly ones*, Na'al? Look at their odd dress, *pale* skin, and *stringy hair!* What are these *miscreant* creatures? Why have you brought them *here?* You must desire to disrupt *and* corrupt our harvest celebration! *Speak up!"* Bydelus would not be made a fool of before his nobility who were pushing in tightly and surrounding him.

"Gladly will I answer you," shouted Na'al. "These are *earthen* ones from another world sent by the Conductor entering in through the Trioptic Giants' realm!"

At the word "giant" a momentary hush fell upon all the noblekin.

Na'al paused dramatically. She then spoke louder over their gasps and renewed whisperings. "Yes, *'through* the giants' realm' and the Conductor intends to have them put a stop to *your* madness, Bydelus, you who have *bewitched* the entire Musselkin people!"

"Oh ... oh ..." Bydelus responded back arms outstretched. "What a

wonderful *fairytale* story!" he mocked. "These creatures are *new* to us—*NEW*! I remember once being told not to trust anything '*new*.' What could they possibly do to prevent our progress as a great nation? They are just ... just *strangely* clad, *gaudy freaks!*"

"That's it! THAT'S IT!" shouted Paige. "I can't *stand* this *insulting* hot air spewing from your mouth! You can't speak about us this way! 'GAUDY!'—well, *YES*, we are. But '*STRINGY hair*'? *A 'FREAK'? 'UGLY,' are we?* Why, take a look in a mirror—*do you have mirrors here? Evidently not!* You're just nothing but a *little* ... a little" she was flustered. "A *little green goblin, a beastly bully!*"

Bonnie was waiting for her turn and didn't miss a step, *"AND ... I* suppose *you* have *never* heard of Salton-suhl, the Giant King? We have met him and spoken *at length. Yes, indeed! And I have even prepared AND served him rock dinner garnished with GEM!"* She lied about this fact, which, if a gem had been present, she would have done. Nevertheless, she proceeded confidently, "We're *friends* of no *MEAN* acquaintance with the Giant King. I only wish his royalty were *here—right NOW—to expose you and put you and your giants in your place!"*

With that, Bydelus instantly looked beaten in word and shamed before all. In front of him stood someone—*or rather some strange, new thing—claiming* to be better connected with the giants *than himself*. Slowly regaining his composure, Bydelus put on his airs once again and said matter-of-factly,"*Well,* I am *quite* certain that this self-proclaimed *King* does not serve you as well as *my* giants serve *ME*, nor does this *Saltron* or *Sullen-face—or whatever his name is!*—create public and architectural *wonders* as marvelous as *mine* to be enjoyed by all. *Away with them! Take them away!"*

Yelling louder, Bydelus added, "And onward my giants, Bryton-duhl and Nimbrik-al. Onward and *upwards!"*

Hilasdem, carried by Wheldon-olt and trailed by Creyvyn and his band, arrived at the Central Coliseum in time to observe the Musselkin nation in the distance on the roadway advancing behind the twin giants pulling the noblekin platform.

Creyvyn commanded, "Stay here, Wheldon-olt, and guard this *despicable* snail. But understand this clearly: *Don't let a word emanate from its shell*. Do you understand, Wheldon-olt?!"

"I will obey my master," replied Wheldon-olt. Creyvyn, of course, took "master" to mean himself. It did not. (Mind you, reader, the importance of proper pause and comma usage.) Contented greatly with the thought of the giant's compliance, Creyvyn raced down to report the events to his father, Chief Governor Bydelus.

Arriving shortly and being hoisted up atop the platform, Creyvyn's mean grin conveyed to his father the success of his expedition to the Narrows in search of the one last Silver Snail. Hugging his father, Creyvyn whispered, "We got it! The *last* one, Father. It's *over*; it's *all* over! Sylvanwood is *ours!*"

"Splendid, Splendid, my son. How is the snail held? I want no distraction during my speech; *this* is our moment of victory!"

"Wheldon-olt has the snail securely—not a vibration will be heard! He will obey! He is stationed just inside the Coliseum and awaits further orders from you."

"Excellent!" He clasped his hands tightly. "Now I'm going to introduce the Central Coliseum and let the kinsfolk enter and then I'll give my inaugural speech. Our trustworthy Tarius is overseeing the final preparations for the fire rock display. Go and confirm with him the timing of its start—precisely as I end my speech *at my signal*—and for the inauguration meet me back up here on the stage with your mother altogether as the royal family." Then Creyvyn rushed away to complete his task so as to return as quickly as possible to the speech that would guarantee his bright future.

As the crowds took in the new sight of the great Central Coliseum, Bydelus positioned himself at the back of the platform facing the masses. The twin giants brought the platform to a halt at the entrance of the enormous structure. Gasps turned to questions and speculations, which turned to shouts of excitement at the sight of such a grand public work, obviously accomplished by the hand of the beloved giants.

Central Coliseum, color pencil by Guinevere Mitchell (assisted by Paige Edwards)

"Noblekin and Kinsfolk," Bydelus waving his hands downward and waited for the crowds to grow silent. "Dear Noblekin and Kinsfolk—Please listen carefully. During our Harvest Festival where you have enjoyed the days of feasting and celebration, I have instead *labored* to produce for you this Central Coliseum which you now see before us. Nimbrik-al and Bryton-duhl have plied their crafts and skill in its construction—*it will seat our whole kinsfolk nation.* I want you to *notice* its particular architectural features, which truly embody and symbolize our *great* nation. This main entrance, which will soon be adorned with the greatest ornaments of our best craftsman, allows access of this rolling stage and attests to the grand scale with which the Coliseum has been made. The symmetrically ascending outer walls begin at no less than fifty feet in height and reach at the opposite center end no less than one hundred and fifty feet! There is seating from top to bottom; and notice the many entrances and tunnel exits for your convenience. This coliseum will be used for our Pojo and Crumkit tournaments and other special events, commencing this *very* evening. So, please find a seat, for I will be making an announcement of *GIANT* proportions for which you will want to be present as I foretell of our nation's *glorious* future."

Cheers erupted at the words "*GIANT* proportions" since the vast majority of the kinsfolk adored anything associated with the giants. Instantly, masses rushed to get the best seats at the far end of the coliseum at its highest height. At the same time, the platform itself was wheeled about as the twins now pushed it to the far central end passing on their way, Wheldon-olt who was standing leaning against the back wall stage right.

At the end of the stage were the most coveted of seats closest to the beloved Bydelus. The noblekin pulled on the platform looked down on the commonkin quite pleased with themselves even in their not-so-elevated positions. It took nearly half an hour for the coliseum to fill up—if 'filled up' was the right expression, for the coliseum was only half full after the masses of Musselkin had pushed towards the center closest to the noblekin platform. Bydelus was baffled as he observed this fact while the last stragglers entered, until a counselor leaned over to him and speculated that the coliseum had been built much larger than had been expected, which relieved Bydelus's ego and gave him another talking point for his speech—*there was room for the nation to grow.* Creyvyn soon appeared proudly on platform's center and joined his father and mother, Harpís.

Currently, Jarwyn, the Governor of the Second City of Kerr, approached the forward center stage and began the official event raising his hand here and there spotting favors friends and family. "Welcome! Welcome indeed to our *Central Coliseum* which is conveniently located near the first city of Nimbyn, and for generations to come will be host to our games, theatrical entertainments, and other national celebrations. As a representative *of* the Noblekin governors *myself*, we have a very important announcement to make. After many very prodigious indications from our holy sedges and altars and after much deliberation, we have found it in our *best* interest to appoint a '*Chief Governor in Perpetuity*'—that is, a *governorship* that is *stable* and *never ever changing*, representing us *ever faithfully* to the Conductor *forever!* And, we are fortunate—*very fortunate indeed!*—to have found such a governor among us who has shown tremendous leadership and remarkable initiative and has always had the best interests of our kinsfolk nation *in his heart of hearts—his heart is as large as a giants'!* (about which, dear reader, let us tell you, Trioptic Giants have no heart), a person whom *we know you would heartily approve* and who has garnered the skillful and beneficial affections of our northern giant friends, a person for whom I now step aside to announce and introduce to you—*Bydelus, Highest Priest, Chief Governor Supreme in Perpetuity!*

Part V

The Venture of Redemption

Chapter 24

Verthana's Ransom

At the evil announcement of Bydelus's ascension to *'Highest Priest, Chief Governor Supreme in Perpetuity'* the coliseum erupted with cheers of excitement and shouts of elation from the kinsfolk. Hearts and minds swelled with pleasure at the decision to have Bydelus rule them forever, to whom they had already submitted their very lives and futures. Reluctantly, or so he made it seem so that the others around him encouraged him on, Bydelus slowly, feigning reluctance, walked to stand in the center with Jarwyn to address the assembled nation, pointing and waving to this and that kinsfolk, smiling as he approached.

"*Thank you! Thank you!* What a beautiful evening! The Conductor bless you! Wow! This is *quite* an unexpected honor! Thank you! I am truly *humbled.* I ... I *simply* had *no idea* that such honor was to be granted me. *I am stunned, truly* ... and before I can even think of accepting, I must direct your attention to these kind friends of our nation, Wheldon-olt, Bry-ton-duhl, and Nimbrik-al, who through fate, were brought our way to bet-ter our Sylvanwood and advance our nation even *beyond Sylvanwood*—yes, even *beyond* our own wooded lands ... because...," Bydelus paused and spoke slowly and strategically to let the kinsfolk take in his statements, "Wheldon-olt here..." he turned around looking, "*Where are you??!*—ah ... *haha* ... he's humbly standing in the back there—Wheldon-olt has just *re-cently finished* creating a *bridge ... to cross the Narrows ... over the Kliffs of Kalm!*"

With this, on cue the noblekin all stood up and clapped heartily; and so also the rest of the kinsfolk instinctively stood and clapped, most of them doing so even despite being uncertain whether they would *want* to cross the Great River or not. Yet some kinsfolk were deeply stirred with hope at what this bridge might hold for their futures.

Turning to his right with out-stretched arms, Bydelus addressed the two closer towering figures of Bryton-duhl and Nimbrik-al and the more distant Wheldon-olt still against the back wall. "Please ... please, let me address these, our giant friends. *Thank you ... thank you!* Truly ... here is only a partial token of our thanks." Bydelus then snapped his fingers, and a curtain on the platform was pulled away under which was piled gems and jewels of various colors, sizes, and shapes nearly six feet high. Bydelus was delighted always to be the giver of the gifts to the giants and urged them to take and eat, "Please ... please, my giants, enjoy *these* our gifts in thanks for all your works." The coliseum once again was filled with clapping and whoops of appreciation.

Motioning Wheldon-olt over to share in their delights, Bryton-duhl and Nimbrik-al were a bit puzzled at his refusal.

"No, I don't want them...." he declined. Wheldon-olt also requested , "Please, Bryton-duhl and Nimbrik-al of the Tumbel-duhl Clan of the Smytstoyne Watchers, meet me outside of the coliseum. I'll follow you out."

Bryton-duhl quickly quipped, "Well *good.* More gems for me!"

And so he and Nimbrik-al greedily began to eat up the gems, which however were never quite satisfying enough since they often worked with limestone. Both watchling giants, however, had noticed Wheldon-olt's hand held behind his back. This caused them some pause remembering something from an earlier incident. Yet, in short order, Bryton-duhl and Nimbrik-al finished grabbed up the rest of the gems, stuffed their palates, and departed the coliseum to await Wheldon-olt.

Meanwhile Bydelus continued his speech, "Now, I turn to address a most troubling matter—we are confronted with challenges, as you know.

For example, we have these trouble-making rebels—not worthy of even naming—who hate our nation and its progress...." Bydelus motioned with his hands and then pointed to Praktor and Dernal along with Na'al, Orín, Bonnie, and Paige, and some others tied up and under guard who were ushered forward beside him. "*These are troublemakers* who resist our progress and do not *like* our giant friends...." at which booing and angry shouts arose, starting on cue with the noblekin; the booing soon continued throughout the crowds. "Yes, *booooo to them*! What *shall* be done with them?!!" Bydelus asked dramatically with his hands raised high in exasperation. The booing continued.

Just then, as the twins exited, Wheldon-olt approached the platform holding Hilasdem out front extended fully in his right hand. Bydelus, amidst the booing, glanced at them approaching. He immediately reveled in his heart at the coming of this final triumph to be rid of the snail and the rebels at one foul swoop since the crowds had expressed such strong and vocal displeasure with them. However, Wheldon-olt carefully placed Hilasdem down beside Bydelus, whose heart suddenly was filled with fright as the giant released his grasp, and strode on out of the coliseum after Bryton-duhl and Nimbrik-al.

Instantly, with all the vigor and resolution of the Conductor aiding him, Hilasdem began vibrating mightily and pitched the ebb and flow of the melodious tones into loud, distinct expressions of articulate speech, "*O Musselkin Nation ... O Forlorn Ones! How low* you have become in your inclinations, thoughts, and aspirations! *Flee from here at once!* Flee from this rocken tomb around you! *Flee!* Those who still have *sense* in your hearts and a *conscience* to direct your souls, *flee* and turn back again to the Conductor's life that is *true* life! Return to the way that is *pure light* and *sure joy*! *Flee*, I say, *into the high lands*, for '*Although there's been a deadly drought, from Heaven above comes a flooding spout*'—your ransom draws near! Its dew will soon be upon you all!"

Now, dear readers, the following segment of this story is *very* difficult to relate, for not only foremost is it dreadful to the very depths of hell in that Hilasdem *dies* but also because so many things happened *all at once.* Confusion and darkness *seized* the coliseum.

Bydelus, in response to Hilasdem, began shouting contrary statements, *"Not true! It lies!"*

Simultaneously, the guards rushed at Hilasdem to stop his vibrating without any great effect.

At the same time, across the whole of the coliseum, some wise Mussel-kin, coming to their senses, began to "flee" darting to the exits in obedience to the snail's warnings.

Just before these events were unfolding within the amphitheater, Wheldon-olt had gone outside to plead earnestly with his clan members. "Listen," he said to Bryton-duhl and Nimbrik-al, "Listen my clan members...."

But before he could continue, Bryton-duhl broke in, "What *did* you have in your hand?! Let me guess ... *a delight!"*

"Never you mind! We giants have already done so much *wrong* down here—utterly *evil*—that we must *leave* this life of indulging ourselves and *cast* Bydelus behind us *immediately!* There's *still* hope for us!"

Just then the pulsating vibrations of Hilasdem had reached the ears of Bryton-duhl and Nimbrik-al.

Bryton-duhl angrily said, "*Aha!* You were holding out on us ... *again!* I knew it!"

The twins looked at each other with desperately wild eyes savoring the final tasty treat awaiting only *one* of them. Bryton blurted its last ditty, *"Last one there's a silly yunt and will have a stomach in want!"* And both rushed back in through the broad coliseum entrance.

But Wheldon-olt, in a crouched stance, prepared met them both in stride. A titanic clash ensued; the twins wrestled at first independently, but soon, once again, plied stratagem together against their elder watcher. Hands and feet maneuvered mechanically and ventured counter-maneuvers. The three separated temporarily. But Wheldon-olt had understood that the best he could do was only to stall their forward motion. So, faking an upper body throw into a double headlock, which he had so often done in their previous matches, suddenly Wheldon-olt dove down between them to clutch each of their ankles. He pulled with all his might and tripped them up into a tumbling pile, his hands clasped hard. It was a stalling move with the Great Mover setting in the western sky. The giants would soon fall into their slumber. With his flailing legs intertwined with theirs, Wheldon-olt leveraged his torso and massive back against their equally massive fighting frames and tried desperately to stop their progress. Nevertheless, dragging Wheldon-olt slowly, the giant twins frantically grasping turf and terrain, crawled their way back into the entrance of the coliseum.

Bydelus, amidst the confusion in a final attempt to regain control of the situation, had given the signal to ignite the fire rock display. Tarius set afire the wick, which snaked over to the makeshift fire rockets like fiery arrows that shot skywards with streams of sparks high overhead concluding with loud booming reports and colorful flashes all around and above the darkening coliseum.

Just as this happened, the three Trioptic Giants wrestled their way into the center of the amphitheater, Wheldon-olt hopelessly failing in his stalling efforts. Many kinsfolk eyes were delighted and transfixed between spectacles and the din both of the giant mêlée and the flashes and booms of the fireworks overhead. This entertainment at Central Coliseum would be its first and biggest, but also the last.

With a sudden coordinated effort and turn, the twins got hold of, lifted, and pinned the struggling Wheldon-olt against the eastern wall.

He wailed, "No! Not *this* one. Leave it *alone*! This is *the Last One*. You must not...." With these last words, the twins heaved Wheldon-olt over the shorter wall of the coliseum. But this structure sent seismic wave all around it such that it began to teeter-totter and crumble like clay.

Simultaneously, Nimbrik-al and Bryton-duhl in full sight of the enraptured audience leaped at Hilasdem, still pleading and warning the Musselkin until his last vibration—*Hilasdem, the Last Silver Snail*—and landing upon the platform, flipping it. Flung in mid-air, two enormous hands simultaneously grabbed the snail tightly and crushed it as the Trioptic Giants, wrestling still, rammed into the back supporting foundations of the coliseum with such a force that the whole rock face fell upon them. The surrounding cliffs also commenced crumbling down from their heights. Quickly then did the whole structure seemingly implode with thundering quakes and multiple avalanches from each side in a pulverizing, smothering mass of limestone rubble. Debris was strewn about as ashen dust whooshed up and flooded out the valley.

Reader, we must tell you that *never* have souls died with such titillating excitement than there and then at the booming of flashing fireworks and the thunderous, fighting furry of three wrestling Trioptic Giants.

From below, nothing moved for several moments; nothing was heard but rocks settling by force of gravity. Dust continued to drift up in all directions. Slowly, moaning and scrambling sounds across debris were heard from the few surviving Musselkin fleeing the catastrophe.

Above in the heavens, the final crackles and two "booms" of the greatest ever firerock display ended their reports abruptly and gave way to a steady, dark rain drops falling and adding pitter-patter sounds all round. The shower contained no joy, nor indication of playfulness. Instead, it bespoke the misery and divine sadness over the utterly tragic events. In fact, never had rain fallen in that world of Verthana. It rained straight for eight hours less than two full days.

In a high cave in the Valley of Turnus overlooking the crumbled tomb of Central Coliseum, Tanner and Guinevere with their Musselkin friends had observed the whole catastrophe of coliseum imploding. In unbelief, the earthen twins looked back and forth at each other and at Gnurl and Ranít. Tanner, weeping asked miserably, "*Who* could have survived *that??! Where* ... are Bonnie and Paige?" He slunked his head into his hands sobbing. Guinevere wept beside him, for they had at one point seen Bonnie and Paige, brightly visible in her wedding dress, on the platform stage.

Further above along the nearby slopes of the two-mile high mountain, another trio of large eyes had watched the whole scene unfold with equal distress. Large, grey tear drops fell to the ground as the giant laid down and fell into a long, slumbering sleep. For the sun had fully set on that fateful day only to be seen again on the morning of the third day after.

Chapter 25

Troyton's Journey Westward

The rain not only fell in the lowlands but washed throughout the mountainous regions of the Giants' land. It was a cleansing rain, a purifying rain that worked its effect divinely with simultaneous chemical and spiritual power and import. The perfection and specificity of the chemical equations and the corresponding divine commentary which would attempt to depict the physical sublimity and holy love behind the rains *could not* be contained even within the Corridor of Time if it were expanded a thousand-fold. Simply put, the rains brought the beginnings of the Restoration of the Giants in that mostly fallen world of Verthana.

But dear reader, you must recall what had befallen Troyton-suhl with Thomas and Archer the previous day. Troyton-suhl, remember, had outwitted Anton-duhl on the night before the rainfall started. In so doing, he had successfully rescued and repossessed the One Gem for the whole Trioptic Giant race.

On this night before the rains, Thomas and Archer worried terribly for their watchling now nearly 40 feet tall. Troyton-suhl had stiffened badly from the calcifying talcum powder that now was impairing his well-designed, graphite joints. Any water would have helped Troyton-suhl, but none was reached before the sun had set that night, and so Troyton-suhl slumbered fitfully even as his frame increased in length, due to the fantastic growth rate of a youngling Trioptic Giant, *to nearly 48 feet in height!*

Thomas asked Archer, "What are we going to do? I don't think that Troyton-suhl can carry the One Gem and finish his journey; we should think of something else."

"Yes. He needs water terribly bad. But we haven't seen very much even when have found some water," replied Archer who growing very frustrated with their situation.

"I can't stop worrying about how this is all supposed to work out," said Thomas. "I mean, how can we ever meet back up with the others? We have *no* idea *where* they are!"

The two friends stared at each other with bewilderment. Tired and hungry, Archer unfolded the yunts' gift of the leathery leaf and they huddled underneath it within earshot of Troyton-suhl and tried to fall asleep.

Thomas eventually had a dream. He saw a crystalline city on a cloud. Above it was the sun. The city sat upon foundations of rich purple and contained beautifully elegant tall buildings of various colors, which moved. Suddenly from the clouds, massive stones swooped up and then down upon the city; a swooping stone met a building and was seen to collapse here, and another collision occurred there as building after building collapsed. Then a wall was erected encircling the city. The dream continued and the stones persisted in their attack upon the city and its falling buildings. More and more of the beautiful buildings plummeted at the onslaught of the falling rocks. Then the sun rose even higher above the city and covered it with a shower of sun rays—a few more stones swooped but were repelled by the shower of the sun. Next a large pair of hands extended from both the sky and the sun and the hands sprinkled water upon the city, and the buildings regained their former shape and brilliance as the sun seemed to shine brighter than it had before. Light brought joy and warmth ... a wonderful warmth ... and a jubilant joy.

"Wake up, wake up, my little watchers! The sun *awakens* us and pulls me *onward*, for today we shall see the Western Sea Tides—I can smell the breezes with water in them." Troyton-suhl loomed over the waking Thomas and Archer, who were blinded by the light refracting through the prism-like Gem that Troyton-suhl held above them.

Rubbing his eyes, Thomas asked, "Troyton-suhl, how are you feeling?"

"Just fine. Just fine.... Watch me jump." Troyton-suhl tried but stumbled and crashed to the ground; he let out a surprising chuckle.

"I don't get the joke. How can you *laugh* at a time like this?" asked Archer.

"Well, I tell you that today we shall *worship* on the Western Sea Tides! Today, I will finish my course, even if I shall need to *crawl* there. I will do it! The Conductor has assured me of this during the night. Today, my watchers, we will look upon the great Silver Sea!"

"But ... but...," began Thomas. "*Who* will carry the One Gem?"

"Never you mind the gem," dismissed Troyton-suhl. "It is *nothing* to me."

Archer spoke up loudly with an idea that had been growing in his thoughts during the night, "Just eat it, Troy! It will be good for you, like any of the giants! The gems are good for giants, right?! This is what you should do. *Eat it* and you will be *better*!"

Troyton carrying the One Gem, pencil by Archer Edwards

"*NO!*" shouted Troyton-suhl. "*No*, you cannot ... *I say again* ... you *must not* even *MENTION* that to me *ever* again. It is *not mine* ... I am Troyton-suhl. This ... this gem belongs to King Salton-suhl and to all the giants. If you do but mention this again, I will leave you behind me, Archer."

Archer shrunk back from his suggestion immediately and remained quiet most of the rest of the journey, so frightened was he with the demeanor that came over Troyton-suhl at the mention of eating the One Gem.

"Come now, my watchers. Let's go! The sun is animating my limbs wonderfully for our journey." Troyton-suhl picked up the One Gem over one shoulder, and began to hobble ever westward along the ancient, cobbled highway.

The clan traveled for several hours before coming to a rest way. Needful of water, Archer and Thomas ran up to the pool and were happy to find a small puddle in it. They eagerly drank while Troyton-suhl hobbled up to the pool and set down the One Gem.

"Is there *any* for me?" Troyton-suhl asked.

The two friends stopped and sheepishly looked up at Troyton-suhl, whose kindly rocken grin betrayed no anger at their selfish actions of muddying the waters before he could wash away the talcum residues from his joints. Thomas was very disappointed with himself, since he knew that Troyton-suhl was much more in need of the water than either of them, especially while bearing the burden of the One Gem.

"Here," offered Thomas, "We can wet your limbs to clean them when this water clears up. Where should we start?"

"With my hips ... here," Troyton-suhl pointed, and they did so. Archer used his leaf to hold and lift the water high up while Thomas wetted his shirt and squeezed out the water now here, now there. The two small boys resembled two fairy nurses attending their huge patient.

The clan stayed there for nearly an hour. During that time when resting, a bouley had come up to the pool with a melon. The wondrous creature looked disappointedly at the low water, left the fruit, and bounded away. Thomas and Archer were only too happy to consume the delicious humin fruit.

Troyton-suhl grew rather eager to leave. So, picking up the One Gem on his shoulder, he motioned for the two others to follow him. His walking was a bit easier and there was less grating of his joints and dragging of his tri-toed right foot along the ground. Still Troyton-suhl hobbled and his gait was uneasy and grew increasingly painful with each stride he took. He continued counting each step.

Awkwardly, Thomas broached the subject of his own thoughts of the previous day. "Troy ... I *mean* Troyton-suhl ... I need to say ... ah, really, *confess* that in Anton's trove when Archer and I found the garnets and other jewels ... I ... I was not *sure* that I wanted to *give* them to you to eat. Today, I've been thinking that I must have wanted to keep them for myself to try to bring them back home and get *rich* and all. I mean ... I think that's what one usually wants to do when holding precious stones, me included. I'm sorry for being *soooo* selfish."

"Is this *an apology*?" asked Troyton-suhl. "None is needed. You readily gave them up to me yesterday, and so no harm to me was done. Had you *not* done so, I think I would be in sorer shape today since this powder has messed up my joints. The gems prevented this from being worse than it is, I am sure." He paused before continuing, "I have been figuring that one needs to distinguish the idea from the *thought-action*. Thomas, you had the *idea*, which one could call a temptation. But then—only God knows for certain—whether you took any *ownership* of the idea to make it a thought-action—a *thaction*, so to speak, as we giants put it. Perhaps it might help us, and you in this case, to think of it in this way, because it is *not* a sin to be tempted, but to *act* on the idea and this *action* starts as a *thaction*."

Thomas sighed, "Well, I definitely owned the idea just now, and so I guess I committed the thaction."

"That may be true. *Regret*, can do that. It's deceptive!!! It's in your grief of the loss, then, that your heart has begun to *own* the idea, and so commit the *thaction*," said Troyton-suhl.

"But" Archer asked, "are *all* thought-actions *bad?* I mean, might not *some* thactions be good? I bet we have thactions all the time, and, surely, they're not all bad and come from having *bad ideas* and making *them* our own."

"You're right, Archer. At least in this view from the perspective of the giants. In this giant body and frame of mine, I am able, as I've told you before, to enjoy the ability to *think* and *calculate* like the giants. It's quite remarkable—and fun!—and yet my *previous* memory and person is the same. I have these elevated abilities and am yet *still myself*. I can see things both from a human's and a giant's perspective, and the views are *mutually* illuminating."

"I don't understand ... you've lost me there, Troyton-suhl. You've been using *bigger* words, more *precise* words perhaps, than before, which are *bigger* than your age," remarked Thomas.

"By 'mutually illuminating' I mean that I can see things from both perspectives, and a lot is gained from this. The saying, 'walking in another's shoes' captures this idea. I'm quite *literarily* in the *giants'* shoes right now and I understand *both* them better *and* my own human life better. I hope I'll *never* forget this!"

"Well, as interesting as *this* is," Thomas broke in, "how much farther do we have to go? Can you see anything?"

"No, not yet from up here. But I smell the ocean and the air is *full* of interesting smells! My mind is trying to sort them all out. But," Troyton-suhl stopped and looked, "*who* have we here ... the poor fellow ... and I believe there's *still* motion in his thactions." He stopped in front of a pile of slumped over rock. Three eyes opened and a glimmer of hope shone on a trioptic face.

Chapter 26
At the Western Sea Tides

"Humble Greetings, O Ancient One. We are from the Mitchell Clan, and I am Troyton-suhl—the last born from the Pool of Emergence." Troyton-suhl waited awkwardly, not wanting to assume that the giant could not speak.

Slowly deep speech gurgled from his throat, "I am ... pleased ... .to ... meet you, Youngling Troyton-suhl. My ... name is Padton-olt, messenger of King Salton-suhl on route to the Western Sea Tides. I'm delayed, is all. Duty first, however. I might ... make it there ... yet with message for the giants assembled around the altar." He glanced at the One Gem and his eyes enlarged.

Troyton-suhl acknowledged the look with a certain statisfaction and nodded in return. "Yes ... this *is* the One." Troyton's eyes flickered with Padton's with deep understanding. "I'm traveling to the Western Sea Tides—Have we far to go? My limping and lumbering have thrown off my stride count."

"One hundred and seventy-six strides to go, or so I have counted—my stride was always seven or so off from the Pool of Emergence. In any case, you are *almost* there." Padton's speech was improving greatly. "And, let me congratulate your seizure and rescue of our majesty's possession. But I observe that this has come at some great cost to you." He had observed Troyton's debilitating bent and awkward posture from seizing up. He shook his head, "Oh, Anton-duhl, Anton-duhl, Anton-duhl Meer!"

Troyton-suhl nodded and raised a fist. It had indeed come at a cost. But he felt that his trouble and pain were nothing compared to the slowing motion that he had many times now observed in the ancient giants like Salton-suhl, the Elders, Tipton-Tyne, and now Padton-olt; and truly only the Conductor knew how many countless others. Troyton queried, "I've been figuring and calculating what to do with this One Gem—and nothing yet has come to mind. Are you able to help me, Padton-olt?"

"Oh, I see." Padton-olt mused wistfully. "Well, you should not *worry* yourself, youngling, with this inadequacy, for the Conductor certainly has determined *how* this Gem will be used for our restoration, *the* Restoration of us all. That you possess it in honor of King Salton-suhl is sure sign that the Conductor's redemption is drawing near. So, I'd say, make haste to the Sea Tides, and I surmise that you should place the gem upon the oracular altar there. The Conductor will speak to you assuredly in *some* way. And, pray, be on the lookout for my companions, Belton-uhl, Ruedton-al, and Gerndon-tuhl—but do *ignore* their mocking manners. Tell 'em ol' Padton-olt is still a movin'!" And with that he itched his slurry pouch.

So, with that send off, Troyton-suhl and his little watchers, who were growing wearier and wearier about being swept up in something much larger than they could comprehend, continued their westward trek. Each step for Troyton-suhl was a burden. His right leg dragged behind him and he occasionally hopped queerly, but nothing could be done for him. Archer and Thomas kept looking for pools of water while staying either well ahead or well behind for fear of Troyton-suhl falling on them.

After two bends in the skyway, the dusty road began a steady sloping downward. Even saw-off ones, like Thomas and Archer, could now see out over the distant cliff edge to the bright shining sun. Before them were three bodies of stone in the midst of the roadway. Before they had reached them, one shouted out, "Hey ... *who* goes there? Friend *or* foe?"

"Friend to King Salton-suhl. How answer you to *that?*" said Troyton-suhl.

"Well asked ... well asked." The voice pulled back into civility. "But what name do *you* bear for yourself?"

"One that was given me by the will of the Conductor as pronounced by King Salton-suhl—*I'm Troyton-suhl of the Mitch-ell Clan.*"

"Well said ... well said. And *what* is this possession of yours you bear? A big burden, I see."

"No possession of mine, mind you, but, in fact, the One Gem from Anton's Trove. I've been chosen, it would seem, to bear it thither to yonder altar, except were *you* to prevent my passage."

"Well answered ... well answered. You *may* pass, for friend of mine you are, and your humble servant am I, Gerndon-tuhl of the Quarrenrok Clan."

"Greetings, then, my elder friend, from Padton-olt who still moves," replied Troyton-suhl and his clan moved forward.

Another voice suddenly arose from the second body of rock, "What there? Padton-olt, you say? Are you *friend* of that *foe* of *his??!* He's a scoundrel and sluggard. Although it may *please* Gerndon-tuhl to let you pass, you must *first* answer my riddle before I'd let you pass."

Fortunately, Troyton-suhl was willing to humor the giant. "Let me guess ... you must be the great and kindly Ruedton-al." This quickly disarmed the giant to have been so easily known.

"Okay, okay ... don't delay ... *answer* me this, what crawls on all fours in the morning, strides on two feet midday, and walks no more in the evening but only scratches its crack?"

Troyton chuckled at this because he understood the joke referred to a giant's front slurry pouch or "crack." He said, "Ahh, I think you meant to end that riddle with 'never is able to walk again always wanting, but unable, to *scratch* its crack... Oh, that's an easy one ... 'Ruedton-al,' of course!"

"Why *YOU! Who's* the 'rude one' now! No, not me, it's Padton-olt, that old slurry bellied, crack scratching braggart!" He then mockingly said in a whinny little voice, "My name is Padton-olt, *the only messenger* of King

Salton-suhl on route to the Western Sea Tides ... blah, blah, blah!" He paused, gathered himself, and stated musefully, "But ... since you can so rightly adjudge a giant and match their manner to their name, and dare I say, quickly judge the character of a giant—excepting, of course, Padton-olt who's obviously blanketed dust over your middle eye—even so, *you* may pass by me!" He smiled ruefully at the clan.

So, the clan moved forward once more. But, as they passed the third body of rock, Troyton-suhl caught ear of a faint whisper, inaudible to Thomas and Archer. Troyton-suhl stopped and stooped nearer the head.

"Closer," it said. "Closer, youngling" until Troyton's ears were beside the frozen head of the motionless giant.

At that, the giant belted out loudly, *"WATCH OUT! GIANTS PLAY TRICKS, YOU KNOW!"* at which Troyton-suhl, terribly startled, tipped, and fell backwards, dropping the One Gem, which began slowly rolling down the steep incline of the skyway. Instantly, the three frozen giants released peals of laughter penned up for years.

"Oh, ... now *THAT* was a good one!" bellowed Gerndon-tuhl.

"Yes, twenty years in the making!" laughed Ruedton-al.

"No one is *LOUDER* than *ME!"* shouted Belton-uhl.

At this, Archer shouted out, "You bullies! Look at you! And to pull such a *prank* on a Youngling, and a *crippled* one at that! Why, if I had a *sledge-hammer*, I'd let you have *it!"* But the giants only belly laughed louder.

"No, Archer," yelled Thomas. "You'd not need a sledgehammer, but a *jackhammer* to get through to these thick-headed *BLOCKHEADS!"* Thomas froze at that insult and looked at Troyton-suhl who had just struggled to stand up. The giants, seeing this, laughed even louder.

"Padton-olt warned me of you three," Troyton-suhl brusquely remarked. "I hope you've not ruined all of our chances at redemption!"

But the three giants belly-laughed louder and louder until they all heard a clear, distinct "pop" and "glurping" sound. They looked, and Belton-uhl indeed had popped his slurry flap, leaking very old and nasty slurry onto himself. While he gasped in dismay, the other two giants laughed paused only to begin laughing on and on until they all continued to laugh themselves silly.

In the meantime, Thomas glanced at the One Gem slowly rolling away. Troyton-suhl saw it too and hobbled hurriedly downward after it, leaving Thomas and Archer behind. The gem's speed increased as its momentum propelled it over the ancient roadway, well worn by years of travel. Troyton-suhl began to calculate its rate of speed increase and his own hobbling and was figuring when he might just jump to grab the gem before it would fly off the cliff to the unknown waters below. Faster it rolled, and faster he chased. Downward the pair went, past the altar to the edge where Troyton-suhl had calculated the jump. And as he jumped, he simply missed it. "*The One Gem is lost over the cliff!*" he thought exasperatedly. Troyton-suhl landed and let out a cry of despair and slapped the ground, "No! No! No!"

Then he stopped amidst the rise of cheering all about him. He looked up and observed hundreds of frozen giants lining the cliff ridge all about the altar, some facing it, others facing westward. He saw then the One Gem sitting right in front of him. "*But how???*" he wondered. In fact, if it had not been for the reach of one frozen giant right there—Muhdol-muhl of the Rumylrydge clan—at the very edge who caught it as it began to plummet seaward, the gem would have been lost in the sea tides below. Right beside him, Muhdol-muhl lifted his browridge and smiled brightly.

The cheering increased as Troyton-suhl worked himself aright and smiled back at them all. The cheers were *indeed* for him, he understood. He proudly picked the One Gem up and hobbled a good number of strides back to the altar and set the One Gem upon it. The brightly shinning, setting sun shone brilliantly through the diamond producing the full spectrum of vibrant colors, warming and stirring all the giants who marveled at the illuminating jewel.

Suddenly, crowd hushed as the Conductor's sure voice emanated like a song surrounding the altar, emanating from the vibrating the gem itself. "Well *done*, Troyton-suhl! You have completed the task before you. As your Maker and Creator and Conductor of this World of Verthana, I commend *you* for your faithfulness despite your own trials. *You* were the Last One born to the Trioptic Giants this one-thousandth cycle of the High Season. Nearly completed *is* the beginning of the Restoration of the Giants' race." He continued, "But your part is but one piece of it, and not even the *actual* beginning. This start is taking place, as I speak now, by the ransom of my beloved last Silver Snail, Hilasdem! Such a sacrifice was needed also on *your* world. But you have received *this* present grace to be here and to experience this. So, learn your lesson *well.*"

None of the giants there, still moving with thactions, fully understood these last remarks since they had forgotten what a Silver Snail was, never having seen one in the flesh. But the Conductor's comments were intended then for the humans and for future recollection of the all the giants.

With these words, when the Great Mover was still barely hanging on the horizon, just then a gentle, steady rain began to fall. It did not stop until two and half days later, during which time the sun was not seen.

As the falling water pelted Troyton-suhl, he felt surges of renewed energy and limberness returning to his joints and frame. Full motion began to return to his digits and appendages. Joy—*true joy of full motion*—filled his heart at release from the deathly, freezing bondage he had felt. A reverent chorus of praise rose around him as all the gathered giants sang out, beginning to receive the same relief as he had. Troyton-suhl gazed in wonder at the beauty of the setting sun over the expanse of the sea tides. From his height, waves were clearly demarcated and seen, yet they remained virtually motionless upon its surface, reflecting the yellow of the setting sun. The expansive view reminded him of that which he had seen once from atop the Sleeping Bear Dunes, but the sea's colors were deeper, richer, and even metallic and the rain only amplified this effect.

In the sky, a prism of colors arched before them, just briefly, catching the falling flood. And then, finally, the sun dipped beneath sea, and the collective chorus of thanks turned instead to snores of slumber. The giants slept, under the pelting of the healing rain and the dense clouds, until the Great Mover's next visible rising on the third day.

Archer and Thomas had never fully caught up with Troyton who dashed towards the cliff. Instead, they watched the spectacle from their vantage point above. As the rain began to fall, they scrambled back upwards to a small cave nearby, which providentially contained dried currant branches with edible berries that a yunt pack had collected. Never did the thought of their warm beds at home seem more appealing to them than during that two and half day stretch. They warmed themselves, ate, and slept securely with hundreds of sleeping giants outside below.

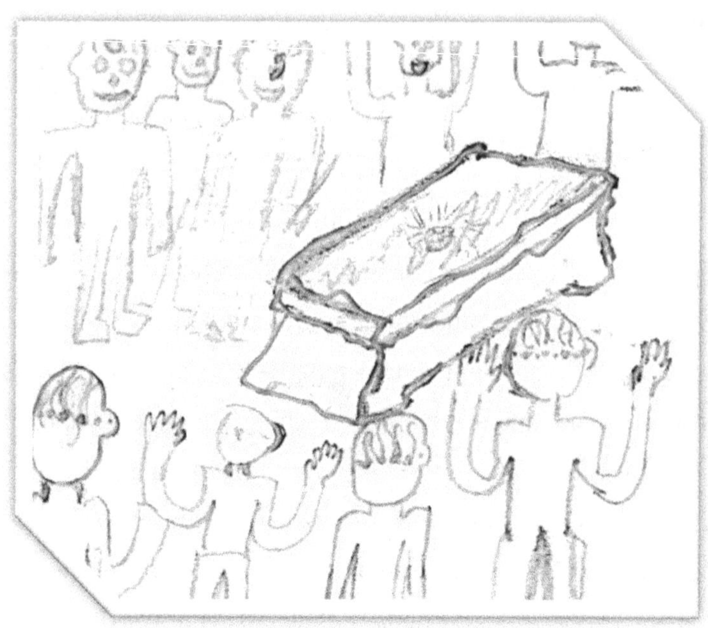

The One Gem on the Western Sea Tide Altar,
pencil by Archer Edwards

Chapter 27
The Tunnel from Within

In the cave high up in the Valley of Turnus, the Musselkin companions agreed to take turns keeping watch and then sleeping. But when Gnurl couldn't sleep, they agreed that Ranít should curl up with the young earthen children. After softly singing some of their own bedtime songs, they then tried to fall asleep. Tanner and Guinevere passed the early part of the night sleeping fitfully with dreams approaching nightmares.

Gnurl kept an anxious eye on the downward slopes looking for any sight of their companions returning to rejoin them at their pre-established rendezvous. He and Ranít did not want to split up looking for them, lest something might happen to the children in their trusted care. Fearful for him were the torrents of water "falling *somehow*" from the sky. "But *how?*" he pondered, "and *why?*" The thought of so much water was abhorrent to the innate sensibilities of the Musselkin. Their fire kept them warm and snug, but even so the dampness outside cooled the cave air.

Midway through the wet night, Gnurl caught sight of Musselkin climbing into nearby caves. His nerves bristled when he realized that any of these parties could be supporters of Bydelus. The companions weren't the only ones, surely, who knew of the many caves in the foothills here, but none was as high and safe from the plummeting "water" as theirs, and so, he reasoned, *"It will only be a matter of time before some party finds us."* So, he urged the others to move deeper into the cave to shelter them from obvious view should others arrive and demand to share the cave, with which he would, by all manner of hospitality given these dire circumstances, be obliged to comply. He even thought of putting the fire out, which surely, he figured, could be seen by others climbing the valley ridges.

Just then, four figures appeared quickly scaling the path that led directly to their cave. Gnurl ran to the back and woke Ranít. But before the two both turned to face the approaching strangers, the four figures, kneeling, spied in through the doorway.

"Sedgénu!" said one.

"Sedgénu to you, too!" replied Gnurl, who with Ranít ran to greet Na'al, Orín, Bonnie, and Paige.

Hearing the joyful excited exchange of greetings, Guinevere and Tanner awoke and staggered over, as like little children at being awakened Christmas morning. They offered their sleepy hugs. These hugs were "abbreviated" since Bonnie and Paige were soaked through and through. The hugs transitioned to exclamations with joy warming their hearts.

"I can't believe it!" Guinevere said. "You're *alive!!!*"

"Of course!" exclaimed Bonnie.

"I *knew* it ... I *knew* it!" Tanner exclaimed back.

"It's raining cats and dogs out there!!!" Paige announced.

"What does *that mean*?" asked Gnurl.

"Oh ... uh ... it's *an expression*. I'll explain later!"

The four wet ones undressed as much of their muddied clothing as possible and sat down to warm themselves around the fire. The two pairs of youth and Musselkin huddled together to get warm

As they warmed a bit, Na'al spoke first, still shuddering, "It *was awful!* ... so many *disappeared!* The Conductor is surely angry with us! But His Hilasdem warned us! He saved us and would have saved others, but they would not listen! It all makes *no sense!* Bydelus deluded our kinsfolk terribly!"

"Yes," admitted Orín sadly, "He kept having us want more and more 'glory' and set aside our heads and hearts to pursue our imaginations, or longings. He's introduced terrible *evil* into our hearts! We needed discernment!"

Ranít asked, "So, did our kinsfolk *die* like our Silver Snails!"

"Yes ... most all did, I think," Orín sighed sadly and put his head into his hands weeping.

"Oh no!!!" Ranít pressed in further, "But how did you all *escape* the falling amphitheater?!"

"In the end," Na'al confessed, "it was Hilasdem. Bydelus ordered our guards to stop him from warning us all—*just how Hilasdem persisted in his audible vibrations is beyond my comprehension!* They climbed on him, hit him, stabbed him completely through his ... his neck ... and ... *still* he would not stop warning them." Na'al wept with Orín.

The others looked back and forth waiting patiently.

Raising his head and wiping his eyes, Orín picked up the account again, "And ... and then there were flashing fires in the sky with loud sounds like *booming* and *this* distracted everyone around! *I thought our sky's stars were falling ... that our world was indeed coming to an end!*" He paused, breathing heavily. "But ... then we were able to flee the stage—*hands still bound!*—and ran off the back to the ledge and into the nearest of the tunnels. I looked *back* and ... the twin giants, wrestling each other ... had jumped and *were ... were ....*" He paused, choked up and could not continue, shaking his head and sobbing.

Na'al reached her arm around his shoulders and squeezed. She continued, "So, we were ... in the tunnel. We all looked back one last time to see the twin giants jump slamming onto the stage fighting to grab *Hilasdem ...* and they *got* him!!!" She was shaking her head. "It was *awful!*" she paused sobbing.

So Orín continued on, "and ... then the tunnel began to collapse ... we ran fast!" He breathed heavily reimagining the scene, "*I will never forget the sight*, though I wish I could. We fled from this *evil* ... all was crashing down ... left and right ... when we climbed up overlooking it all, we saw the coliseum—even the upper levels—had collapsed and water began falling from heaven!!!"

"It was awful!" Paige agreed.

Bonnie added, "We kept scrambling up and away. We stopped only to untie our hands."

Gnurl broke in urgently, "But ... did *Praktor* and *Dernal* make it out? How about any *others?* Did you see how many *others* escaped?"

"In the coliseum? I don't know ... I doubt many survived that stayed ... maybe some," said Orín somberly. "On the stage, Dernal and Praktor with others ran off too, when we did, but they must have taken another tunnel out. We didn't see them after that. It all happened so fast!" He squeezed Na'al's hand firmly to reassure her that she would hopefully see her family again.

Finally, the hard question had to be asked. Ranít braved it, "Did you *see* ... um ... were there any *others* from the stage that escaped?!" The last question was very difficult to put into words since it was terrible to conceive of even holding out the possibility that Bydelus also might have escaped to continue his cruel hold on the Musselkin.

Bonnie responded solemnly, "I *did* see a few others of the well-dressed nobility leave ... on the way here we've tried to figure out how many."

Na'al replied also, "Yes ... a group around Creyvyn also ran towards the tunnels as the rocks began to fall, but they were separated from us by crashing debris. I'm unsure whether Creyvyn would have been able to escape ... but it's possible." With a sigh she concluded somberly, "But *Bydelus*, none of us saw *him* leave the platform probably because he was so pleased to be *orchestrating* the events! I don't think he survived."

Paige took a turn, "Earlier we saw a good number of Musselkin leaving at Hilasdem's final warnings, and no one was preventing them. Later, while coming up to our cave, we also saw different groups climbing among the hills, but I'm pretty sure they didn't see us since we kept low and stayed quiet."

"Are we safe then?" asked Ranít with some anxiety.

"Yes, I believe so," said Orín. "Everyone surviving this ... this ... *evil—for I think this has been the worst EVIL ever!*—would not be in any hurry to harm anyone since enough harm has been done to weep on and on *with no end!"*

Still sniffling with tears streaming, Na'al reflected, "I believe that heaven is crying *right now!* Bonnie and Paige told us that this falling water is called 'rain.' But I'm convinced it's the Conductor's tears for our broken world ... *tears, I tell you!* They also say that these heavenly *tears* are common in their world of *earth*, which must be a *very, very sad* place to live *indeed!* But in our Sylvanwood we have never had any such *tears*." She paused and with anger said, "But these *be-damned* giants—is this rightly said, Bonnie?—and *especially* Bydelus brought this evil and these tears upon us!" She broke down sobbing again.

After a few more words of the origins and explanation of the earthen rains—and the expression 'raining cats and dogs' which they decided with some chuckles would be 'raining yunts and bouleys'—the party huddled together and slept with intermittent brief sobs as happens after a child has been crying hard.

It was not until the morning of the third day that the sun of Verthana finally was seen again. The rain had continued steadily until then and suddenly began tapering off, leaving two new visible things in the high sky—*clouds* and a massive, prismed, colorful *arch* not unlike seen here and there in the misty mornings along the streams and at the various waterfalls, but now fully spanning north to south opposite the rising sun. The Musselkin did not like the new white cottony fluffs pillowing the sky, now here and now there, that broke up the deep aqua blue and at times blocked the shining warmth of the sun. The idea of "water afloat in the sky above them" in these clouds would take some time for them to get used to.

On the ground below, easily seen from atop the high cave entrances, could also be observed something new across Sylvanwood—large bodies of water pooled along the uneven, rocky slopes and flooded all across the wooded terrain further below. Steady flowing and gurgling streams from the heights pushed constantly lower and lower seaward where no streams had been before. The high-water level greatly worried the Musselkin, but the earthen youth explained that the water would eventually drain.

Eager to leave their high cave and enter into the brightness of the sun, the collective group agreed that before all did so, a scouting party would descend in search of other surviving Musselkin to ensure the safety of all. It was also agreed that over the next few days all would prepare for the journey northward to King Salton-suhl and the Pool of Emergence. They were hoping in the journey up the mountains regions there somehow to find Thomas, Archer, and Troyton-suhl, or perhaps, by the aid of King Salton-suhl, to be reunited with the only other earthen teenagers in Verthana.

Paige wondered herself how the other earthen creatures faired that she had secretly brought along, unbeknownst to the others.

The scouting party was comprised of Orín, Na'al, Bonnie, and the twins, Tanner and Guinevere, who both insisted on going; the latter took the place of Paige, happily for her, who complained of foot cramps and was very content to stay put and improve her otherwise quite disheveled appearance while attempting to clean up her muddied wedding dress. *"Never before have I looked so bad!"* she worried.

The party left quickly before the sun had reached its zenith. The sun felt unusually hot, and by the end of that day, the Musselkin would have a burning sensation on their skin, which the earthen youth called a "sunburn." Other Musselkin were peeping out of various caves along the descending trail, and on many occasions the old greeting was offered once again, before Bydelus had risen to power, to the party as it passed. The greeting "A Conductor's day to you" was to be met with "And the Conductor's blessing to you, too." Instead of this, Bydelus had insisted on replacing the words "Conductor" with "Giant."

Presently, the group was able to navigate through the rushing streams, which broadened and became more foreboding and impassable as they neared the bottom of the valley just above the crest of the partially sunken coliseum. "*Fortunately,*" thought Bonnie "*there are no signs of Musselkin corpses; how terrible it would be for Guinevere and Tanner to see such a sight!*" She figured that if there had been any dead Musselkin outside the coliseum, they had been long washed out to the seas by the rapidly flowing waters, or, were covered up with the sediments left behind them—graves of mud.

Enough of a clear path remained that the party could make their way safely to the upper section of the crumbled coliseum. As they worked across its northern crest westward, it still was quite tall. When they reached the western side, which was banked by a swiftly flowing stream, they were confronted with an odd sight—it only made sense after the fact. A massive tunnel, which appeared to have been burrowed, not from without but from within, faced them originating through the debris of crumbled rock.

Orín asked, "*What* is this from? *How* could such a tunnel be made?" The questions gnawed at the party.

"The tunnel," answered Tanner, who had begun to sketch the scene in his notebook, "reminds me of a night crawler's burrow—a worm from our world. About this big," he wiggled his index finger to show them. "We've seen this lots after a night when the ground is softened enough by rain ... uh ... the *falling water*."

To the Musselkin's knowledge, however, no such "worm" creature existed in Sylvanwood. The thought of one gave Na'al the "creeps."

Furthermore, the tunnel was not upward like a worm's on earth would've been, the youth agreed, Instead, it was horizontal from within the very bowels of the collapsed coliseum itself.

In an instant, Tanner suddenly rushed inside, notebook in hand, with Guinevere right behind him. Bonnie almost caught Guinevere's hand but missed and stood staring into the black entrance to the cave.

"*Tanner?! Guinevere?!*" she called several times but heard nothing.

The Tunnel with Sedges added, color pencil by Guinevere Mitchell

Chapter 28
The Great Rising

The whole scouting party kept yelling, as loud as they dared, for Tanner and Guinevere to come out. They waited for many minutes until finally the two appeared with large grins on their faces.

"I understand it now!" Tanner exclaimed. *"I get it.* I believe *completely!"*

"Go in, Na'al and Orín," pointed Guinevere excitedly. "Please, go *inside!* You *need to see this for yourselves!"*

The two Musselkin, very puzzled and afraid, felt compelled to go into the dark tunnel. Once inside, they could make out a faint green light source far ahead and walked some distance to reach it. The light unmistakably began to take the shape of not one but two Silver Snails. Stunned, the two Musselkin stopped.

One of the green glowing snails addressed them, "Blessed are you, faithful creatures of the Conductor, who is to be praised *forever and ever!* Behold, here lies the very spot of the death of the *Last* One, who is also the *First* One who sets free those held in captivity. *'Where is Hilasdem?'* you are well wondering. We will tell you—He is alive and will see you again soon. Go now! Prepare for your ascent up the mountains, for your new friends must soon return to their world. Their role here is now being completed along the Giants' Skyway. You shall meet Hilasdem Triumphant at the Sedge shrines at Willowbough before heading upward. You *must* not delay but go straightway with the aid of Wheldon-olt, the redeemed giant.

Fear him not. And finally, fear not the *Gilded One*, who has *also* arisen but will come to a sure end once its destruction is complete."

Before they could ask any questions, the two glowing figures vanished in front of them. Na'al and Orín ran out of the cave, and explained all to Bonnie, Guinevere, and Tanner, who listened carefully with the glint of awe and recognition in their earthen eyes.

The party thought it best immediately to return to the high. The sun had risen quite high now, and as they turned northeastward around the crest of the fallen coliseum, the sun was blocked completely from their sight. A towering giant had arisen over them, so they instinctively began to fall back and tried to scamper away.

"Fear not! Fear not! I am no longer an enemy by the Maker's mercy! I'm Wheldon-olt come to do the Conductor's will and the will of His First One. I have seen Him even this morning. I've come to take you directly to Willowbough."

And so, after gathering provisions and collecting the others, which took some considerable time, since Paige had serious doubts about Wheldon-olt, the party was set a top the giant's shoulders, who moved carefully and steadily over streams and furrows towards Willowbough.

As they did so, a trio of eyes followed their every progress, keeping in stride with them from a distance.

Before the hidden sun returned once again to be seen rising in the southern parts of Sylvanwood, a gilded giant had also arisen on the sunset of the last night of the Harvest festival as the rain began to fall from the heavens. This giant had laid abandoned near where the Musselkin had initially set it up in their northern washlands. After that, they then avoided it like some evil with its failure to impress Therndon-al. Bydelus, of course, wanted to forget the failed effigy.

But, if observers had continued to keep an eye on it, which a few Musselkin claimed to have done (as later reported), they would have noticed over days, weeks, months, and a year a slow and meticulous transformation of its carriage—by day sometimes shaking and quivering and at night sometimes illuminated by balls of light like fireflies. Moreover, they would have heard clanging, clunking, wrenching, and whining of a "mechanical" sort emanating from *within* and *beneath* it. Although initially carved from wood, hollowed out, and gilded with gold by the Musselkin, the giant now had "mysteriously," or even "providentially," developed a capacity for "motion." And, with the start of the rain, the Gilded One indeed *did move ... and with a vengeance.*

The intent of this gilded giant was set upon destruction as reflected in its whole demeanor and particular actions. As it arose, it ripped and pulled out trees without care and cast them aside sheering off others. It then began to rampage across the rain drenched forest until it crossed Bydelus's southern highway. At that moment, it set its trioptic eyes upon the roadway and ripped and pulled and pried and disrupted the laid rock with a determined fervent frenzy that was frightening to behold. And, the few Musselkin who did behold it over the next two and half days, to escape it, even fled through the swelling streams, braving and forging newly formed creeks to move to higher ground as far away as possible from the wrecking, Gilded One.

During the steady deluge of rain, reports began to circulate amongst the surviving Musselkin to the effect that a terrible gold giant was "undoing" the works of Bydelus's with destructive precision and uncanny resolve. Meticulously, roadways, homes, shrines, fields, wells, statues, and virtually everything else constructed by the will of Bydelus through the agency of his giants—Wheldon-olt, Bryton-duhl, and Nimbrik-al—were demolished throughout the eastern and southern parts of Sylvanwood.

The Gilded One worked furiously along the roadways, not missing one item to kick over or bludgeon with its massive fists. As the rains continued and the waters rose, it then worked back northward to the center of Sylvanwood and followed the western road to the coast and from there moved northward along the shores of the Silver Sea destroying the famous Dome House of Bydelus. It moved then to Roetin's Bay where many noblekin homes had been built. Then, it followed another road leading to the Central Coliseum wreaking havoc all the way, sloshing through torrent and tempest, swelling and blowing about it.

It arrived at the coliseum just before midday of the third day as the rains slowly began to abate. In the far distance, the Gilded One caught sight of another giant its own size, animated by the arising Great Mover, walking away eastward. It followed at a distance, stopping here and there to kick over this or that structure as it went.

On one occasion, when the golden brute razed a market center nestled in the foothills, the noise of the destruction became audible to Wheldon-olt, whose ears were otherwise overwhelmed with the rushing of streams all about him. He turned slightly to catch sight of the Gilded One which followed persistently behind them.

The others riding on his shoulders had also heard and saw it then too but were so frightened that they kept utterly quiet, only looking intensely at each other with great distress wondering what sort of giant this was.

With the sun rising higher and higher, the Gilded One's golden exterior blazed brilliantly against the stormy sky in the west, reflecting the morning light and flashed eerily like a massive mirror in the distance.

This was indeed too close for comfort even for one taking giant strides. Wheldon-olt quickened his pace, which, however, was slowed from carrying his companions with care. They were now but two hundred and fifty-one strides from Willowbough.

The companions said nothing to Wheldon-olt, who had enough to think about. They kept turning back again and again to keep track of the Gilded

One's persistent progress, at times even holding their breaths as if to lighten themselves to help their giant move more quickly.

As they travelled eastward, from afar above another trio of eyes watched them closely. These eyes, upon seeing the Gilded One tracking behind them, filled with a resolve to act rightly—*a watcher returning for good.*

Upon reaching Willowbough, Wheldon-olt carefully disembarked the party on high ground. *"There you go! Take cover!"*

The Gilded One (aka the Destroyer) at Willowbough, photograph by Bonnie Mitchell

"What *is* it, Wheldon-olt?!" asked Orín finally able to breath normally.

"It's the Destroyer of Bydelus's making. He had forbidden us to see it, but one day I ventured upon the gilded effigy and stayed well away, for it's covered with gold, a sure death to me or any giant of my race who might touch it!!!" He continued, "But, I fear it is up to me to *face it now* since I am *solely* responsible for everything and have brought this plague of evil and death into Sylvanwood—*the blame is all mine!*—and I must bear the consequence before any more kinsfolk are harmed." He sighed and said,

"Hilasdem *has* forgiven me—*I know*—and showed me how to have courage *to face my stoppage* squarely in view of the hope of the Conductor's grace."

Resolutely, then, Wheldon-olt turned to face his gilded foe who had continued advancing upon them. He hastened forward to meet the destroyer *head on* in the clearing outside of Willowbough where in safety the mixed party of Musselkin and humans watched ill at ease.

Upon meeting, calculatingly, the two giants slowly circled each other at a distance as cats before a wrangle, sizing each other up. Tension filled the air. Suddenly, the Gilded One pounced at Wheldon-olt. But, at that very moment, a sudden rush from the sloping north mountainside crashed down at the two opposing giants so that the Gilded One never reached its intended mark. Instead, it was met midair by yet *another* giant of the exact same stature, but tawny copper rather than gilded in gold. Upon hitting the ground, the two giants maneuvered fiercely with holds, grips, grabs, and kicks.

The companions watched amazed. It indeed dawned on them that the two were, in fact, *perfect mirror images of one another* except in color.

Wheldon-olt stepped back stunned. He reeled with the sudden revelation and yelled, *"Therndon! Therndon-al! No, Therndon!"*

But Therndon-al Byrl maintained his determination and muttered out, *"I'm* to blame—*I* came down here first. *I'll* bring this to an end *here and now!"* Unwavering, he wrestled his golden image, the Gilden One, spinning, leveraging, and wheeling about, as they stumbled along the bank of the swollen river there.

As he watched, Wheldon-olt leaned this way, then that, wanting to enter the fray, but frozen to do so.

Soon it was evident that Therndon-al began slowing, as if tiring, and that his copper color was softening to a deathly pale yellow. With a renewed final effort, Therndon-al then engaged his foe to form an inseparable clinch with clasped hands in an ever-holding bear hug. The pair toppled over along the bank with a splashing thud, rolling about in the fatal hold. Therndon-al squeezed and squeezed the motion out of the Gilded One with crumpling and crinkling, even as his own motion of life ebbed out by the poisoning of its gilded exterior.

Then, just as suddenly as the match had begun, its participants stopped and laid still partially submerged in the overflowing stream. After a couple moments, the water and bank about them began to quiver and tremor as like from an earthquake. Steam hissed from beneath and around them. All this was seen and heard for several moments until the two forms seemed to quiver and mold together as one golden figure half sunken in the misty stream. Moment by moment further, this golden exterior gave way to a pallid coppery exterior of the fallen, stiffened Trioptic Giant of Therndon-al. Wheldon-olt approached the still form of his former watcher now half submerged and fell at his side, sobbing.

However, a scurry of bouleys came to the misty bank. They playfully ran up and patted Wheldon-olt's foot and coaxed him to look up, and as he did so, the party on Willowbough could just barely perceive through the mists that he was nodding as if in conversation.

Wheldon-olt stood up and strode over fully sound in mind and himself once again, relieved and somber and at peace. He said, "*Come!* There is One who must see you now. His presence has given hope to my rocken frame, for he is *alive* and the *First* One, who has started the restoration of this falling world of ours!"

Suddenly on the bank appeared Hilasdem with silver shell shimmering brilliantly with green hue as the sun peaked down into the clearing.

Na'al and Orín and the others, amazed, fell at his side caressing and rubbing his soft, leathery skin and beautiful shell.

Fully extending his scar-filled neck and eyes lengthening out, a pulsation resonated, pitching and ebbing, into audible speech, "My friends, how *good* it is to see you and for you to *have seen me!*"

"Oh, Hilasdem, how can this be?!" exclaimed Na'al.

"My protector and dear, dear friend! You *know* how—the Conductor's hand has *fashioned it!* Although I was the *Last* One, He has made me the *First* One to start the Restoration, to set many aright and to bring them home again."

He paused looking at them all with purpose. "Our mission has *just* begun, and I will need your brave hearts, stout hands, sturdy feet, and keen minds to see it through. You must go *throughout* Sylvanwood and give testimony to what has happened—*The Conductor forgives as surely as I live!* And you, kinsfolk, must live as you have always lived—but *now* with enduring and increased *griefs and pains, sorrows and strains including one's stoppage in physical death."*

He continued, "Moreover, the Silver Snails will no longer be present with you as before. However, with this next youngling season our remembrance will be all over the woods for you to see and to reminisce. I too will be ever with you, especially on your darkest nights and in your deepest fears. You must live on bravely!"

He paused and said further, "I have more to say to you, but it will wait for another occasion, for before his Great Mover sets this day, Wheldon-olt must bring these earthen ones back up to the giants' land."

The vibrating stopped and his eyes and neck retracted. And without a word, Hilasdem, still glowing green, withdrew himself into the stream, disappearing in the misty swirls atop the water, color-filled in an arching prismed mist, dropping beneath and vanishing.

Chapter 29
The New Giant King

On the morning of that same day, the great arising continued with the Great Mover's steady march across the sky. This morning was much happier—we shall tell you *now*, dear reader—than what had occurred below with the flooding waters and the destruction of the Gilded One. For two and a half days the rain had come and had hidden the sun, but, at last, the rain ceased and the sun rose powerfully with vibrant yellows and oranges streaking throughout the heavens. So too did a nation of once frozen Trioptic Giants *arise*—not just Troyton-suhl, nor only Ruedton-al, Gerndom, Belton-uhl, but every stony soul of the giants' race who had received the benefits of the healing rain that had so mysteriously fallen. This acidic ionized water cleansed the giants of their impurities of calcite, gold, and other compounds that had poisoned them such that their restored graphite interior lubricated their motions once again.

At the Western Sea Tides, over four hundred giants were singing. Their melodic praise well sounded like the chorus of several thousand. Giants, who had just three days prior completely stopped moving except for their thactions, now rolled and leaped and danced while singing and clapping. A wondrous and thunderous sight it was.

To Thomas and Archer, waking up to these sights and sounds was rather frightening, quite beyond anything they could ever have imagined. The saying *"Fe-Fi-Fo-Fum!"* kept coming into Archer's mind and he half-figured that by the end of the day he would be ground up and baked as bread to be eaten. The two friends had, until then, become quite accustomed to being in the presence of one giant, and on a few occasions two or three of them, but to see *so many* at once and moving so agilely and gaily was nearly beyond their capacity to comprehend. The scene was thoroughly *surreal.* Fortunately, the ground upon which they stood was very firm and steady; but, nevertheless, out of fear of a cave-in collapse, the two left the cover of the cave even moving a bit closer to the thunderous stomping and dancing.

The collective giants danced in large circles around the altar in a rave. Troyton-suhl was taken up in the dancing. One giant, Tipton, with the aid of others, hefted Troyton-suhl aloft and the representative contingent of the giant nation marched joyously carrying Troyton-suhl, crowd surfing, upon a flowing sea of their arms held high above their shoulders.

The dancing came to an end when a giant stood on the altar until all stopped; this giant offered a final prayer of thanks to the Conductor. Then, he addressed the joyful assembly, “Fellow Giants of the Conductor’s realms in the Highlands under King Salton-suhl! We are privileged to have in our throng a *champion* of mathematics, a mathstatition who has freed the One Gem and, in some way or other, has brought these falling waters to restore our stony frames and purify our clogged inwards. Our praise—*so long bottled up!*—has erupted for our Conductor! May the Conductor’s cleansing extend *thoroughly* inward wholly to our *thactions*! We must now accompany Troyton-suhl and the One Gem to the Pool of Emergence. *He* is the last of our younglings to emerge, and we must help him complete our ancient custom since it appears that he has had no watcher over him....”

Troyton-suhl interrupted suddenly, “But ... *I do* ... *I do* have *watchers.*” He had nearly forgotten Thomas and Archer but had caught sight of them huddled outside a cave overlooking the throng and pointed. All gathered of the giant nation turned perfectly in unison towards the direction of his gaze, and so all the giant eyes fell upon the two cowering earthen boys less than one-tenth their size.

“Yes, these *two* are among my watchers. We are of the Mitch-ell Clan from the world of earth from beyond the Great Mover." All the giants listened in astonishment.

"You said '*among* my watchers.' But are *these* the *only ones* of your watchers here now?!" asked the presiding one.

"Yes, they are, as you see. I ran westward, as a foolish youngling, leaving my other watchers behind me in order to fulfill the urging of King Salton-suhl. And, I have managed thus with the help of Tipton and the Conductor to find and rescue the *One* Gem." Troyton stopped and made an important statement, "But now, we must *somehow* meet back up with my other watchers to return to our own world, for we have even more clan members *there* who would miss us terribly should we never return there again. And so, I declare before you all, I believe that I have fulfilled my purpose and obligations as a giant."

"No, you have not!" the presiding giant objected. "Not quite, youngling. After this 'Course of Growing' that you have now accomplished over these several days—*and more, no doubt!*—there is yet for *you* to return to accomplish the 'Journey of Vocation' with precise strides from this Western Sea Tides starting at this altar hence directly to the Pool of Emergence which can be done in one day, even *yet* this very day!"

Tipton-tyne offered up, "I *volunteer* to be the accountant!"

"Very well, this is needed!"

"And we, his assistants," said Ruedton-al, Gerndon-tuhl, and Belton-uhl. "If Troyton-suhl will but forgive our tricks played upon him, which was nearly disastrous to us all. *We* are in his debt and so his service. Our *giant* apologies extend to you all!"

"I will forgive," said Troyton-suhl. "And I would like Padton-olt to be with them."

"My pleasure," offered Padton-olt who had finished his journey. "Ruedton-al, Gerndon-tuhl, and Belton-uhl will need someone to look after them to keep them out of trouble, and I am the one. Also, I have a *timely* and *urgent* message from the King—*but I have forgotten it!*—it's been twenty cycles."

"Well, perhaps it will come to you as we journey!" said the presiding one. He finally asked, "Are all these attendants acceptable, then?"

In unison, his query was met with a corporate pronouncement, *"So be it!"*

"Then, it is agreed. I am Roldon-nuhl, the King's Accountant! I will oversee this momentous trek. So then, *let us proceed!*"

Troyton-suhl pointed up and strode to gather Thomas and Archer onto his shoulders, who were happy to have his special attention after their misery in the cave.

Roldon-nuhl motioned them down and positioned Troyton-suhl at the foot of the altar. He them gave these stern instructions: to stride normally on his course with no unusual strides, neither was he to stop, while always accompanied by his attendants the whole course. Tipton was to watch and count his every step to ensure accuracy. It was thought best to let Roldon-nuhl carry the One Gem, while at the same Thomas and Archer were carried by Troyton's assistants "to assure for stride accuracy." Then the march commenced, Troyton-suhl striding wonderfully consistent midmorning across the giant skyway towards the still rising, animating Great Mover followed by four-hundred strong with others joining throughout the day's march.

The giants sang the following song as the procession made its day long journey eastward. Each sang recollecting the joy of recounting their own Journeys of Vocation.

Nine-Thousand Strides to go,
One less now, not to slow,
Five more now as we stroll,
Accountant, mark the toll.

Eight-thousand nine-hundred ninety-four strides to go,
One less now not to slow,
Five more now as we stroll,
Accountant, mark the toll.

You can image, earthen reader, how this song might continue on and on and on! Fortunately, it had variations at the announcement of certain special numbers, which the giants loved for various reasons due to their perception of the physical universe; however, the rhythm of the singing helped one to pace out one's strides consistently. Tipton kept careful watch of Troyton-suhl as Roldon-nuhl oversaw Tipton's accounting.

Ascending the mountain range, Wheldon-olt made balanced progress, even carrying the six travelers on his head and shoulders. He slowed only when the sun ducked behind a cloud. Only Na'al and Orín accompanied the four earthen youth, who were *beyond anxious* to find Thomas, Archer, and Troy. Wheldon-olt calculated the best way and worked steadily upwards. It was a quiet scary journey, but the riders held on tightly to crevice and cracks upon his shoulders and head, which were especially necessary in the more difficult vertical stretches of the steep climb uphill.

Yunt while ascending on Wheldon-olt's Shoulder, photograph by Bonnie Mitchell

With the passengers, the giant was somewhat slowed. But soon his own clan's slurry ridge was in sight, and as Wheldon-olt and the party approached the top, they heard a round of singing echoing past. Wheldon-olt hurried his pace and popped up and over the ridge to see the rear of the column moments before having just passed. He was relieved to be among his kind once again, and with such great numbers he had never seen, singing a song that he knew. He, however, had sung it only once for Bryton-duhl and Nimbrik-al—the very thought of them brought great sadness. The ringing of singing, however, pulled him out of his reverie of remorse into the celebration of one's completion of the Journey of Vocation.

Wheldon-olt hurried safely up to the first giant he could reach, "Pardon me, *who* is taking the Journey of Vocation?"

"Why, Troyton-suhl of the One Gem!" replied the giant, who upon seeing the Musselkin and earthen riders and the urgency of Wheldon-olt to continue frontward, with excellent foresight of calculation began to go ahead of Wheldon-olt saying, "Open up! Excuse us ... catching up here ... urgent watchers here. Special Guests! Other-worlders aboard! Excuse us ... Here come the rest of the clan of the Watchers of Troyton-suhl!"

Heads turns and odd-looking grins (from a human vantage point) greeted Wheldon-olt and his companions. Eyes met them in wonderment. *Such softlings had never before been seen*, and the giants being passed each enjoyed a closer inspection of them—popping their heads in and up close and back again)—since those in the rear of the parade had not been able to inspect Thomas and Archer close up.

At first, these giant massive heads closing in and backing back out frightened both Musselkin and the earthen youth. The gawking giants were indeed fearful such that Tanner and Guinevere closed their eyes. The silly song, however, lightened the atmosphere making it more "light-hearted." At the same time, Bonnie and Paige were somewhat relieved to hear mentioned Troyton-suhl although not understanding what was happening.

As the companions progressed forward through the throng, now some seven hundred giants strong, Wheldon-olt explained to them this ancient custom of the journey. After many more strides weaving in and out working forward, the party riding on Wheldon-olt finally saw Thomas and Archer carried by a couple of giants who followed another giant carrying above his head a huge clear gemstone. And, in front of this giant were finally two giants leading them all. After several more bends of the skyway, it widened into an opening with many hundreds more giants gathered around the Pool of Emergence. Yet, very oddly, no giant stood southward of the pool. And just beyond the pool eastward sat King Salton-suhl on his throne.

The lead giant, Troyton-suhl, took one last step right to the very edge of the pool. All eyes looked at him as his final stride fell. Cheering erupted simultaneously and led to one repeated chant, "*Nine-thousand strides! Nine Thousand Strides! Nine-thousand strides!*"

After a few moments Roldon-nuhl cried out, "*Order! Order! COME TO ORDER!*" But it was nearly useless. Finally, the chant stopped with giants chatting to one another being reacquainted with old friends. Roldon-nuhl continued, "Accountant of the Journey, Tipton-tyne, *what say you!*"

"By my accounting," Tipton answered loudly, "under the authority invested in me by the Conductor under King Salton-suhl ... Troyton-suhl of the Mitch-ell Clan has walked most worthily of the Conductor and has given nine-thousand *PERFECT* strides!"

"Nine-thousand strides! Nine Thousand Strides! Nine-thousand strides!" erupted once more over and over again.

Then, Salton-suhl stepped down from his throne and stood opposite Troyton-suhl across the pool. A hush fell upon the gathered giants, which numbered now over nine hundred. He bowed low and said to Troyton-suhl, "At your service."

All bowed down before King Troyton-suhl. Even Wheldon-olt bowed down, and his riders disembarked. Troyton-suhl *stood there dumbstruck.*

Part VI

Farewell to the Giants' Land

Chapter 30
Kingly Prerogatives

"King?" Troyton-suhl asked. *"Me?* The *king* of *what?!"*

"Sire," said Roldon-nuhl from his knelling position, "you have perfectly completed the Journey of Vocation with the accuracy that only the Conductor can grant—exactly *nine-thousand strides* with *no* variation, from the altar at the Western Sea Tides to the edge of the Pool of Emergence! To you, therefore, has fallen the kingship over giants' domain."

"But ... but ... that's *impossible!* I'm not *worthy!* My home is on another *world.* I'm still but a youngling, a boy, and this does not match *any* calculations or hopes of mine."

"That it does *not* match your calculations is perfectly fitting, Sire, since it is of the Conductor's *doing.* And, who needs another world when you are King and Master of these *glorious* giant highlands?"

Salton-suhl approached the new King Troyton-suhl from around the north side of the pool and bowed again. He spoke earnestly, "Sire, there are two very, very, *very* urgent points of business before us." His eyes diverted to the south side of the Pool of Emergence where there lay a golden form the size of a watermelon in the shape of a ring. On it was set the most exquisite clear stone nearly the same size as the ring itself. No giant dared to stand near it.

"First, This ... this hideous, poisonous band with stone" Salton-suhl pointed, "Must be dealt with. "And, second," Salton-suhl paused, having earlier noticed Wheldon-olt's softling passengers approaching, "I humbly request that I be allowed to perform one last function of a king, though not *as* 'king,' if I may, Sire. I see we have guests, greenish softlings of a kind that I've never seen, but from our *own* world, no doubt. May I please extend to them hospitality as is befitting of a king of the Trioptic Giants?"

"Why yes," replied Troyton-suhl who eagerly turned himself to see the visitors approaching from behind him.

Just then that mixed party of companions comprised of humans and Musselkin alike, who had ascended the mountains upon Wheldon-olt's mighty frame, finally reached Thomas and Archer and Troyton-suhl; earthen friends and family were joined together once again.

Paige rushed to Archer, and Thomas eagerly received hugs and kisses from Bonnie, Guinevere, and Tanner. The reunited party hugged each other with joyful weeping and then realized that one was left out of their celebration.

Thomas and Archer directed them to the giant standing there. They gazed up at Troyton-suhl, astonished at his full-grown stature towering above them. At this Troyton-suhl himself experienced a mixture of feelings, being both a giant and human at the same time.

"Troy?" asked Bonnie, "is that *you?!"*

He nodded and they went to hug him around his monstrous ankles.

Salton-suhl extended greetings to the group, "Welcome! Welcome *all* to the Northern Highlands, Watchers of Troyton-suhl! I am at your service." He bowed once more. "And I see that you have brought visitors. Are they *not* from the *lowlands?* Please introduce them."

Bonnie commenced with the introductions, "It is good to see you King ... ah ... Salton-suhl. This is Na'al, daughter of Governor Dernal of the Musselkin of Sylvanwood in the lowland washes and beyond, and her companion, Orín, the son of Zaren. They are very dear, *dear* friends, and are loyal to the Conductor. We have so many things that have happened! If we only had all night to talk, I might only *just begin* to tell you of their bravery! But Wheldon-olt here will be able to tell you about these things much better than I when he is able."

As Bonnie and the others continued to make introductions and talk, Thomas took Tanner aside and asked urgently, "Do you *still* have *the rings?* We've got to get out of here fast!"

"Yes ... yes," he dug in his backpack for the trinket box. "Right here. I've not even pulled it out since we arrived here." Tanner then more excitedly flashed to Thomas his notebook, "I've also been taking *notes!*"

"Never mind *that*," chided Thomas. "The *rings* are what we need to get out of here. Can you get the golden ring ready?"

"Alright," whispered Tanner back.

By now the Musselkin visitors had conversed briefly with Salton-suhl and Roldon-nuhl after having been introduced to the larger giant assembly which marveled that such intelligent creatures, who also served the Conductor, existed on their world, even if they were softlings living beneath them.

Presently, an announcement was made: "King Troyton-suhl, you must ascend to the throne and take your seat to ratify your Kingship." It was Roldon-nuhl, the King's Accountant, who was very interested to formally finalize the ascendancy of the new King according to their custom. He feared some mishap might result amidst all the irregularities of the recent events and due to the presence of the other-worlders and the green lowlanders.

"Yes," responded Troyton-suhl. "I will address the giant nation from the throne. But I must first attend to this *poisonous* ring and take counsel with my watchers in my clan."

So, it was that Troyton's first action as king of the giants was to rid their highland world of the poisonous gold band, which the cleansing rains of the previous days had flooded and purged from the Pool of Emergence, depositing it plainly for all the giants to see one last time as a reminder of the idolatrous and grave misstep that the giants had committed as a nation many centuries earlier. Na'al and Orín agreed to take the ring back to the lowlands with the aid of Wheldon-olt, who was brave enough to bear on his shoulders the Musselkin who bore the insidious ring, makeshift, with large plant leaves provided for them. After wrapping the baneful gold band inset with the clear gemstone thoroughly, the two Musselkin readied themselves to depart.

Orín started, "Goodbye, *ugly* ones with *stringy* hair and *gaudy*, colorful clothes. *You* will be missed!"

"Goodbye," said Paige with a forced smile. "I see that the *evil* words of the one—whose name is *unworthy* to mention—*still* lives on! Some people *never* learn!" The words hurt her even though offered in jest.

"I hope you're wrong, Paige. We must not *ever* mention that name ... but I agree with Orín that your hair *is* stringy," said Na'al. She and Orín eyed each other, as the levity of the joke faded into a question of what the future held for the Musselkin nation.

Bonnie, looking past the jabs, perceived the anxiety of the kinsfolk. "What will you two do now?"

Na'al sighed. "Search for our family and friends as we obey what Hilasdem has commanded us to do." She continued, "There's *much* work to be done!"

Orín eagerly asked, "We know you must go home, but will we see you in Sylvanwood again?"

The earthen youth looked at each other doubtful, but not wanting to answer "no"—the thought had not even crossed their minds, so eager were they to reunite with one another and return home.

Na'al repeated Orín's question. Still the youth gave no answer until finally Paige spoke up, "Only if I have shoes and nicer clothes. I'll have a new haircut, too."

And so, the two parties made their final farewells and offered up hugs. Tanner and Guinevere held up their arms as if surrendering, "Bye, Bye!"

They all laughed.

Wheldon-olt then picked up the Musselkin and their poisonous package and descended over the ridge wall out of sight down to the lowlands of Sylvanwood. They would arrive below just before sunset of that same day. The giants above murmured as they left.

Troyton-suhl and his royal clan then made their way to the side of his throne, and he knelt down in quiet counsel with them.

Thomas spoke first urgently, "Troy, you *cannot* accept this position as King! We must get back home! I'm afraid that we could get separated again. You *again* hold matters in *your* hands!"

"Yes," urged Bonnie. "You can't be king. Perhaps you can make Salton-suhl king again or to someone else. Or, if you can't do this, then somehow you must exercise your right *as* king to take the journey with us back home." The clan talked for some time about these matters and finally decided on a plan of action.

Then Troyton-suhl, walking over and pulling aside Roldon-nuhl, asked him privately, "If I *am* King, then can I *do* whatever I please?"

"Well, yes, Sire, within the limits that the Conductor has established."

"I am permitted to move freely about and travel, even *off* of this world?"

"Yes. Certainly. It has been done, at least as recorded in the Corridor of Time, but only on special occasions." Troyton-suhl was surprised to hear this but regathered his thoughts and continued his line of inquiry.

"Okay ... So, if I were to go away, may I then also appoint someone to rule in my place?"

"No. Absolutely not!"

"But, what *if I were* to travel and *not* return?"

"I should hope *not!*" retorted Roldon-nuhl shocked. "But if this *should* happen, I would think that the former King would assume rule; but, in any case, the Conductor would make that clear."

"Alright then," Troyton-suhl responded as he pursued his final line of questions, "Are giants allowed back *into* the Pool of Emergence?"

"Well, this is likely how a giant would travel ... but ... in our recent history such a thing has occurred *once*, and it was *very, very bad*—you have already dealt with the golden ring! How it came to be located in the Pool of Emergence is a long story, but it started with...."

Troyton-suhl stopped him mid-sentence. "Not now, please. Let me continue ... so, a giant has entered the Pool *legally?*"

"Well ... *yes* ... but *wrongfully*," Roldon-nuhl said with hesitation. "It is safe to say that typically giants only *emerge* from the pool and are appointed a watcher, and they do *not* re-enter the waters; the water is only otherwise used for drinking or dipping stones for eating."

"I intend," declared Troyton-suhl, " to re-enter the waters again *right now*. They have been purged and purified and are henceforth to be used for *cleansing*." Troyton-suhl spoke beyond himself and understood these last words were under the direct influence of the Conductor.

"As you wish, my King," said Roldon-nuhl bowing uneasily.

Ending the interview, King Troyton-suhl went to the throne and stood facing the entire gathered giant nation. "Fellow giants, I ask for all of your ears. Providence has brought me and my Mitch-ell Clan into this world. By instinct and Providence, I have journeyed to the Western Sea Tides only to journey back again to find myself *your King*. I say forthright that I am unworthy of this honor and title. I am a *fallen* creature of a *fallen* world, like yours. And so this honor is not *mine* to enjoy."

But note you, dear readers, that Troyton *misspoke*, for Verthana was not a *fallen* world, but a *falling* one.

Nevertheless, the giants rejected this statement outright. "No! You *are* Worthy! You *are* the King!"

"Okay, then," Troyton-suhl continued strategically, "As your King, with all the authority I have, I will now depart from this world to return to my own. Therefore, because of my absence of undetermined length, I hereby *return* the Giant Kingship through my own royal right until which time I may—*or may not*—return to King Salton-suhl, who has served you and the Conductor so faithfully during his entire reign."

All the giants were visibly disappointed and a bit puzzled. But no one of them dared either to object to the actions of the new king by his own stated right or to insult the worthiness of the former King Salton-suhl to rule in his place.

With that, Tanner was ready with the rings, box open, and the earthen youth stood hand-in-hand with Thomas touching Troyton-suhl by the pool. Bonnie had found Troy's clothes, but the scabbard that he had brought from their attic was missing. The party was ready to go home.

At the sight of the open box, Salton-suhl immediately erupted, "*Wait! Wait!* Are *these* the gold rings that I have forbidden to enter the Pool of Emergence!?"

The youth's triumph of departure had turned to sudden despair. It was jump then into the pool or perhaps never be able to do so!

However, several giant attendants quickly rushed them and one grabbed up Tanner firmly with ring box in hand, which broke their hand-to-hand connection. "Bring him to me!" insisted Salton-suhl. He then began a very close inspection of the box and its golden and green contents. "Tip-ton-tyne!" he shouted, "Is Tipton here? There is none better for this sort of work with his eye." Tipton-tyne made his way quickly to the old king. Poor Tanner remained suspended some forty-five feet up in the air, himself holding out the tiny box while standing in the flat palms of a giant. Leaning closely to his tiny body were the two massive heads of Salton-suhl and Tipton-tyne.

"The golden rings are ... *they are*, I think ... Barinium and the green ones Kairynium," mused Salton-suhl.

"I ... I ... would respectfully, Sire, disagree," firmly replied Tipton. "The golden ones are Chronymium."

"No. *Barinium.* Your eyes fail you!" interposed Salton-suhl insultingly.

"No! *Chronymium,*" insisted Tipton. "I've actually *been* to the Caverns of Time and Travel, Sire, more than you have, let me remind you!" This was, in fact, taken as an insult, although only Tipton, of those giants present, had ever visited and knew the precise location of the two caves, the only places from where these precious metals were to be found.

An argument erupted between the two giants but five feet in front of poor Tanner. He sat and closed his eyes and tried to shrug his shoulders to cover his ears.

Like a mother bear, Bonnie freed herself and ran over shouting and screaming. Surprisingly, her outcry and jumping stopped Salton's and Tipton's antics. "How *dare* you?! Is this what you call a *giant's* hospitality? In your hand *stands* a frightened youngling and you carry on such like younglings yourselves. The golden rings, it is clear, are *not* made of gold. So, put poor Tanner down."

Then turning to Troyton-suhl, Bonnie feigned to continue her chiding speech, "Perhaps, King Troyton-suhl," she winked, "there *is* another giant more fit to be king than these two, but, if not, then perhaps you should stay because I truly fear for the fate of giants' nation under the rule of such giants as these!" Her words hit the mark.

Tanner was quickly lowered to return to his fellow clan members by the side of the pool.

Salton-suhl and Tipton melted into a rumble of deep apologies that ended with Troyton's uplifted hand for silence and with their forlorn looks of shame.

Another voice broke out urgently, "But, what of the *One* Gem, the Diamond, Sire?" asked Roldon-nuhl worriedly. "Would you take *that* with you, King Troyton-suhl?"

Troyton winced at that question. He had hoped all along that the One Gem would not be brought up again as a temptation to him. "No," Troyton-suhl said slowly. He fought against the thaction that would lay claim to the gem only for himself. "No," he repeated again and decisively. "The One Gem belongs in the giants' realm as a symbol of the Conductor's Mercy and sustaining Grace. I know not exactly what its use is for the giants, but that it should stay here I would thus now command. Let the Conductor's will be done with it!" *"There I have done it,"* he thought, and meant it, too.

Now, dear readers, one further distraction occurred before the earthen youth were permitted to leave. It came again from King Salton-suhl who had resumed his place on the throne looking contentedly at them ready to jump in to depart through the terracotta pool. He had a smile on his face again, somehow quickly recovered from the recent scolding words of Bonnie and stroking a rather large furry mottled creature upon his lap. It was like an earthen rodent in shape, but not in size. When Paige glanced at Salton-suhl one last time and saw the creature, she did a double-take. To make things worse, to her surprise Salton-suhl nodded at her and said, "Thank you for this *wonderful* pet, young lady—so *cuddly* and *conversant*, too." And at that same comment, the creature winked at her as if to say, "*Thank you! Goodbye now.*"

Paige shook her head, straitened her clothes, then fidgeted a bit, being even more eager to go. She looked at the other youth looking at her with puzzled faces. She shrugged in feigned denial and blurted, "Let's get out of here *quickly*, please. Okay? *Let's go!*"

Nodding their heads, they and the towering Troyton-suhl stepped into the pool all touching. At the count of three, Tanner put on the golden ring, and rather than immediately vanishing as like from the Mitchell's basement, they sank peacefully down out of the sight of the gazing Trioptic Giants of the Northern Highlands of that strange world of Verthana.

Chapter 31
Home Again

Through the green waters the brothers, sisters, and friends passed. They surfaced in the wood to other worlds. Most notable, when they emerged from the pool, was the fact that Troyton-suhl was Troy once again somehow clothed. Their plan of departure had worked! They had reasoned that since Troy had become Troyton-suhl through the terracotta pool, he should become "normal" *again* when they exited through the *same* pool. And so, they had decided, to stand in the pool before putting on the golden ring to leave that world. Most impressive for Paige, however, was that her wedding dress had been washed clean from the journey; all of the youth were cleaned, in fact.

When they first entered the Wood, the party was dazed—remember that this is a side effect of such celestial travel—but slowly they recovered their wits, which was made faster by the scurrying guinea pigs that reminded them of earth and who they were. Then, without delay they gathered again hand-in-hand as Tanner put on the green ring this time, and they jumped into their earth pool.

It was still 10:34 when the youth popped back into the basement of the Mitchell's wearing the same garb as they had exited. Only three items did not make the return journey—Troy's scabbard, Archer's bow, and Paige's slipper, which she immediately tripped over in the basement when they returned. Despite this, all were elated to be back. They jumped up and down and screamed, at which Mrs. Mitchell yelled back down to them in response, *"Hey, keep it down, would you!!!"* They hushed immediately into giggles.

Tanner first put the ring away safely into the trinket box and shut it.

Thomas pointed to the clock on the wall, and they all marveled that no apparent "earth time" had passed (really it was but a few seconds) yet they had experienced a whole week in another world.

Bonnie stretched out on the carpeted floor and began making carpet angels. Following Bonnie's lead, they all did the same, so glad were they to be dry, comfortable, and safe at home again.

Then the two parties—each separated for most of their journey—each took turns telling their stories as they remembered King Salton's initial riddle from the Conductor of which every word had come to pass. The boys wrestled like the giants and gaited monkey-like around like the yunts while the girls walked gracefully around like the Musselkin or hopped around and cheeped like the bouleys. The three older boys mounded themselves together transforming themselves into a huge snail upon which the twins hopped aboard to ride. For the rest of the morning and afternoon the youth continued their playfulness with a sparkle in their eyes since the Mitchell kids had all pleaded successfully to have the Edwards stay past lunch until dinner—"it's Saturday after all!"

At one point during lunch, Mrs. Mitchell complimented Troy on his improved behavior, "You've not called anyone a 'blockhead'—that's quite amazing!" She also noticed that the three older boys, Thomas, Archer and Troy, were getting along exceptionally well.

After lunch, the youth went outside and were huddled around Tanner and his notebook consulting also with Guinevere's drawings.

But here is an oddity, fine reader, that we must mention to you. After coming into the giants' land, Tanner and the others, unbeknownst to them, adopted that world's language conventions for all their communication, including writing. Back on earth, Tanner stared in vain to decode those portions of his note taking and narratives which he so carefully and "naturally" related while running around Sylvanwood and the giants' land, but which was in the tongue and manner of the giants' and Musselkin's world. And so, you understand our need to relate them now. But lest you become disappointed to think that those youth had lost all their own intelligible written description of those wonderful events, you must remember that Tanner and Guinevere drew a good number of pictures—some of what they had seen and some of what their siblings described to them shortly after—and although even the perspective of the drawings was peculiar to a Musselkin or giant from that other world, these were quite relatable to earthen perceptions, if not also quite pleasurable to see even from an earthen point of view. Additionally, please know that Tanner also wrote in his own *idiolectic* language, which, since it was native to his mind's eye, would always be intelligible to him whenever and wherever he might be. Consequently, those sizeable portions of the notebook were still quite readable to him, if, however, not to the others or his parents who might happen to pick up the notebook to read, which Tanner deeply hoped *would* happen. Even that very evening, it, in fact, did.

The crowning moment for the youth, before Mr. Edwards arrived to pick up Paige and Archer, was when Bonnie remembered about her digital camera. They huddled around Mrs. Mitchell's laptop to view the pictures on the camera's memory card.

"Why didn't you take more!" chided Thomas.

"Geez, we were running around here and there! I forgot I had it, and I didn't want the Musselkin to ask about it!"

Nevertheless, viewing the dozen pictures Bonnie took confirmed to them just how *bizarre* and *terrifying* the events of their otherworldly travel had truly been.

That night, after their children were in bed, John and Dora had their late-night snack with some decaf coffee. Chips and salsa were a favorite of John's even though it could on occasion give him heartburn while sleeping—it was a particular weakness of his. He was just then reviewing his translation of the Septuagint of Psalm 18:6 and asked Dora about it.

"Dora dear, I'm *stuck* with this odd metaphor in the Greek translation of Psalm 18:6; it reads, 'And he, going out like a bridegroom from his bridal chamber, will rejoice like a giant running his course...' What's *that* referring to? I mean, when does '*a giant run his course'?* This is a *confusing* metaphor, I mean, metaphors compare two *knowable* things."

"Well, dear John, what does the *original* text say? Isn't that what you *always* ask? It was originally Hebrew, right?" She opened up her Facebook account and began scrolling.

"Well, Yes. Let me see. Oh, ... it's simply *gibor*, 'a strong man' which is what most translations have, I see...." He was looking on his laptop. "Hmmmm ... but why did the Greek translators of the Septuagint use *gigas* 'a giant'? I mean, *gigas* occurs elsewhere, too, like in Gen 6:4 where the *Nephilim* 'fallen ones' are also at the end of the verse called 'mighty ones' translated by the plural *gigantes* in the Greek, *yadda yadda yadda.* This verse forms the basis for First Enoch's description of some 'giants' who corrupted humans. There's some relationship to that, I'm sure...." John paused lost in thought and then became present once again.

Dora hadn't noticed his delay.

"But," John continued, "in Psalm 18:6, I'm still left wondering what's *particularly* in view here ... *I just don't get the metaphoric reference!* It's *odd.* I mean, Greek mythology features 'giants' ... but there's nothing *specific* about 'a giant running a course' that I'm aware of, only that they battled the Olympian gods ... the *Gigantomachy....*" He trailed off again.

Dora noticed his pause and yawned, "*That's so very, very* interesting, John, on a Saturday night."

"Ah, *okay ... yeah*, I'll stop working." John, self-aware, shut his laptop.

"That's nice, honey," and she realized that *she* should herself get off of social media.

The couple sat there in silence for a moment before she perked up again.

Bouley on Boulder, pencil by Guinevere Mithcell

"Hey, dear, did you notice how well the kids played together today? From breakfast to lunch, John—I kid you not—it was as if they were a different group of kids from a different planet! Troy was his pleasant self again and the three older boys were 'good ol' buddies.' And take a look at *this*." Dora handed John Tanner's notebook.

He began leafing through it, "Very imaginative, and ... ah, I recognize Guinevere's drawings here and there ... well, all over actually... she's getting quite good.... but, this here ... and this is very odd to me—here's Tanner's own language script; he's shown it to me before, but I still haven't deciphered it—but over here ... and on this page ... and over here ... this other writing looks very similar to proto-Phoenician script, but I can't make it out; see this portion in Tanner's hand as if written in verse." And this is what he saw:

Dora leaned over and looked closely. "But I tell you, John, *this* is the *least* of it. How *long* would you guess Tanner worked on *this particular* notebook?"

"Well, since it's filled up with scripts and pictures ... I suppose a week ... well, maybe a few days if that's all he did." He leafed through some pages. "Hmmm.... look at *this* strange creature ... and here. That's a *very* large snail!"

"Well, *that's* just it," Dora pensively replied. "He asked for a new notebook this morning *after breakfast—this very one!* And after the Edwards' left, he left it on *my desk* for me *to find*."

"Hmmm...." John surmised. "Well, sure he would ... he's proud of it if it's *indeed only* a day's work. OR, maybe it was a group effort? OR, maybe this is not *the exact same notebook* and he's playing a trick on you? OR, maybe he's simply a little genius, that Tanner of *yours* ... creative, bright, and beautiful *just like his mom*?"

At that, she punched him gently on the shoulder. "You're b-*OR*-ing me *to death* tonight, John. And your obvious use of flattery just when I reminded you it's Saturday night ... I'm not unaware. He's *our* child anyway—his looks are *yours*—the *poor* kid!"

John returned the friendly touch by gently kicking her shin under the table. "We're *EVEN* now." He then asked seriously, "Dora, have you seen that trinket box with strange decorations? It's not on its display shelf where it normally is."

"Oh, yes. Tanner asked for it a week ago. Why?" Dora began looking at facebook again on her laptop.

"Oh, probably nothing ... but the writing on the outside ... it looks like ... well ... I just want to have a closer look at it. It's *very* peculiar."

But Dora was not fully listening. "Sure, ... ah ... I'll ask the kids about it tomorrow." Her left index finger just then skimmed the side of the laptop. "Ah ... *interesting* ... there's a memory card in here. It's Bonnie's from her old camera. She forgot to take it out ... *again!* She's as *absent-minded* as her mother! Earlier I found them all riveted, looking at her pictures." She mused, "John, would it be *wrong* for us to have a look?"

Na'al (left), Ranít (right), Hilasdem (center bottom), photograph by Bonnie Mitchell

www.ingramcontent.com/pod-product-compliance
Lightning Source LLC
LaVergne TN
LVHW020507100826
845148LV00003B/714

* 9 7 8 1 6 3 6 6 3 1 3 8 7 *